Stephanie Butland has written two books about her

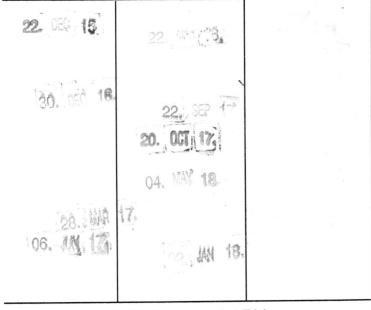

Also by Stephanie Butland

How I Said Bah! to cancer
Thrive: The Bah! Guide to Wellness After cancer
Letters to my Husband (*originally published as*
Surrounded by Water)

THE OTHER HALF OF MY HEART

OF MY HEART

Stephanie Butland

BLACK SWAN

TRANSWORLD PUBLISHERS
61–63 Uxbridge Road, London W5 5SA
www.transworldbooks.co.uk

Transworld is part of the Penguin Random House group of companies
whose addresses can be found at global.penguinrandomhouse.com

First published in Great Britain in 2015 by Black Swan
an imprint of Transworld Publishers

A CIP catalogue record for this book
is available from the British Library.

ISBN 9780552779166

Typeset in 11/14pt Giovanni Book by Falcon Oast Graphic Art Ltd.
Printed and bound by CPI Group (UK) Ltd, Croydon, CR0 4YY.

Penguin Random House is committed to a sustainable
future for our business, our readers and our planet. This book is made from
Forest Stewardship Council® certified paper.

1 3 5 7 9 10 8 6 4 2

For my parents

'Arise, and eat bread, and let thine heart be merry'
I Kings 27:7

Prologue

Missingham, 1993

HOWARD AND HIS twins, Sam and Bettina, are sitting in the front row of the audience. It's a privilege accorded to them as they are the family of one of the show's stars. Also, Howard says, as he's the one who has to turn up early to put out the chairs he doesn't see why he shouldn't give himself a perk and bag them the best seats in the house. He smiles as he says it: Tina, sitting between him and her brother, feels warmed.

'I feel like I've seen this a thousand times,' Sam says. 'In fact, I feel as though I'm in it.'

Tina laughs. She knows what he means: since their mother was cast as Beverley, home life has been dominated by *Abigail's Party*. Alice has even been found smoking in the garden. 'I have to get used to it,' she'd explained. 'It has to look authentic when I do it.' Tina had agreed, although taking up smoking didn't strike her as particularly normal behaviour for a mother. But one of the things that's wonderful about Alice is that when she decides to do something, she really does it.

'If someone doesn't show, you might have to take part,' Howard says.

'Over my dead body,' Sam says, and goes back to his book. It's a biography of Stalin, something he asked for at Christmas. His fringe flops forward as he reads. There's a crop of freckles on his cheeks; Tina's own face has the same markings. They will be fourteen soon. She is going to ask for new riding boots for her birthday. Sam will want more history books, and he has his eye on some New Balance trainers.

'Let's be proud,' Howard says. He's one of the quiet heroes of the Missingham Amateur Dramatic Society. As well as putting out chairs, he paints furniture for sets and brings wine and crisps from the cash-and-carry for performance nights and last-night parties. He photocopies scripts and counts the money. If he ever gets tired of it, he doesn't show it. Tina smiles. She can sense how proud he is. It comes off him like aftershave or the smell of a clean cotton shirt when he moves. She loves her father, but she envies her mother her bright spirit, her fearlessness; she sees the same thing in Sam, but not in herself. She is her father's daughter, she knows, and not only because her mother says it so often, and with such satisfaction, as though there is nothing better than being steady and quiet. ('We're only quiet,' Howard had said just that morning, 'because you and Sam won't let us get a word in edgeways. It's learned behaviour.' And Alice had shushed him, and then told them all off when they wouldn't tell her what was funny.)

Someone at the back of the hall throws the light switches and there's darkness. And then there's Alice, smoking in a way that's definitely authentic, bright eye-shadow, long green dress cut low. Sam touches Tina's hand and when she looks at him, he winks a wink that says, yes, let's be proud, but that is our mother up there, and I do know exactly how you feel.

When the applause starts at the beginning of the interval, Sam leans across and says, 'Let's have a pizza and watch a film tomorrow night. She's great but we deserve it. Compensation for the embarrassment.'

'Deal,' Tina says, and she wonders how people without a twin can possibly navigate their way through the world.

Part One: Throckton, 2013

THE THAI TAKEAWAY is sweating on the passenger seat of the car. Rufus knows that the food won't be worth eating by the time he gets back with it; his daily ten-minute drive home from the office has already taken three-quarters of an hour. He remembers that he is learning to be patient, and tweaks the volume of the Rachmaninov symphony he's listening to up a little.

The horse and rider that passed his stationary two-hundred-and-fifty-five horsepower BMW convertible ten minutes ago are making their way back up the hill. Rufus clicks the stereo off, turns the key in the ignition, slides the window down and feels the March breeze chill his face, despite the early evening sun, as he leans out to hail the rider.

'How's it looking?'

'Not good. There's a lorry stuck on the bridge,' the rider says. 'It's got halfway round, then—' She shakes her head, makes a you-know-how-it-is face. 'I'd go the other way if I were you,' the horsewoman offers. 'The fire brigade is still scratching its head down there. It's going to be a while, by the looks of it.'

'I think I will. Thanks.' Rufus waits until the horse has

got well away before starting to shuffle the car out of the queue and turn round. He might have nine points for speeding on his licence, but his years of squiring his daughter from pony club to gymkhana means he knows how to treat a horse when he meets one on the road.

'Oh well,' Bettina says, half an hour later, 'we'll just have to have one of your famous omelettes.' She's arrived at her neighbour's for dinner to find him still taking off his coat, and the two of them have taken one look at the contents of the cartons, limp and tepid, before deciding to put them straight in the bin. She smiles: sudden sunshine. 'Well, it's not the end of the world, is it?'

'I suppose not.' Rufus is still shaking off the disruption to his evening. 'I could go downstairs and get something,' he offers, half-heartedly. It's not that the food from the Italian restaurant he lives above isn't good. But he's home an hour later than he meant to be already, and because Bettina gets up at four, she'll want to be in bed in an hour and a half. He rubs the inner corners of his eyes, hard; shadows jump behind his lids.

'Don't be silly,' Bettina says, putting a hand on his arm, drawing it away from his face. He thinks, for a moment, that she's going to kiss him, but she doesn't. She is cautious with physical contact, as though she has only so many touches to give and must give them wisely. Either that, or it takes an effort.

Her smiles, though, are unlimited. 'There's nothing better than your omelettes, if you don't mind making them.'

'Of course not.'

'I'll go and get some walnut bread, shall I? I made it this morning.' And she's gone before he's had time to answer: to say, yes, thank you, and might I just add how wonderfully easy it is to be with you. But I wish you'd stay the night. Just once.

She's back before the butter foams in the pan. In her absence Rufus has taken off his suit and tie, put on his cords, loosened his shirt collar, rolled up his sleeves and swapped his Italian leather shoes for his Italian leather slippers. He's opened a bottle of Viognier, put plates in to warm, sliced some tomatoes, remembering the time he and his ex-wife spent in France as he breaks the fruit from the vine. He's checked that the bedroom is in good order. (Which it is, because he left it that way this morning, and as it isn't the day for his cleaner, no one has been in there since. But still.) He pours the eggs into the pan and as he waits for them to set he watches his neighbour, friend and sometimes lover (not-as-often-as-he'd-like lover) set the table.

The flat is quiet. This is a silence that Rufus likes: he doesn't think he's ever had a relationship with a woman when silence means, simply, that in this moment there is nothing I want to say. This is wordlessness without waiting, or punishment, or heavy unsaid words. Of course, part of the reason that it is so uncomplicated is that Rufus is held a cautious arm's length away from real intimacy, and he knows this. But he hopes he can wait. He thinks he is learning to be careful, at last. He mulls their relationship over, often; he knows it would be foolish to rush in, and he reminds himself that there's no hurry, pushing his resentment away. He does this more often than he'd like to admit, because he knows – he tells himself – that he is a better man than he used to be. But he wants to say: you're lovely, Bettina, I wish you knew how much I think of you. He wants to be able to look at her, fully, properly, drink her in. He wants to gaze. But if she sees him gazing she stops what she's doing, uncertain, as though he is a stranger in the street, looking in at her through a window.

He puts the first omelette in the oven to keep warm – he will eat it, so that Bettina will have the fresher one. He pours the eggs for the second into the pan and adds an extra twist of pepper, which he knows she will like.

Rufus watches Bettina as she puts out knives, forks, glasses and the unsalted butter that he keeps in an antique cheese dish on top of the fridge. She's absorbed in what she's doing – this is something else he likes, her thoughtfulness, her focus – so he can watch her, out of the corner of his eye. And he likes watching her move. She isn't graceful, exactly; a slight limp means that she always seems unsteady. Unless you look for the limp, Rufus thinks, you wouldn't know it's there, but once you've noticed it you can't help but see it, like a spelling mistake on a business card. She's a little too thin for her own good, too, which worries him; it's not that she doesn't eat, more that she's never still, nervous energy constantly eating everything that she eats, and more. He makes a point of feeding her, brings her gifts of chocolate and the French cheeses from the deli round the corner from his office. She eats them all, but she never seems to gain any weight. He wonders if she realizes that he offers these small gifts from his heart, even though he wraps them in friendliness and gentlemanly consideration.

Bettina's hair waves and curls as though it's been set by a hairdresser who trained in the 1940s. She has it cut into a blunt, unfussy line that sits halfway down her jawline, her parting on the left and her right ear usually exposed by the curls tucked behind it. Her skin is clear; her mouth is, if anything, a little small in her face; her teeth are small, too, and when she smiles her lips tend to stay shut, so seeing them is an oddly intimate experience. It's as though the rest of Bettina's face knows that it can't compete with her eyes, which are a sort of buttery walnut colour, with bright amber highlights. In the half-light across dinner tables or in bedrooms, they shine a blackened bronze. They might be the most beautiful eyes that Rufus has ever seen. She glances up at him and he feels his heart falter as he returns her small smile. If the contents of her bathroom cabinet are to be believed, the only make-up she ever wears is brown mascara. Her eyebrows are thick arches the same pale mouse-brown as her hair.

As the second omelette sets, Bettina puts out the bread. She's brought it wrapped in a cloth, in a basket. She puts the basket in the middle of the table, pulls back the corners of the cloth, takes the loaf in both hands, then breaks it, slowly, gently, her attention on the freshly exposed shards of crust, then moving to the soft bread within, which she inspects with the same expression that Rufus's daughter has when she looks at her own

21

little daughter's fingernails. When the bread is in pieces, she wraps it again. Rufus has watched Bettina perform this ritual many times, whether the bread is a breakfast baguette, the accompaniment to an omelette, or one of her complicated, ornate plaits, glazed to the colour of good, rich coffee on the outside and pale as milk within. It seems to him a prayer, a grace, although he doesn't think she knows what she is doing. He'd joked, once, that breadmaking was a religion to her; she'd said, seriously, that if religion is what makes your life bearable, then she supposed it was. She'd added that it had rescued her, once. He hadn't said anything else, but he'd filed her answer away. Attention to detail is what makes Rufus Micklethwaite a good architect. All of the problems in his life have arisen when he's allowed his attention to wander. He wishes Bettina would let him give her his true, undivided attention.

She turns her face to him. 'All set,' she says, and she smiles.

'Me too,' Rufus says, 'I'm ready for something to eat.' When she looks at him he knows it's nothing special, to her. He's seen her give her full attention to a loaf of bread just a minute or two ago, after all. But he feels chosen by her look, and something in him responds with a choosing of his own. I choose you, Bettina May, his heart says, and if I can do enough, and be here enough, you will choose me too.

Bettina chose Rufus – insomuch as it was a choice – as part of a bigger decision, to settle down at last, to try to find a semblance of a life, in the hope that the sadness that trailed and sometimes engulfed her might diminish at last. Almost a year ago, she had started her business in the bakery and moved into the flat above it, and very shortly afterwards she had seen movement in the flat above the Italian restaurant next door. There are two windows at the back of the flats, next to the second bedrooms, that overlook each other: Bettina had found seeing an occasional presence, passing the window carrying a box or pulling on a jacket, comforting. She recognized him when she saw him in the shop, and stopped to chat when he introduced himself. An evening or two later found them both eating in the restaurant, at two tables-for-two placed a little too close to each other. Rufus had struck up a conversation, and Bettina had been reticent at first, but when he asked her about her plans for the business she'd found herself saying all the excited thoughts in her head out loud. After that, Rufus had become a regular customer at the bakery and an occasional dinner companion, if they happened to be in the restaurant at the same time. Bettina ate early, and sometimes she would see him walking past the restaurant window on his way in from work; she'd know that within fifteen minutes he'd be taking a seat at the table next to her. She would order before he came, not wanting to be committed to anything like a date; but it was nice to see him, and have someone well mannered, interesting and interested to talk to.

Rufus did ask her, once, if she would like to make a plan to meet rather than leaving it to happy chance, as he put it. She explained that she never knew how tired she would be, and that getting up at four most mornings made her odds-on lousy company in the evening. Rufus had said something gallant in reply but things had stayed as they were, and Bettina felt proud of herself, for making a friend.

But then, after six months, on the first evening that really felt like autumn, it all changed. It was the evening when she decided that she was, definitely, going to extend the café, rather than being frustrated by the current set-up and thinking she really must do something about it. Bettina spent the time after the shop closed that day thinking and pacing and measuring. She'd already done the maths, studying the spreadsheets on one of the grim train journeys she made every month, so she knew she could afford it, if she made her mind up. And if it was possible. Which was something Rufus might know about.

So she knocked on his door and asked if he might have time to pop over to the shop one evening and give her a bit of advice?

'Why don't I come now?' he asked.

She said, 'That would be fantastic, but I don't want to interfere with your evening. If you have plans.'

'I have plans now,' he said with a warm smile. 'Just let me get my keys,' and soon they were standing in Adventures in Bread. Even with the shelves empty, the place still smelled bittersweetly of sourdough, and there was, too, the trace of hot, fresh bread in the air, or at least the memory of it, which amounted to the same thing. Bettina never got tired of it. She took a deep breath when she unlocked the door, and saw Rufus do the same. She smiled, and thought about how, if she was

24

the sort of person who touched other people easily, she would touch him now, just squeeze his arm or rest her hand on his shoulder for a second, to say, I'm so glad you understand how wonderful such a simple thing as bread can be.

'The thing is, I'm halfway there,' she said instead, waving an arm at the shop side of Adventures in Bread. There were wooden shelves, wicker baskets, a stone floor, a marble counter and a stack of brown paper bags ready to put her wares into. There was the smell of bread everywhere, the blackboard with the baking schedule for the week, the community noticeboard and an old French bread crock where people could – and did – donate their change for charity. Bettina found Throckton a generous place.

'But – this.' The café that was also part of the lease had been a feeble effort of the last owners. It was barely a café at all, just a couple of folding metal tables and ornate and uncomfortable metal chairs. Bettina had decided to get the bakery up and running before she turned her attention to the café, but she found herself cringing at the sight of people squashing themselves around the tables, no one looking comfortable. She wanted wooden tables, scrubbed pine or maybe with red gingham tablecloths, not-necessarily-matching wooden chairs, hot tea in brown teapots, milky coffee in bowls, toasters on the tables, proper homemade jam.

'I've been thinking about this for a while,' Bettina said, 'and I'd like to know if you think it could work.' She had opened a door marked *Private*, on the left of the double doors which were the entrance to the shop. Rufus had peered into a storeroom that was home to two half-empty metal shelving units and a pile of disconsolate-looking empty cardboard boxes.

'This must be half the floorspace of the shop again,' he said.

She laughed. 'It took me the best part of half an hour to work that out,' she said. 'I suppose this was useful if you bought a lot of things in, but as you can see, I don't really use it. And I'm wondering about pulling down the dividing wall and making this a proper café.' She outlined her plans, trying to sound businesslike and practical, but feeling as though she was serving up her heart on a plate. Suddenly, she was uncomfortable and wished she had kept her ideas to herself, or asked someone she didn't know at all, paying them for their time and their separation from her. 'What do you think?' she asked, not meeting his eyes.

This was the first time she'd spoken about her plans out loud, and in doing so she'd realized how much she wanted them to work. It was less that she had a burning desire for a tiny teashop in keeping with her bakery; more that she had grasped that what she was doing was submitting to the idea that Throckton was becoming her home. The need that had been growing in her lately was the need for a life more unchanging, more solid, than it had been in fifteen years. And although there was a time when the fact that she felt like staying was enough to make her move on, it seemed to be different now. Standing watching Rufus assess and think, she'd allowed her mind to drift back to her own mother, who was a great believer in the ritual of teatime. It wasn't an elaborate ritual so much as a space in the day where everyone in the house would – must – gather in the kitchen and sit and have a mug of tea, and a slice of cake if there was something in the tin. And they'd talk, about nothing much, and then when Alice stood up and took the teapot to the sink they would disperse. 'As you were,' she would say, 'back to your lives,' and she would smile, and if Tina's friend Katrina happened to be there she would say, 'I love your mum,' although Tina often suspected that it was the chance to sit down with her brother Sam for half an hour that Katrina really loved.

Of course, that had been when her mother still had a grasp of what teatime was, and of who she was, and of who her daughter was. Bettina had leaned against the counter, taking the weight off her aching leg as Rufus assessed her dream with his architect's eye.

She held her breath as she watched Rufus measure up, tap at walls, walk from the shop to the storeroom and back again. He'd waited until she looked at him, full in the face, and he held her gaze and smiled, as though he was telling her that he understood. Or perhaps she was too tired to think straight. It had been one of those weeks. She looked over to the window, as a car drove past.

'It's certainly possible,' he said, 'and from what I can see, it should be straightforward. This wall,' he rested the tips of his longest three fingers against the partition, 'is wood and plasterboard. Someone has put it in to make the storeroom, but it's not part of the original build. You could take it down, and I don't see any reason why you shouldn't bring the stone tiles right through. We can even off the floor first, if we need to.'

'Good,' Bettina said. 'How long will it take, do you think? How much will it cost?'

'What's your budget, if you don't mind me asking?' His voice was businesslike now, and hers matched it.

'I've got the details here,' she said, tapping the closed lid of her laptop, which sat on the counter. 'I'd like to see what you think. If you wouldn't mind.'

'I'd be delighted.'

'Thank you,' Bettina said. She reached out to pick up the laptop, but Rufus misunderstood and assumed that she was going to take, or shake, his hand. So he took her right hand in his own right hand, his palm against her fingers, and grasped it for a minute; it was an awkward half-friendly gesture, perfectly suitable, it seemed to Bettina, for their awkward half-friendly relationship. 'Of course,' she added, 'I'll pay you for your time.'

'Surely that's not necessary? We're friends, aren't we?'

She looked at him, and said, 'I don't know. I don't really have friends.' Hearing how peculiar this must sound, she moved away into the storeroom. She looked around it, wishing she could see what Rufus could see, a job already completed, the new reality sketched on top of the old.

'When I say "you" can make these alterations,' he said, following her, 'I mean that I can find you a good builder who can do this. It's not a weekend-DIY job.'

'Of course,' Bettina said. 'I know my limits.'

'I like to check,' Rufus said. 'You'd be amazed how many people think taking down a wall is as simple as swinging a hammer.'

'I bet,' she said, surveying the storeroom and the existing café.

'If I could make one suggestion,' Rufus continued, 'have you considered one large table rather than small ones? You'll get better value from the space that way. Although—'

'Yes,' Bettina said, 'yes!' And suddenly her plans leapt into life. She had spent hours trying to work out the logistics of fitting tables in. There needed to be enough for the place to feel a little bit buzzy, but not so many that a double buggy or a badly placed walking frame would bring everything to a standstill. She'd puzzled over how to get a toaster on to every table without having cables taped to the floor or taking floorboards up. She'd come up with something, in the end, that sort-of worked, but Rufus had given her a solution so shimmeringly obvious that she couldn't imagine how she hadn't seen it herself. Because in that moment she had seen it, really seen it, for the first time. She had seen mothers with pushchairs gathered at one end of a long oval scrubbed wooden table, a couple of skiving sixth-formers playing at sophistication with double espressos at the other. In the middle, enough space for someone with half an hour to kill to take their teacake, spread out a newspaper and fill in another couple of clues on the cryptic cross-word someone else had started.

She saw that she was making a place for conversations that could be easily and harmlessly overheard, for tea and cake and a few words swapped with near-strangers. There could be a few small tables, too, of course, for quiet conversations, or solitary types. But the café at

Adventures in Bread would be something special. It would be, she realized, exactly the sort of place that she would have run a mile from five years ago, which might be why she hadn't been able to visualize it herself. Excitement was popping at the surface of her stomach; her face was tingling. If she was a dancer, she would pirouette. So much of the last few years had felt like a day-by-day plodding: in that second, she'd felt giddy at how far she'd come. It was as though she'd raced a thoroughbred to the top of a hill, but been so focused on the animal's ears and the sound of his hooves that it was only when they stopped that she saw how high she was. She felt reckless, dizzy at her success, although no one looking in would see that knocking down a dividing wall and creating a space for people to share a pot of tea was quite the breakthrough that she knew it to be.

'Rufus,' she said, 'you're a bloody genius. I could kiss you.'

'Don't let me stop you,' Rufus said.

And, giddy still, she had.

Now, six months after the night she had first kissed Rufus and three months since the new café opened, Bettina is getting into the swing of being a little more public. The most challenging part of this is the bread-tastings she holds once a fortnight. The big table is perfect for them. Sometimes she's trying out a new loaf and needs to know whether her customers will like it, and sometimes tastings are more of a PR exercise, with nothing new to trial but the chance to get some customers to taste the breads they haven't tried before.

Today, at 10.30, there will be one of these informal tasting sessions. Before the bakery and café start to get busy, Bettina puts aside a sage and saffron loaf, some rye rolls, a plump, purple Merlot bread and a cheese and bacon plait. On a tray next to them she lays out plates, knives, napkins, unsalted and salted butters, and jam. Then, from the kitchen she brings small bowls of grains, flours and the homemade yeast starter that is the basis of all her baking, and one of her first baking notebooks, pages and pages of notes and sketches and scribbles. Her idea is to help people understand what goes into something that they more or less take for granted, in the hope that they'll see beyond the price to the value. Bettina doesn't think that her bread is expensive, but she knows that her own perspective might be different to that of her customers. And even though Throckton gives every impression of being a well-heeled little town, she hears the chatter in the shop, about redundancies at the print works in Marsham and the gift shop closing. She knows that, however she feels about good bread being a necessity, for many her bread is a luxury and she wants to do all she can to make sure that, if money is tight, hers is the luxury people keep rather than the one they do without.

The tasting is from 10.30 to 11.15. Bettina will sit at the table and talk, and encourage people to toast and taste, and by the time the event is finishing the coffee crowd will be arriving in earnest, and she will leave out the leftovers for them to try. The talking, the being on show, is not a comfortable thing for her to do. She isn't really comfortable anywhere out of the kitchen, although behind the counter she feels protected. As soon as she steps away, she feels nervousness creep out of her bones where it's been hiding and surround her, a clammy cloud of wishing she was somewhere that no one would speak to her. But she knows that this isn't the way to live, and so she perseveres.

At her beautiful scrubbed-pine table, surrounded by a hotchpotch collection of wooden chairs – all bought from an auction house and costing more to transport and have re-sanded and varnished than to buy – Bettina is exposed. She's not good at small talk; she never has been, even in her teens before her life veered off the road. One of the things she likes about Rufus is his ability to make conversation smooth and simple, whereas what comes out of her mouth often seems awkward, or off-key. Even last night, when she had turfed him out although she'd known he was unwilling to go, he'd managed to be polite and make it less awkward than it might have been. He had called in on the pretext of dropping off a takeaway menu for the Indian restaurant near his office, and she'd invited him to stay for a drink.

Although, now she comes to think of it, he hasn't been in this morning. He often pops in to get a sandwich to take to work, or half a dozen croissants to drop off for his daughter and granddaughter. Bettina's mind and memory are suddenly full of her mother's voice, ticking Sam off for giving a classmate a Valentine's card when the girl he had intended it for gave him the brush-off. Don't start something that you can't finish,

Sam, she said. It's not good manners. You've been brought up better than that. For all her playfulness, Alice had standards, and rules. You did as you were told, in her house. Bettina suspected that her advice about Rufus would be the same, were she in a position to give it.

Bettina drags her mind back to the here and nearly-now of today's tasting. It's an effort. Part of the reason she tries to stop herself from thinking about the distant past is that, given the choice, she would rather stay there than be here, most of the time. Of course, her memory is selective, and the memories – especially the ones that wake her screaming – aren't all good. She takes a breath. There's a rosemary cake baking, and it smells so good that she could cry. But she doesn't because, she reminds herself, this is business.

She knows that she has to promote her products and that, for now at least, the best person to carry out that promotion is herself, so she just gets on with it. People buy people first, her father used to say, and she has worked in enough bakeries and boulangeries to understand how important a face for the business is. For her first tasting, she'd prepared a series of prompt cards for each section and she'd learned by heart what she was going to say, delivering it in a voice that seemed brittle even to her own ears. Now she's learned that if she can only get through the chat before everyone settles down to the tasting, she can manage the rest, because when she's talking about baking she's on safe ground. Last time, she had sixteen tasters, four of them new customers; with the exception of one person, they'd all bought something, and she's pretty sure that all of them have been back at least once. Angie will look after the shop and the rest of the café, and in the kitchen Simon will keep the hungry ovens fed. And so this morning, all is well at Adventures in Bread.

There's a mellow ring from the cluster of brass bells that hangs on the back of the door, and Bettina looks up. She recognizes the newcomer from her photo-byline in the local newspaper, and the world tilts.

Oh, hell.

She has forgotten – well, not so much forgotten as pushed to the side of her mind, into the area labelled 'things to think about later when I am feeling up to them' – that this is happening today. Verity Ross of the *Throckton Warbler* is here, right on cue, to do the interview that Bettina has been trying to ignore. She looks at her hands and they're shaking. It's one thing to cope with feeling exposed, sitting in your own café; quite another to be written about in the local newspaper, where anyone and everyone can read about you, and judge you, or recognize you. Bettina swallows. She tastes bile at the back of her throat, burning the skin and leaving a sourness that will linger all day.

'Morning,' Bettina says, feeling her customer-smile make its way to her face, and willing her voice to sound brave. It shakes, a little, but it manages to hold. 'You must be Verity.'

'Bettina? Yes, I am. Hello.' The journalist is a neat, smart woman, dressed in a tweed jacket over a white blouse and a black skirt. A deep pink silk scarf is knotted at her neck; her smiling lipstick matches it. She might be fifty or she might be seventy, and she probably won't change at all in those two decades. Bettina feels herself shrink inside. She wishes she had inherited her mother's talent for acting: then she could play the successful, confident bread-shop owner. Right now there's a good chance that she will clam up and be able to squeeze out only yes or no answers. She feels as she used to feel when she was plagued by panic attacks: she's waiting for the feeling of time stopping, the air closing around her and suffocating her. But she comes out from behind the counter, and she keeps smiling because she doesn't know what will happen if she stops. She shakes Verity's hand, her own suddenly cold, and says, 'Welcome to Adventures in Bread.'

Her leg aches. The old injury is the place where her tiredness and stress always make themselves known. It's an outward manifestation of a pain that's as familiar and constant as birdsong in the dawn. She shifts her weight and remembers what her father used to say about how the hardest part of anything is to begin. 'Shall we get some coffee and cake and go upstairs to the flat, where we won't be disturbed?'

'That sounds lovely,' Verity says, her glance roving along the baskets of breads, the trays of cake. She lets out a little sigh. 'I wish I hadn't had breakfast.'

Angie, Bettina's assistant in everything except bread-making, laughs and says, 'We hear that a lot.' Once the drinks are made and the cakes chosen, Bettina leads Verity upstairs, trying to remember what state she left the place in this morning, focusing on the flat as a way of suppressing her emotions, which she is managing to punch down like dough after a first proving. They'll rise again, she knows, but she needs to be able to put off dealing with them until later.

'Your nomination for the Heart of Throckton New Business Awards is proving very popular,' Verity says with a smile when they are settled on two small sofas, facing each other across a coffee table cluttered with recipe books, notebooks, a jug full of peonies only just on the wrong side of ripeness, but nothing worse. Rufus brought the flowers a week or so ago, wrapped in yellow tissue tied with a green ribbon, 'because I thought they were cheerful and you'd like them'. Bettina had been ungracious about them – for no reason other than the fact that she doesn't know how to accept gifts, especially when they are surprises, although she had said something about how she didn't like cut flowers much, by way of an excuse. She's felt guilty about her ingratitude ever since, so she's kept the flowers too long, as a sort of penance: every time she looks at them, she thinks of how complicated even a casual relationship seems to be. Bettina scans for anything she doesn't want the journalist to see, but she thinks she's safe. And the coffee, the cake, give them something to do, and give Bettina a chance to breathe deeply. Verity, after much wondering, had chosen a Tartly Lemon Slice; Bettina had stuck with her old faithful Kickin' Coffee Kuchen, although she eats only a bite before she puts the plate down on the table.

'Well, it's good to be popular,' she says, before subjecting herself to small talk that makes her squirm when she is on the receiving end of the questions: what she thinks of Throckton, whether she lives on her own, her unusual name.

'May I call you Tina?' Verity asks.

Bettina, shocked into abruptness by the remembrance of the time when that was the name everyone called her, says, 'No.' She adds, 'My name is pronounced to rhyme with "retina" – my mother was always very firm about that – and so "Tina" feels . . . unintuitive to me.' This is true, although everyone outside the family had short-ened her name in the same way that they shortened Samuel to Sam, and Bettina/Tina quite liked it. Alice didn't. When Bettina's friends or teachers used her shortened name Alice would smile and say, 'I don't know a Tina, I'm afraid. My daughter's name is much more beautiful, and unusual, like my daughter herself.' Teenaged Tina would cringe and her mother would wink and smile and say, well, if you stuck with the name you were given I wouldn't be forced to embarrass you, sweet-heart. She'd go back now, in a heartbeat, and please her mother by using her name – or at least she would wink and smile back, instead of sulking off to her room, and leaving it as late as she could before going down for tea.

Still, Bettina embraces 'Bettina' now, and she has told her mother so. She'd like to think that Alice understands, and sees loyalty as well as expediency in her decision. There was a time when she'd considered changing her name altogether. She'd even picked out a shortlist of not-unusual, serviceable names that she thought suited her – Annie, Karen, Claire – but when it came to it, something stopped her. The happy parts of the past, perhaps.

Bettina wishes she'd had the courage, or the insight,

to duck out of the interview – out of the whole Throckton Business Awards. But then she has never been brave. She is happiest out of the way, in the kitchen, mixing and measuring, surrounded by yeasty earthy smells and sweet, plump tastes. Publicity makes her nervous, sitting in her guts like dough left out in the cold. She's afraid that the article will be seen by someone she doesn't want to see it. She tries hard enough not to brood about the past: she cannot bear the thought of it confronting her.

She supposes she must have thought that she would manage it better than this. After all, Verity – who is now wittering merrily about her figure and how much one of her granddaughters likes baking, although eating her scones is a labour of love – is, plainly, no threat to Bettina. Yet her palms are cold and her hairline prickles, and she could, so very easily, cry.

This interview won't even be the end of it. If Adventures in Bread turns out to be one of the three businesses with the most votes, Bettina will have to stand on the rickety stage at the Throckton Spring Fête in May for the awards ceremony, smiling whether she wins or loses. She hates the thought of her quiet, busy-enough life being disrupted, and she cannot bear the idea that she will have to look at her picture in the newspaper, even if it is only the *Throckton Warbler*. The thought of it makes her shake. She puts down her cup and holds her hands in her lap, each steadying the other.

She focuses on Verity. This woman isn't going to do her any harm, despite the way her instincts are rearing up and warning her of danger. Breathe, breathe, she tells herself. 'Bettina it is, then,' she says. 'I'm afraid I always want to shorten names because it's impossible to shorten mine.' She smiles at Bettina.

'I suppose not,' she says.

'I'm tempted to lick my plate,' Verity says, and smiles again. Instead she dampens her finger with her tongue and uses her fingertip to collect the last crumbs. 'I'm surprised that you don't have more cakes. When they're so good, I mean.'

'Well, I see Adventures in Bread as being primarily about bread,' Bettina says, her words coming fast, 'and everything I sell is made on the premises. But of course I wanted to sell cakes too, so I have a dozen tried-and-tested cakes and I bake three of them every day. My customers know that they will get a small choice of fresh cakes alongside the breads. They seem quite happy with that. And when people come to the café they can't resist the toasters.' The refitted café is everything Bettina hoped it would be.

'And where do you get your ideas for breads from?'

'Well,' Bettina says, 'I've always liked the thought that, if bread can be the thing that you put interesting flavours on, there's no reason that it can't also be the thing you put interesting flavours in.' To her surprise, she finds that she is starting to feel lighter, supported well by this familiar ground. She is answering questions that she answers in the shop, a couple of times a week, more often when the tourist season is in full swing and the hotel and the holiday cottages are bursting with people new to Throckton who come in exclaiming over the smell, the look of the place, and want to know more about it. This journalist, she tells herself, is just a customer with a notebook, really. And a rather nice one, at that. She makes the effort to slow and steady her voice. 'You eat bread with meat and cheese, but also with jam and honey,' Bettina continues, then pauses and waits for Verity, who is nodding and scribbling, to catch up, 'so I try to make breads that incorporate some of those tastes, which are adventurous. Hence the name of the shop.'

Verity smiles. 'But I notice that you also cater to those with more traditional tastes?'

'Of course,' Bettina replies, 'those people are my bread-and-butter, if you'll pardon the pun.' Verity laughs; Bettina smiles – perhaps she can play this game, after all – and continues, 'My best-selling loaves are the plainest, but some of the others have what you might call a cult following. And I have a suggestion box, where customers can suggest a bread and I'll do my best to make it. That's how my Scarborough Fair loaf came about.' Every time Bettina takes these aromatic cobs from the oven, she feels as proud and glad as she's ever been. In this life, at least. 'Parsley, sage, rosemary and thyme,' she adds, although she suspects it's unnecessary.

'I've tried that, it's lovely,' Verity says, nodding, 'not very local, though – and you're not local, either? I'd like to emphasize the Throckton angle, if there is one.'

'No, I'm not local,' Bettina says. 'I grew up in the south-east of England, in a little town no one's ever heard of, about a hundred miles from here, and I trained in France, mostly small boulangeries, where I learned everything I could about breadmaking.' And that, she thinks, is all you're getting of my past. 'I moved back to the UK two years ago, and soon afterwards I started to look for a suitable place to start my own bakery. Throckton is that place. The business is one hundred per cent local. I use local water and flour to make my own yeast, I use Throckton people's suggestions for my breads. Even the water makes a difference to the finished loaf, so the bread I make here I truly couldn't make any-where else. I consider myself to be a Throckton person now. I have no plans to be anywhere else.' Bettina realizes her voice has risen, quailed. She stops talking, hopes that her tone has gone unnoticed.

It looks as though it has. Verity is flicking back through her notes, several pages of what Bettina thinks will make very dull reading. Verity looks up with a smile. 'I think I have everything I need. Thank you for your time, Bettina.' She pronounces the name carefully, as Bettina had explained it, which makes her interviewee give a small, real smile. 'I appreciate that you're busy.'

'Not at all,' Bettina says. 'Why don't we go downstairs, and I can show you around and make you up a hamper? I'll be doing a bread-tasting in a little while, too, and you'd be very welcome to join in.'

'I'd love to, but I have to get back,' Verity says apologetically, 'though I'll take the hamper, if I may – it will go down very well at the office, I'm sure.'

'Of course.' On their way towards the door of the flat – just as Bettina is catching her breath and thinking that the worst is over – Verity stops at a bronze sculpture, not even ten inches high. It's a horse. He looks exactly the way he used to look when Bettina called his name

41

– alert, ears sharp, sense of readiness perfect in every line and curve. Her heart quickens as Verity picks it up. 'How beautiful this is,' she says.

'Yes,' Bettina says. There needs to be a better word than beautiful, really. When she feels the cool bronze in her hands, it's as though she can also feel the firm, true muscle of a horse's croup under her fingers, and smell the warm leather of a well-used saddle. It's strange how a tiny lump of metal can act as a conduit to her younger self, making her remember – whether she wants to or not – the thrill of letting an animal bred for speed run as fast as he wants to. Sometimes, her heart leaps up the way it used to when her mount cleared a fence and they were airborne; sometimes she feels sick with longing. Rufus has admired the bronze too. She had told him that she was given it as a gift and braced herself for further questions, but he'd just said, 'How lovely,' and put it down again. It doesn't look as though Verity will move on so easily, though. It's only the fact that Bettina doesn't know whether to panic or cry that stops her from doing either. She thinks about her breath, the way a nurse taught her to, long ago: feels it pass, cool, into her nostrils, notices how it's a little bit warmer as it leaves her body.

'My husband deals in art,' Verity says, 'and you can't help but get an eye for good things. Do you know who made this?' She's turning it over, looking for the maker's mark. Bettina's fingers twitch, as she quells the urge to snatch the bronze back.

'No, I'm afraid not,' Bettina says. 'It was a gift. A long time ago.'

'Well, it's beautiful,' Verity says, holding it at arm's length to take in the wholeness rather than the detail, and so giving Bettina the opportunity to take it back into her own hands, 'so lifelike. My daughter-in-law is a bit of a horsewoman, her house is full of paintings and photographs and ornaments and whatnot, but it's not often that I've seen something so . . .' Her words run out, and Bettina wants to agree, but she can't speak. She knows exactly what Verity means. This little statue could be breathing. It's the one thing in the flat that she cares deeply about, and one of only two mementoes from her past that she's allowed herself to keep. Her leg is throbbing again as she makes her way down the stairs. She feels her foot start to drag across the kitchen floor, as she explains her processes and introduces Verity to Simon, her baker.

For once, it's a relief for Bettina to throw herself into the tasting; what she usually dreads makes her feel safe by virtue of being at least familiar. From there it's not long until the lunchtime rush begins – Angie makes the sandwiches, while Bettina deals with everything else. At two-thirty Angie leaves, and at three-thirty Josh arrives from college to do his afternoon shift until five. Bettina heads for the kitchen once Josh is in the shop, and shapes the loaves that will prove overnight and go into the oven tomorrow morning, in the half-light.

Tomorrow is croissant day at Adventures in Bread, so she puts the ingredients for the dough into the mixer, and while the hook slowly turns the flour, leaven and water to something smooth and stretchy, she beats the butter flat with a rolling pin and puts it into the fridge.

In the morning she will roll the dough, lay the butter on to it, fold dough around butter, then start rolling, rolling, rolling it flat, doing the whole thing again, until the dough is the right colour and has the right give and all that there is to do then is to cut it into triangles, roll the triangles into crescents and bake them. She wonders how many croissants she has made over the years. People always exclaim how light they are, how flaky and soft. Well, she always says, I did more than ten years in French bakeries, so if I couldn't make a decent croissant I'd be in trouble.

Bettina's times alone in her kitchen – first thing in the morning, before Simon comes in, then after Josh arrives in the afternoon – are her favourite parts of any day, a safe, warm space that nurtures her. Today, though, there's no magic and no healing as she works. Her leg aches and so does her head. Her heart and lungs seem too small, so that there's no finding evenness of breath. The skin on her temples feels stretched. Her head is stuffed with heaviness; she hasn't eaten anything since the bite of coffee cake, so her stomach is an acidic lightness that aches. Her mind goes back to all the parts of the past that she usually makes such an effort to keep it away from. A day that began as the new, happier, more settled normal for Bettina has thrown her back into the past. If she worked for anyone else, she would make an excuse, hand in her notice and pack her bag tonight. Tomorrow she would find a place that had none of today's feelings in it and she would start again. But all she can do is go upstairs, move the bronze to the bedroom, close the curtains, and hope that the world will leave her alone.

* * *

It does. After two quiet days, working in the kitchen and going straight to bed at the end of the day, Bettina feels better: or, at least, her sense of perspective has returned. She has been remembering the times at the beginning of her recovery, when anything and everything could send her spinning off into chaos and despair; the feelings triggered by Verity were no more than a pale echo of those times. Of course, she has told herself when she's been awake and working in the morning, there will be bad days. The fact that you haven't had a bad day in a long time is, really, a good thing.

On the third day, Rufus is her first customer. He comes bearing gifts – two pewter planters, brimming with lavender.

'I was going to bring you flowers,' he says, 'but I remembered what you said. I thought you would like living things.'

'Thank you,' Bettina says. She feels awkward; she threw the peonies away last night.

'I'm learning,' Rufus says, with a smile.

'I'm grateful,' Bettina says, and she is: she knows that she doesn't deserve such consideration in view of her verging-on-rudeness. She reminds herself of how lucky she is to have someone like Rufus to be so thoughtful and full of care for her. She can sense that Angie is all agog behind her, as she kisses Rufus on both cheeks. When Angie first discovered that Bettina and Rufus were having what she insists on referring to as 'a thing', she had spent several mornings in the shop regaling Bettina with the complex history of Rufus's love life and the

45

reasons why he ended up living in a flat above a restaurant while his ex-wife is happily ensconced in the former matrimonial home with a policeman. Bettina had half listened – she'd already had versions of the story and its backdrop, the most shocking thing that had happened in Throckton for many years – but refused to join in the gossip, and so Angie had eventually given up. Bettina knows that all Angie's friends will know about Rufus's gifts before the week is out. Although she'd like to think that they cared as little for gossip as she did, she's lived in enough small communities of one sort or another to know better. 'You have to decide whether you care more about what other people think, or what you think,' her father had said to her once, when she had been teased at school by people who had seen her mother in a play. He'd wrapped her into a hug as he'd said it, and she'd known that he was right. He was still right, later, when it got more difficult: when the know-ledge that she and the people she loved were being talked about had made her sick to her heart. But, she reminds herself, a little bit of chatter about some lavender is not going to do her any harm. Not every-thing about the past has to colour the present.

Rufus looks as smart and dapper as always. Bettina likes his hands – his fingers are long, and his nails clean and cared for. His eyes are the unrepentant blue of the first July cornflowers and his hair is short and a little grey, something that he doesn't trouble to hide. She thinks what she likes best about him is his confidence. He never doubts himself, or if he does, he doesn't show it. He expects to be successful, and he is. Bettina cannot imagine him lying in bed at night, awake, wondering about the places in his life where he went wrong, worrying about the future.

He takes half a dozen croissants. 'I guess these are for Kate and Daisy?' Bettina asks as she hands them over.

'Yes,' he says, 'I just called. I'm dropping them in on my way to work.'

'Would you like to meet in the restaurant, later,' Bettina asks, 'about seven?'

'That would be lovely.' Rufus positively beams. He has good teeth, too.

'Great,' Bettina says, 'and thank you again.' Already she is wondering what a sweet lavender loaf would taste like. It would be easy enough to make a lavender cake – unrepentantly sweet and finished with orange drizzle and brown sugar crystals – but a bread would be better, for lavender. She imagines the semi-sour rind on her tongue while the sweet scent fills her nose. It will be a grown-up loaf, good with cheese: the sort of thing that Rufus would like. She might talk to him about it later. She promises to text him to confirm their meeting for dinner, and waves him off to see his daughter and granddaughter.

'Morning, Rufus,' Richenda says, when she lets him in, 'are they croissants? You'll be popular.' She's wearing a plain blue dress that grazes the top of her ankles. There's a pashmina that he remembers buying her thrown around her shoulders, fastened with a silver brooch he doesn't recognize. She smiles in welcome, as usual. It's as though he is a visiting neighbour. He wishes he could feel the same way. Having to knock on his own front door still pinches at his guts.

'Good morning,' he says. He doesn't respond to her remark about popularity, as he can't always tell if she's being sarcastic or not. Of late, the shrewishness he associates with her has been replaced by a confidence that is both galling and sexy.

To begin with, on Rufus's morning drop-ins on Kate and Daisy, who live in the family home with his ex-wife, Rufus had gained great satisfaction from seeing his wife's lover standing, unshaven, in the kitchen, and felt all of the confidence and superiority provided by his good tailoring and freedom from his unhappy marriage. But he had got his comeuppance: there came the time when he arrived unannounced to find Richenda barefoot in an eau-de-nil satin dressing gown that Rufus had never seen before. She had been all politeness to him, and had told him the latest news of Kate and Daisy, who were still asleep. And she had been leaning against Blake as she talked, her lover's hand curving the side of her waist, and Rufus had realized that, maybe, the reason his marriage was unhappy was not because he had married the wrong woman but that he had treated her badly. If he had been more like Blake, more considerate, more kind, perhaps he and Richenda would have been happier. And he had known that he was the one at a disadvantage, gold cufflinks or not. Since then, he has always called ahead.

Not that he regrets their divorce. Not really, not now; although on some days he wonders how he could have been stupid enough to think that moving out was a good idea, on others he blames himself for not making more effort to fix things way earlier. He can admit that the speed with which Richenda has moved on to a new relationship galls him. He wasn't sure why he'd been surprised when she asked him to leave. Their marriage had been long but unhappy, his infidelities frequent and intense, their relationship barely more than a mostly civil habit.

And then the bombshell had struck. Their daughter, Kate, eighteen at the time, was headed for Oxford one minute, then pregnant the next, in the worst circumstances imaginable. The baby's father, Mike, was a married policeman who drowned pulling her out of a lake before anyone knew about the baby. So he and Richenda had struggled on for the sake of Kate, but before baby Daisy was six months old his wife had taken him to one side and said, quite matter-of-factly, that she thought he should go. He was no help with the baby, and having Caroline drop him off at the end of the road rather than outside the door didn't actually count as discretion. Caroline had been a fling, a respite from their complicated life at the time, little more; she'd been, he thinks, just part of his habit of faithlessness. And his marriage had been like the sky in the morning, so unremarkably present that he had never bothered to wonder how the world would look if it wasn't there.

Rufus thinks now that if he'd had time to see it coming, he'd have been able to do things differently. Richenda had threatened to leave him so often that he hadn't taken it seriously. It had always been a possibility, but, like winning the lottery, not a possibility to be planned for. They were all tired by baby Daisy's crying and worried about her future. They seemed to be scrabbling through one day to the next. He did, anyway. Richenda had lost no time in moving on. He remembers going to collect the rest of his clothes, a couple of months after he moved out, just after he had moved into the flat, and feeling the shock of seeing a glass of water on each of the tables at either side of what had been the marital bed. He hadn't said anything to Richenda, but she'd read him like a book. 'I'm in a new relationship, Rufus,' she'd said, 'and it's very early days, and it's Blake, and it didn't start until after you left, and you cannot possibly object.' He'd opened his mouth, but before he'd had a chance to say as much as a word, she'd held up her hand and said, 'Actually, Rufus, not only do you not get to object, but you don't get to say anything about it at all.'

It was one of the few times that he had cried. He'd gone back to the flat and sobbed with shame and a belated, useless guilt. He had tried to resent Blake, to be furious with him, and it had been easy in the brandy-soaked darkness of 2am, but harder in the morning, through a hangover, with all of his faults staring at him from the bathroom mirror.

And now there is Bettina, who makes his life so much brighter. He has just extended his lease again so that he can stay in her eyeline, although if she knew this she would be horrified. There are better flats he could rent, closer to work, quieter, flats where the bathroom skirting boards weren't like the ones that annoyed him every morning, because they were made of plastic and not even properly attached. He will build his own house, one day. But he knows that his only chance of having a real relationship with Bettina is to be close, to barely move, to be the man in the garden who sits in silence, day after day, until, one morning, the song thrush lands on the arm he has draped so casually along the back of the bench.

But that is for later. Today is today and the immediate challenge is the discomfort he still feels around his ex-wife. Sometimes he wonders whether telling Richenda about the wave of regret that swelled through his life when they divorced would make a difference. But at worst, she would be dismissive, at best, sympathetic: and as Rufus doesn't want to be dismissed or sympathized with by Richenda, he keeps quiet. He follows her into the open-plan living and dining room that had been three rooms until he had had the walls between them taken down.

'Morning, Blake,' he says to the man sitting in his place. It pleases him to be civil, because it fits with his idea of himself as a mature man who has moved on – and because he suspects it annoys Richenda no end. One day, he knows, he will give up this pettiness: he knows that he's being petty. One day. But not yet. Perhaps when he has built his house, or when he and Bettina are really a couple.

He had taken today off work to drive Kate and Daisy to Daisy's appointment at the cystic fibrosis clinic. Then the appointment had to be moved, but Rufus was booked on a client visit on the new appointment day. So after much overly polite textual to-ing and fro-ing between himself and his ex-wife, they had agreed that

Richenda would move a meeting of her own so that she could take charge of transport to the hospital, but Rufus would take his day off anyway and take Kate and Daisy out on the original date. They were going to the soft-play centre and then out to lunch. That was the plan, anyway.

But then Kate comes downstairs in her pyjamas and says, blearily, 'Sorry, Dad, we had a terrible night. We're running a bit late.' The most obvious sign of Daisy's cystic fibrosis is the cough that convulses her little trunk as her lungs try, and fail, to clear the too-thick mucus that her body makes. She was on antibiotics for most of the winter, including three weeks in hospital on a drip while her lungs fought an infection that made her pale and subdued. She had seemed stronger for a while, all the physiotherapy and exercise starting to take effect, and then she had picked up a spring cold from some-where, and the great hacking horror of a cough that belonged in a body much bigger and more broken than a two-year-old's had come back with a vengeance.

Kate goes to have 'a quick shower and wash her hair' – this means a wait of forty-five minutes at least, Rufus knows – leaving him with Richenda and Blake. And Blake is in his civvies, which means he isn't likely to be going to work. Rufus curses shift patterns and prepares to stretch fifteen minutes' worth of uncomfortable chit-chat to fill three-quarters of an hour. Either that or he could offer to take Beetle, Kate's beagle, for a walk. But Beetle is flat out with Hope, Blake's greyhound, in the puddle of sunlight by the doors that lead on to the garden. Rufus can't take Beetle without offering to take

Hope too, and he knows his limits. Picking up after his ex-wife's lover's dog is way beyond them.

As he rounds the end of the sofa, Rufus sees that Richenda is working, laptop on lap, legs stretched out and toes tucked under Blake's thigh. Blake is holding a sleeping Daisy. Of all of them, he seems to be the one with the magic touch where Daisy is concerned. She will abandon everything else – including her mother – when Blake is in the room, climbing up on to his lap with a book. She will nuzzle into his body and go to sleep, and look more relaxed than she seems to with anyone except Kate. She seems to sleep longer in Blake's arms, so after a fractious night he will be the one to hold her while Kate sleeps, or tries to catch up on her Open University course.

Rufus isn't good with babies, but he wants to be a good grandfather, and a good father too. So he has assigned himself practical roles. He's a driver, arranger of appointments, financial provider. He isn't really hands-on, but he's happy that no one seems to expect him to be, and that, as far as Daisy is concerned at least, they can all appreciate each other's efforts.

Every time he's presented with the reality of Daisy, Rufus is a little bit taken aback by her loveliness. Before he sits, he takes a moment to absorb her as she is now, pale white-blonde curls and smooth even skin, pale golden eyelashes and eyelids so fine that Rufus can see the blue-green veins in them. Her eyes, when she opens them, will show themselves to be the same colour as her mother's, ice-blue or grey depending on the light, huge in her face. Kate likes to dress her daughter in brightly coloured dresses and the pastel cardigans that Patricia, Daisy's paternal grandmother, knits. Today, she is also wearing striped tights and a pair of navy leather shoes with pink gingham hearts on the top. Rufus remembers buying them. In the shoe shop, Kate had led Daisy by the hand to see how she walked in them, then said, 'Go find Pops' (the least-worst grandfather name that Rufus could find), and ten seconds later, there had been a laughing, stumbling toddler at his knee.

'She gets lovelier,' he says.

Richenda looks up. She seems a little bit startled. Rufus wonders whether he has said such a thing, unbidden, before, and braces himself for Richenda to tell him, if he hasn't. But she just smiles, and says, 'Yes.'

Blake says, 'She sure does.'

There's a moment. A good moment. A moment of: none of us is quite sure how we are making this work, but we are, and we can be glad of that, despite all the reasons, good reasons, there are to dislike each other and to wish that we weren't all gathered around this sofa.

It passes. Richenda is all business again. 'If you don't mind, Rufus,' she says, indicating her laptop, 'I need to finish this.'

'Of course not,' Rufus says.

'Why don't you make yourself a coffee?'

Kate won't be anywhere near the shower yet. He may as well. He nods.

'Would either of you like one?'

'Thank you,' says Richenda.

'If you don't mind,' Blake says.

54

I will do my best not to mind, Rufus thinks as he walks into the kitchen. There's a coffee-pod machine, which wasn't here the last time he came, and new mugs, floral ones, a bright contrast to the grey and cream and moss-green ceramics that he and Richenda had always used. The fridge is now covered in all sorts of family paraphernalia. There's a swimming certificate for Daisy, a page of Waitrose coupons, a shopping list. And there are photographs: Daisy, Daisy and Kate, Daisy and Beetle, Daisy and Kate and Beetle, Daisy and Kate and Richenda, Richenda and Blake, Richenda and Blake and Daisy. Swings, parks, ice creams. The London Eye. Rufus realizes that he has no photographs on display in his flat. The one of Kate in his office is years out of date, a studio portrait of her at sixteen. He resolves to bring his digital SLR with him the next time he takes Kate and Daisy somewhere, and start making a photographic record of his own. He can photograph Bettina, too; it can be a reason to get her away from her flat or his, and take them both out into the world. He imagines them standing outside a cathedral, or in a park, having taken a day trip one Sunday. He'll ask a stranger to take a photo, and they'll both smile, and Rufus will have a tiny anchor to keep him steady on the waves of his new life.

Rufus hasn't heard Richenda come into the kitchen. He's forgotten how she goes barefoot everywhere. 'Let me know if you want copies of any of them,' she says. 'I came to show you how the coffee machine works.'

'I've got one at the office,' Rufus says.

'Of course,' Richenda replies, as though this has slipped her mind, although she was never a regular at

55

the office, not even when they were married. Rufus feels humoured. He takes mugs that he recognizes from the shelf, leaving the new ones where they are.

Kate is ready an hour and twenty minutes after Rufus arrived to collect her. Daisy has slept for most of that time, and Rufus read the *Throckton Warbler* from cover to cover once the conversation ran out. They switch their plans around and go to lunch first, where Kate is quiet and bleary, spending more time coaxing Daisy into eating than eating herself. Then they go on to the soft play, where all Daisy wants to do is to sit in the ball pool with her grandfather, who feels both honoured and humiliated. Kate drinks tea and reads a book from the sidelines, and so Rufus doesn't get the thing that he really misses – the conversations with his daughter. Though it had been tempting to see Kate's accidental pregnancy as a disaster, Rufus knows that he still has a child he can be proud of. There never seems to be a good time to tell her just how very impressed he is with the way she champions Daisy's well-being, and admires her pragmatic change of direction from a degree in geography at Oxford to an open degree at the Open University.

On the way back to Throckton, Kate and Daisy both fall asleep in the car. The traffic is slow and ill-tempered. Rufus doesn't dare put the radio on for fear of waking his two charges.

'Sorry for being such lousy company, Dad,' Kate says when they get back. They are standing on the pavement, putting off the moment when they need to disturb the sleeping toddler. 'I just had such a rough night.'

'What did the hospital say about the cough?' In the same way that Rufus often forgets how lovely Daisy is, he also forgets the relentless hacking cough that has been the backdrop to their day. It's awful to listen to, and is made worse, somehow, because Daisy barely notices it herself.

'We're going to see what the antibiotics do.' Kate sighs and rakes her hand through her hair. 'It's not really a worry as long as everything else is OK and it doesn't get any worse. I'm keeping an eye. And I've asked to see the physiotherapist again, before her next clinic. We need to see what else we can try.'

'Well, if you need lifts or anything just let me know.'

'Thanks, Dad.' Kate puts her hand on his arm. He pulls her to him; they are the same height, now, but she hugs him the same way that she always did, sudden and tight.

'You're doing a great job,' he says.

'Thanks,' she says, 'I try.'

'I know you do.' Rufus manages to manoeuvre Daisy out of the car seat without waking her. She lies against his chest, heavier sleeping than waking.

'Are you coming in?' Kate asks.

'I'd better not,' Rufus says. 'I think your mother and Blake and I have probably seen enough of each other for one day.'

'OK. Thanks for a nice day,' Kate says, and kisses his cheek as she takes Daisy, who slumbers on, settling her cheek against her mother's shoulder with a snuffling yawn. She coughs, and both adults watch to see if she'll wake: Rufus puts his hand on her back and feels the little ribcage buck and shudder. Daisy sleeps on.

'I'm glad you enjoyed it,' Rufus says. Blake opens the front door as Kate walks up the path. Rufus heads for home, for a bath, for dinner with Bettina, for the new life that isn't, yet, all that he had hoped it would be.

Bettina is at their usual table in the Italian restaurant, by the fireplace filled with a bundle of fairy lights. There's a lamp on the end of the fireplace that means the light is good enough to read by if she's on her own, which is why she always chose it, to begin with, and now it's 'their' table by default. She stands when she sees Rufus; leans; kisses him on both cheeks, sits, and puts her book – one of her many tomes about breadmaking – under her chair. She watches him as he takes off his jacket and hangs it, carefully, over the back of his seat. The front of his shirt is a little crumpled. She likes him looking less than pressed, but has the sense not to say so. 'How was your day?' she asks.

'Tiring.' Rufus watches her as she settles down again. Her eyes are really beautiful, and he knows how her hair feels under his hands: springy, strong. He catches himself thinking: I suppose, if I'm middle-aged, my girl-friends are going to be older, too.

'Me too,' Bettina smiles, 'but nothing new there.' She pours him a glass of wine. His bathwater had taken an age to run hot, he'd nicked himself shaving, he'd spent fifteen minutes on the phone calming an irate client because, as he'd said to his office manager afterwards, it seemed that he couldn't even take one day off without everything going to hell in a handcart.

'It's not a competition.'

'What?'

'It's not a competition to see who had the most tiring day.'

'I know that, Rufus.' Bettina is smiling at him still, bemused, and he realizes that she is puzzled by his behaviour because she's never seen him like this before. He takes a deep breath, and resolves to be the Rufus that Bettina recognizes. Because he really wants to be that man.

Bettina gives him just enough to make him long for her, but not quite enough to satisfy him. And so Rufus has remembered what potential there is in love. Something more fixed between them would seem, to Rufus, to be a deeply desirable and happy arrangement. At their ages, a twelve-year gap is nothing to write home about: Bettina is thirty-five, Rufus is forty-seven, but their intelligence, their quiet ambition makes them equals. Adventures in Bread might not yet have the scope or reputation of Light and Shade, Rufus's well-established architectural practice, but there's no reason why it shouldn't, in their shared future. They would make a well-matched, happy couple, he is sure. Tonight, he's frustrated that she can't see it. Tonight, his feet are cold and his arm is cramping as he waits on the bench for the indifferent song thrush, whose music might not, after all, be as sweet as he's hoped.

A prosciutto and artichoke pizza and a house salad later, Bettina asks, 'Do you want to come back with me?' and he agrees, despite himself. They get the bill, which they split, scrupulously, down the middle – Bettina will never hear of anything else. She leads the way out of the restaurant and down the alley that separates the two buildings, then opens her own door.

'Coffee?' she asks when they are upstairs. She makes it in a silver percolator on the hob. It's good coffee, for sure, but it keeps Rufus awake.

'No, thank you,' he says, 'I'll be awake all night. I don't know how you drink it so late.'

She smiles. 'All bakers are the same,' she says. 'We work such crazy hours that we do everything we can to stay awake, and nothing stops us from sleeping. Do you want something else?' She opens cupboards, curiously, as though she doesn't live here. 'Peppermint tea? Brandy? I don't know how old either are. I don't know if it matters. Do they go off?'

He finds himself smiling, properly, at her efforts to make him happy. Decides to push it, just a little. 'Am I staying?' he asks.

'I'd like you to,' she says. His heart preens: at last! But then he realizes how easily she's said it, and so he knows that he's been misunderstood.

The first time Bettina had invited him into her bed, two things had surprised Rufus. The first was that she'd done it at all: she didn't really flirt, and so he hadn't thought it was going to happen, right up until the moment she had taken him by the hand, led him to her bedroom and said, 'I haven't misread you, have I?' And the second was being sent home afterwards. He'd assumed that he would stay, sleep, wake with her. But no: 'I have to be up early, Rufus, I'd only disturb you when I got out of bed,' she had said firmly. While he dressed, she had put on a charcoal-grey towelling dressing gown with a silk paisley lining that had seen better days, and somehow was all the sexier for it. Her feet, bare on the polished floorboards, had looked all the more naked next to his reluctant shoes as she had walked him to the door. 'You won't disturb me,' he had said, aiming for nonchalance but hitting something closer to pleading, and she had smiled, and kissed his cheek, and said, 'I'll see you soon. Thank you.' And so it has been ever since: friendship, yes, affection, yes, sex, yes, sleeping, no.

'I meant,' Rufus says, 'I'd like to spend the night here. Sleep.'

Bettina, standing over her coffee, tenses for just a second before she looks at him and says, 'I've told you. I'd disturb you. I get up at four.'

'I don't mind,' Rufus says doggedly. 'I'll go back to my flat at four. Or I'll go back to sleep and let myself out.'

The coffee is ready. She pours it into a mug, broader than it is tall. Rufus knows that she will leave it until it's almost cold then drink it, black, in one go. He wonders if she ever thinks about how he drinks his coffee, although he knows that she doesn't. He tries to make himself stop doing this before it's too late. He's been in enough tricky relationships to recognize this territory, this conversation. God knows, he's often stood where Bettina is, trying to remain just committed enough without actually committing to anything.

'Why does it matter so much?' she asks quietly, sitting next to him, not touching him, not looking at him. 'The sleeping?'

'Why does it matter so much to you that I don't stay?' he asks. His voice isn't as quiet as he thought it would be, and he tries a joke to soften the effect: 'Do you snore? I've slept next to people who snore before.'

She sounds annoyed when she responds, 'I don't, it's not that.'

'Well, perhaps you should tell me what it is,' Rufus says, because he's too tired to be patient any more, 'because this isn't really fair, Bettina.'

'Fair?' She repeats the word, her whole face a question mark. 'Are we not old enough to know that life isn't fair?'

Her hand is resting on her thigh and he puts his on top of it. She doesn't take it away, at least.

'Life might not be fair,' he says, 'but we can be, can't we?'

'I am being fair,' she says, not looking at him. 'You asked to stay. I said no. I don't see what's unfair in that.'

'No,' Rufus says. His voice is matching hers in sharpness now. 'I don't suppose you do.'

She looks at his hand as she says, 'Rufus, I did a real relationship once, and I did it badly. Very badly. I promised myself that I wouldn't do it again.' The irritation has gone, not just from her voice but from the lines of her body; she's all sadness.

'We've all felt like that,' Rufus says. He knows he can't compete with an unspecified past. But he can appeal to her logical side.

'No, really,' she says, 'I can't be your girlfriend, and I'm afraid that's what you want. I like you, Rufus. I like that you're clever, and you're kind, and I can see what an effort you make. Believe it or not, I'm closer to you now than I have been to anyone for a very long time. But I'm afraid that if you're hoping for more—' She shakes her head. She hasn't looked at him while she's been speaking, her eyes fixed ahead.

'It's not just the sleeping,' Rufus says. His irritation has dissolved like mist over morning water; he can see more clearly now, to the bottom of the lake. He might be a better man than he used to be, but he's not the man he'd like to think he is, either. Suddenly he's tired. Suddenly the smell of the coffee is too strong, the scent of Bettina's rose perfume, more noticeable now that she's next to him, makes him want to sneeze. But he tries to explain: 'I know almost nothing about you,' he says.

He knows that her mother, who has dementia, is in a care home. He knows that Bettina worked in France for a long time, until her father's death and mother's illness brought her back. He knows that she has scarring across her hips, up the side of her ribcage and down her thigh; when she'd seen him looking at the scars, she'd asked him not to ask her about them, and he never has. Not that she seems embarrassed by them. She is gloriously unselfconscious about her body, her unshaven legs and armpits and her willingness to walk naked from bedroom to bathroom, lie naked on top of her bed or his, never scrabbling for cover, never doing anything but let her body be itself. She has strong shoulders, a waist that he imagines hasn't grown since she became an adult, and a spine whose vertebrae bump-bump-bump when his fingers run down them, as though he is driving over cat's eyes in the road. Rufus wonders about trying to tell her that how she behaves with him, physically – the nakedness, yes, but also the way she knows what pleases her body and how to get it – is completely at odds with her closed-down, shut-off emotional self. But he doesn't quite dare: or rather, he doesn't trust his tiredness, his own need, not to get in the way.

Bettina is tired, too. When she had texted him to confirm their meeting she'd known almost immediately that she shouldn't have, because it was less about wanting to see him and more about not wanting to be alone. And now look where they are. She shakes her head, as though that will make her thoughts settle and clear. She can see how she must look from Rufus's perspective: inconsistent, wanting it all on her own terms.

The difficulty of every damn thing in Bettina's life wells up inside her. She wants things to be fair, though, even if they aren't, so she tries: 'You know more about me than anyone has, for – a long time,' she says. She feels him lean towards her, and realizes that her voice must be hard to hear, as she is looking away from him as she speaks. She moves her head a little closer. There are unshed tears in her voice. 'Honestly, Rufus,' she adds, 'what I give you is the best I can do. All I can do. I'm sorry if it's not enough—'

'So much seems to be off-limits,' he says. He's quieter now, too.

'It's not off-limits,' she says, and then wishes that she hasn't because she feels him take in a breath, and realizes she's offered hope, 'it's more that that part of me doesn't exist. What you've seen of me: that's what there is. That's all.'

He is quiet; she decides not to look, in case she cries, or in case he wants to say more about this, when she really has nothing more to say.

He sighs, and waits. Then: 'I think I'll go,' he says.

'Of course,' Bettina replies, and she leans towards him and puts her head on his shoulder for a moment, before getting up. As she looks down at him she sees how disappointed he looks and realizes that he had been hoping she would ask him to stay. She's so tired. She drinks her coffee as she waits for him to put his jacket on, which he does, slowly, as befits the man who just put all of his winnings on red and watched the ball fall on black.

'I'll see you,' she says.

'Yes,' he says. He reaches for her hand and she's ready for another protest, or to be told how badly she's behaving. She braces. But Rufus surprises her. He says, 'Whatever you think, you're allowed to be happy. And you aren't too badly damaged to try. Remember that.' She nods, although she seems to be shaking her head at the same time.

'Thank you,' she gets out. And she means it. When she goes to bed her hands and feet are cold, even though the flat above the bakery is always warm.

Part Two: Missingham, 1994–1997

TINA RANDOLPH STARTS helping out at the stables at the age of fourteen, when she realizes that a room full of horse posters and a weekly riding lesson is as close as her parents are going to be able to get her to a horse of her own. After a cautious enquiry of one of the friendlier grooms as to whether she would be welcome, she began turning up and making herself useful: lugging bales, sweeping down the yard, making tea, cleaning tack. She leaves the house while her parents and brother are still sleeping, and she walks the half-mile to the stables that sit among the hills above the quiet village of Missingham, and she works, quietly, with the clatter and hum of the yard around her. Two hours later, she returns in time to shower and get ready for school.

To begin with, her parents had tried to make her do this only two or three days a week, afraid for their daughter's school results and sleep. After all, Tina's twin brother Sam had to be dragged from his bed every morning, and he was only two minutes younger than his sister; it seemed impossible that she could really be so different in her needs. But Tina proved that she could keep up with her homework. She hovered around the middle of the class in test rankings, as she always had. Sam, on the other hand, was expected to be top at everything because he was So Very Bright. The phrase was whispered between adults, like a holy secret.

'I wish I was the practical one,' Sam would moan as Tina finished her homework a good couple of hours before he did, 'then I wouldn't get all this extra stuff to do.'

'Don't forget you're Bound For Oxbridge, history boy,' Tina would reply, repeating another of the phrases that followed Sam wherever he went, 'and you love it, really.' She would pack up her books and go to bed early, tousling Sam's hair as she went – it was finer and longer than hers, pleasingly different in her fingers – because she knew how much it would annoy him.

She and her twin are different in almost every respect. Sam is broad where she is wiry, academic where she is practical, sociable and easy where she is self-conscious and awkward. They have long since got used to people pointing this out. 'The twins are so different' is not a whispered phrase, but one loudly broadcast at parents' evenings, family events and social gatherings everywhere. Their eyes are the only things that meet everyone's expectations of how well matched they should be. 'Of course we're different,' Tina mutters to Sam, 'we're basically a brother and sister who were born at the same time.' Sam is better at answering the twin questions than his sister. Yes, they are close. No, they can't read each other's minds. They suppose it is nice, but they've never really known anything different. What is good about it is feeling that there is always someone who, when it comes down to it, is completely on your side.

At sixteen, three days after her last GCSE, Tina starts her full-time job as a groom at the stables. Flood Farm is a riding school and livery, well thought of and busy, with stabling for twenty-six horses, six of which belong to the Flood family, the other twenty spots being for guest and liveried horses. There's always a waiting list for places, but Frederick and Fran Flood refuse to expand their operation, believing that getting to know all of their horses and riders is key to their success.

For the previous year Tina has been paid for her weekend work, which was mainly mucking out, grooming, and tacking up horses ready for lessons. Her anxious enquiry of Fred, about whether there might be any more work for her when she'd finished school, had been met with a clap on the shoulder and a laugh. Fred had said, we thought you'd never ask, Tina, we could do with more of your sort. Tina had been delighted, although she wasn't sure what 'your sort' might mean. Her mother said reliable, her father said hard-working, Sam said dedicated. Tina had joined in some of the chatter around the stable yard about the professional riders the Floods trained – words like 'brilliant' and 'brave' and 'unbelievable' used and overused – and tried not to be disappointed with the more prosaic words that applied to her. She knew that they were true, and that her dreams of being another Mary King, who she had idolized throughout her childhood, were not realistic. But when she mounts a horse, that doesn't matter. First there's the feeling of being high up in the world, then there's the moment of settling-in in the saddle, while she makes sure she's balanced and correctly placed, and she feels the horse shift and adjust to her weight. There are the smells of leather and flesh and heat and hay, which make a sweet whole that can only be horse. When they move, it's a wonder to Tina. She loves the sense of flow and purpose: she's fully aware that the horse is doing the work, but her whole world becomes reins and hoofbeats and whatever can be seen between two pricked, perfect ears.

Most of the staff at the yard live in. Tina, who lives at home and walks to work, is something of an outsider because she isn't sleeping and eating at work too, but she doesn't mind. She suspects that even if she was sharing one of the bedrooms in the old stables, she would still be an outsider to the likes of Stella-known-as-Ells, Theresa-known-as-Tippy and Fiona-known-as-Fudge, who are kind and welcoming enough, but grew up with their own ponies and wear jodhpurs every day while Tina has to save hers for her riding lessons. They are older, too, old enough to live easily away from home and smell faintly of cigarettes and talk about sex in a matter-of-fact way that makes Tina turn away to hide her pinking face. Bettina-known-as-Tina is the wrong way round, an odd name made into a commonplace one, but that seems to suit.

And anyway, Tina isn't there to make friends. She has Katrina, who had all the same lessons as her at school and lives two doors down, and she has her twin, who gives a daily tug to her unruly ponytail or points out her freckles or spots to remind her that she is half of a strong, solid unit, and that is all she really needs. Tina is at the

Flood stables for the times when she is first into the stalls in the morning, when the horses will look at her as she rakes her eyes up and down them, and she is amazed and delighted once more by the smell and the sheen and the gentle noises of greeting. Tina soon develops what she thinks of as her 'practical voice' – 'Morning, Blaze,' she calls cheerfully to the horse as she latches a door behind her, in the way that she hears the others do – but she still takes a few seconds to gaze and admire, a starstruck fan meeting her hero at the stage door.

Most of the horses will have been woken by the morning hubbub of the yard, and so a heavy head swings towards her as she unlatches the lower door and goes in. She will go straight to the horse's head and rub her palm down the long flat face, curl it under the muzzle where hair tickles her hands. The horse's lips, softer than they look, will move across her palm on the off-chance of a treat. Tina runs her hands over the horse's neck, over withers and back, feeling the warmth and the smooth-ness and the easy strength as the animal shifts its weight or starts to move. She's checking for anything unusual, any strange tensions or signs of sickness or damage. If she doesn't find any, she'll give the horse its feed and leave it to breakfast in peace. She'll be back later, for mucking-out and grooming and doing whatever prepar-ation is needed for the horse that day, leading it out to the paddock if it isn't going to be ridden in the morning. But the first moment is the best part of Tina's day, better even than the feeling of an easy canter on an animal that she knows she is lucky to be exercising, or good news about the stables' latest success. She holds this morning pleasure as a guilty secret, although it becomes less guilty after her ride out with Fred.

Whenever any member of staff is going to start riding his horses, Fred invites them to come for a hack with him. They can choose their mount. Tina chooses Snowdrop, one of the Floods' younger horses, a chestnut Dutch warmblood with a sweet, calm nature and a phenomenal jumping ability that he rarely displays when away from Flood Farm. He doesn't seem to like competition, which is a great source of frustration to Fred, but rather endears him to Tina.

'I can tell a lot from the horse someone chooses,' Fred says. 'You're not trying to impress me, because you didn't bring Bob. You don't care about status, because you didn't ask for Foxglove.'

Tina is feeling quite pleased with herself, until 'Snowdrop is a lovely animal, but he won't do anything spectacular. With the right handling, though, he'll do well enough.'

Fair enough, Tina thinks. That's me. Steady. But she knows that she is happy. Steady people don't have spectacular successes, but they don't have spectacular falls either. She's come off once or twice and often thought of the visceral fear of the seconds between broad, warm back and broader, colder earth: she is amazed at how the others laugh and bounce up after their falls, while she is left cold and shaken by hers.

'I often think, you know, Tina, that we have it all wrong with horses,' Fred continues. 'We talk about breaking them, and training them, and working them, and racing them. But everything we do, we do only because we have their permission and we have earned their respect. Look at these animals. They are a thousand times stronger than us, more capable, more beautiful. So, Tina, while you are here, I hope you will do one thing for me.'

They pause at the top of one of the hills that loom over Missingham. It is early, still, and there are some fingertips of darkness clinging on to the western horizon. She and Fred loosen their reins. He is riding Bea, his grey Arab mare, too old for competing now but his favourite. The two horses crop the grass.

'Of course,' Tina says. She is only just able to stop herself from saying 'anything', but that's what she means.

'Will you remember that it is my wish that you will always ask my horses to do what you want them to do? That you will ride them with respect for their greater power? That you will request, and not compel?'

'Of course,' Tina says again. Below them, the world seems silent. Their breath is clouding silver in the air.

'Thank you,' Fred says, tipping the edge of his hat to her with his leather-gloved hand. Dismounting in the yard, she feels disorientated to be back in everyday life, and not just because Fred has led the way back down at a pace that Tina would have thought reckless had she not both survived and enjoyed it. Fudge touches her elbow, and says, did you get the request not compel speech?

Yes, Tina says, yes I did. She braces herself for a joke, but Fudge just gives her arm a squeeze and says, good, isn't it?

Yes, Tina says again.

And she feels as though something momentous has happened: more momentous than, later, losing her virginity or fracturing her collarbone flying over Snowdrop's head when he refuses a jump. Perhaps it's that she's arrived at her place in the world, and found the future that fits. Whatever it is, it's palpable; she can feel her eyes shining, sense a new bounce in the balls of her feet as she walks across the yard. She thinks nothing could be better. And it isn't, at least until the afternoon when she and Roddy work on Foxglove together.

On the evening of her ride with Fred, Tina has another go at explaining to her family why she loves horses, and loves to ride. There don't seem to be words for how it is to get up on Snowdrop and feel every muscle primed and ready to roar into smooth action. She tries to articulate the way that he had seemed to pay attention to every move of Tina's, inside and out; whether it was a twitch of a finger or an extra beat of her heart, Snowdrop sensed it, and reacted to it. Riding him is, she says in a sort of despair as she looks around the dinner table at her family's blank-but-encouraging faces, the best thing that has ever happened to her.

'Wait until you meet the right boy,' her mother says with a twinkle, and her father tuts and shakes his head at his wife.

'Let her have her career before you have her settle down,' he says.

'Haven't you been paying attention, darling? It's the 1990s. She can have both.' Alice pokes Howard in the arm. Tina and Sam roll their eyes at each other.

She tells them what Fred had said to her, with some trepidation; she doesn't want to be misunderstood. They listen, and they nod, and they don't say a lot but Sam squeezes her hand under the table.

So the Randolph household is calm and settled, although it bobs a little in the waves when Sam starts university and Howard, Alice and Tina have to learn to be a trio. Sam seems as happy there as Tina is at the stables, and that makes it easier for them all to adapt. 'It's great here,' he enthuses to Tina in one of his rare emails, sent from the university library and read at the computer in the corner of the living room. 'I'm not very bright any more, I'm pretty average, and so I can get on with my life. At Oxford, I'm you!'

And it seemed that he was good at being at Oxford, his friendliness and social ease making up for the gap between his background and that of many of his peers there, the opposite of Tina's experience at work. But Tina had her horses, so she didn't mind about the people so much.

And then comes Roddy Flood. And she finds that she really, really minds about him. Of course, the son of Fred and Fran has always been part of stable life. But when he pulls her into his orbit, nothing is the same, ever again.

Roddy is the closest thing Missingham has to a rock star. He's tipped for the 2000 Olympic showjumping squad, and when he's riding, he is immaculate, polished and pressed and clean-shaven. When he's working in the yard, he wears old jeans and boots and T-shirts like the rest of them, but he somehow wears them better. If he goes out, it will be in much smarter, much tighter jeans, cowboy boots with pointed toes and a silver band around the top of the heel, a white shirt with silver tips on the collar, and a bootlace tie with a horse's head that fastens it. Next to the other young men in the Green Dragon, all in loose pastel shirts and low-slung jeans, he looks smarter, and sleeker. And one hell of a lot sexier. But if Roddy notices the effect he has on women, he doesn't show it.

Everyone at the stables admires Roddy, according to their lights. Some of them lust after him. Some envy his untroubled grace on horseback, some his fearless assaults on any jump, and his ability to make any horse fearless with him. The family dogs follow him, one Labrador nose to each knee. His memory is legendary; he knows the genealogy of every horse in the yard. ('Would you know if he was making it up?' Sam asks one evening, obviously bored with Tina's non-stop stable yard talk. 'Of course I would,' Tina replies, and their mother tells Sam not to tease her and Tina blushes.) Those who are immune to his good looks and way with horses long for a ride in his car, a Sierra RS Cosworth that, apparently, is quite something, although to Tina a car is a car and that means travel sickness and not a lot else, whether or not it has a spoiler on the back.

What Tina has always liked best about Roddy is the way that, when he is with a horse, he ignores everything else. While the rest of the staff, mucking-out or grooming in pairs, gossip and laugh, Roddy just focuses. Tina notices, and copies, and her understanding of these animals that have absorbed her all her life grows.

Of course, because away from the horses Roddy is easy company, generous and funny and full of stories, his quiet concentration on his horses becomes a part of his legend. Tina, who has never got the knack of being in a group, although she can talk very happily to one or two people she knows well, finds that her emulation of Roddy just adds to her outsider status. But, as she reminds herself on the walks to and from work, she is in it for the horses. And she intends to be a yard manager one day, which she knows will be another isolated position, if Charlie, who manages the yard for the Floods now, is anything to go by.

'Give me a hand, will you,' Roddy calls across the stable yard sometimes, and everyone holds their breath to see if theirs is the name he will call. The first time he calls Tina, Fudge has to prompt her, because although it had sounded as though he was asking for her, she didn't see how he really could be. She feels invisible among the louder, more confident girls. Although Roddy is on speaking terms with everyone, Tina doesn't compete for his attention the way that the others do. She doesn't think she crosses his mind, unless she happens to be standing in front of him. But he has called her name.

'I need to give Foxglove a spring clean,' he says, 'and you always do such a good job.' Tina blushes at the thought of being noticed for her work, but she isn't really sure what to say. Roddy is looking at her and she realizes that he's waiting for assent. His closeness makes her world warp a little, at the edges.

She nods and smiles. 'Of course,' she says.

'Good,' he says, and smiles back. It feels as though he

forgets to look away, or perhaps that's her imagination. They set to work. Roddy's favourite mount is a chestnut thoroughbred who is quick to respond and fast over jumps. First Roddy checks his hooves over. The horse lifts his feet automatically when Roddy runs his hand from knee to pastern. Once all four hooves are picked clean, Tina and Roddy take a curry comb each and start rubbing circles from the top of Foxglove's neck to his chest, shoulders, back, belly, rump and finally haunches. To begin with, Tina slows if she starts to get ahead; she doesn't want Roddy to think her too casual. But they soon find a rhythm that matches, and by the time Foxglove is groomed with the stiff brush, then the soft, they are working as a single unit, tick and tock. Sometimes they catch each other's eyes and smile. They talk about nothing except the work in hand, a murmur here and a 'could you pass' there.

Foxglove is a handsome horse. As Tina works she admires the slope of his shoulders, the length of his neck, and the white markings on his lower legs that Fred calls his go-faster stripes. He is almost always the fastest round a course, but in his haste he can be careless. Roddy is keen that he does better this season, and is spending a lot of time with him.

The horse is wiped down with a cloth, and his eyes and nostrils cleaned, then Roddy takes the mane while Tina takes the tail. As she rakes her fingers through it to separate the tangles before she begins brushing, she catches Roddy looking at her again, but there doesn't seem to be a reason for it: he doesn't offer advice, or say anything, he just looks until she looks away.

'Foxglove likes you,' he says to her, quietly, as they come out of the loose box, eyes stinging in the bright February sunshine. Ells and Fudge, who have been standing outside, murmur to each other and giggle as they walk off.

'I like him,' Tina replies. Roddy nods, as though she's just confirmed something important, and then he's off through the stable yard, joking and chatting, and Tina is wondering what just happened, because it felt like more than just grooming a horse. That is as much of a conversation as they have, but it's enough.

Over the weeks and months that follow, her name is called more often than all the others, and there is no hope of this going unnoticed. 'Roddy wants you,' the others grin, not unkindly, but are still delighted when Tina blushes, her freckles no longer brown, but becoming a pale dapple across her skin as her face reddens. The attention doesn't last long, though. As the months move, and Roddy has another stellar season, the yard finds other things to gossip about. During the summer, when other riders come for training, she barely sees Roddy at all, or if she does, he's with at least one of his fellow riders, most often the beautiful Aurora, who can't seem to be close to Roddy without touching him or leaning against him. He seems always to catch Tina's eye when he passes. Or maybe she imagines it.

'It's funny, your hands are a lot more confident than the rest of you,' Roddy says one day as he and Tina sit in the tack room. Autumn is here and the yard is getting quieter again with the summer visitors gone. He is cleaning bridles while she is working on a saddle, deftly pulling the straps from their fastenings so that she can make sure that every part is clean, soft, supple, as it should be.

They so often work in silence that she is a little surprised by the sound of his voice. She thinks that, maybe, she bores him. When Roddy is with other people he seems to have a lot more to say. She looks up into his face and finds herself studying his mouth. It's a bit too full to be properly handsome; twisted, slightly, by a small scar from an old fall, when he had bitten through his lip. It's the most interesting mouth that Tina has ever seen. She goes back to her leather. Roddy was right: her hands, still steady, are not betraying her, although she is shaking inside at the attention, and at the idea that he is thinking about her.

'Did you hear what I said?'

'Yes,' she risks a glance, 'but I wasn't sure what to say.'

Roddy laughs, mellow and low. 'My mother is always saying, "Roddy, if you've nothing to say, say nothing," but I've never been able to. She'd love you.'

Tina is glad when they go back to silence. But then:

'My father says that he can trust you more than he can trust anyone else who works here. He says because you've earned your place, he knows you mean it.'

Tina feels her blushes spreading up from her neck. She wiggles her toes; Katrina read in a magazine that that's a good way to stop yourself blushing, because it sends the blood to the other end of your body. Tina thinks it might be working. She cannot believe that she's a topic of conversation around the Flood table, or that she has been so noticed, so praised. But then Roddy makes her blush again.

'I think you should be more confident than you are.'

Tina finds her voice. 'Why do you think I'm not confident? Being quiet isn't the same as being unconfident, is it?' This is something that Sam said about her, once, when her school report had said that she needed to have the confidence to speak up in the classroom. Her father had nodded and said, well, empty vessels make most noise, you know. And Alice had made a little pursed mouth and said, guilty as charged, and they had all laughed.

'True,' Roddy says, then, 'I suppose because everyone else pushes themselves forward you look as though you're holding yourself back.'

'Maybe,' Tina says. Roddy is partly correct. Tina also knows that she doesn't have that spark, part courage, part instinct, that marks the great riders like him out from the ones like her. What she really wants to do is manage this yard, but she hasn't met a yard manager yet who isn't male, forty or fifty, and hasn't had an accident that put paid to a serious riding career. She's too in awe of Charlie to ask him what her chances are, and anyway, he always says that they'll carry him off the farm in a box. She almost asks Roddy, then, because she thinks of him as a friend. But: we never talk, she reminds herself, this relationship is all in your head, he likes you because you don't talk.

And then Roddy changes direction.

'Have you always been travel sick?' he asks.

She has got the hang of travelling to events in the

front of horseboxes and Land Rovers. She takes her tablets well beforehand, gets in, sits tight and stares at her hands, placed in her lap as though she's holding the reins of the steadiest Shire there's ever been. So long as she doesn't look up, or try to talk, she should get there without being sick, although sometimes she retches with relief as soon as she feels the ground under her feet again.

'Always.' One of Tina's earliest memories is being stripped out of her travel clothes, washed, and stretching up her little arms to have a bridesmaid's dress slid over her head by her mother, who had hugged her, kissed her head and said, it will get better, sweetheart, I promise. It hasn't, really. She manages not to vomit, if she concentrates and medicates, but there's the same feeling of roiling, the panic, the sense of her insides flailing for solid, unmoving ground.

'But you're OK when you're on a horse.'

'Yes.' She thinks of Roddy polishing his car on a Sunday afternoon, stripped to the waist if the weather is warm. He must think she's ridiculous.

'I've seen the colour of you when we get to an event,' Roddy says, glancing at her. 'I feel for you.'

'I'm used to it.' He feels for her. Tina lets this thought expand; she tastes its sweetness. He has moved to sit next to her; holds her hand. Her fingertips pulse. She wiggles her toes. She smells leather, straw, CK One. Her own perfume – rose oil from the Body Shop – seems too simple against it. She feels like a little girl.

'I suppose you've tried all sorts of things.'

'Yes,' Tina says. A homeopathic remedy had worked,

briefly; it seemed to take the edge off. She likes to be tightly belted in. It's easier if there's no talking. The smell, though not the taste, of mint soothes her. Anti-sickness tablets work, but only if she gets the timing right. Roddy is still holding her hand. Her fingertips are pulsing, but her toes are still and her cheeks cool. Perhaps he's right and her hands are confident.

'So if I want to impress you,' Roddy says, 'taking you out in the Cosworth isn't going to work, is it?'

'I suppose not,' Tina says. She looks away from his hand and into his face: he's smiling. She's smiling.

'I'll have to think of something else, then,' he says.

He stands up, stretches and walks back out into the afternoon's activity. Tina sits there in the quiet for a minute or two longer, wondering, absorbing, trying to calm the flutter behind her solar plexus. Roddy Flood wants to impress her. It's too good to be true, but she likes it.

There is a joke in the Randolph household that Flora, their sweet and sociable tortoiseshell cat, always knows which family member needs her most, and from the day in October when Roddy asks Tina if she wants to 'come up to the house for supper on Friday', a week after their conversation in the tack room, Flora has followed Tina as a seagull follows a plough.

Katrina says it's definitely a date. Unsure, Tina asks Sam when he makes his weekly phone call.

'He's giving up a Friday night, and he's inviting you home, and his parents will be there, and no one else has been invited?' Sam asks.

'As far as I know, it's just me, Roddy and his parents.' You can never quite tell who will be in the Flood farmhouse. But visitors – buyers, sellers, prospective livery clients, trainers, riders – are written up on the blackboard in the yard office; Tina can't recall anyone in for Friday night.

'That's actually a fourth date. Maybe a fifth.'

Flora jumps into Tina's lap. Katrina beams and says, 'We need to decide what you're going to wear.' And Tina wishes that she'd kept the whole thing quiet. She refuses to wear heels, but borrows Katrina's new lilac top to go with her smartest jeans, and consents to mascara. Nervous of taking the wrong wine, instead she bakes a gingerbread with her mother, and in doing so remembers the days when the best treat of the week was to stand on a chair by the kitchen bench and help with mixing and measuring. As Alice was a devotee of teatime, they baked at least twice a week: cut-out biscuits that Tina would decorate when they cooled, tea-loaf, chocolate sponges baked in separate tins and sandwiched together with coffee buttercream icing. This was Tina's time to have her mother to herself; they talked of everything and nothing, drama group and Flood Farm, the starlings and the fuchsias. As they made the gingerbread for the Floods they talked about holidays, and how, this year, for the first time, Howard and Alice would be caravanning – or 'hitching the wagon' as Alice called it – without Sam and Bettina. Everything changes, Alice had said, but I think it gets better. Even when it was good to start with.

And now, after a few days that have both dragged and

flown, here is Tina, sitting in the Floods' kitchen, watching Roddy's mother Fran take a loaf of bread from the oven, turn it upside down and knock on it. Seeing Tina's face, she says, 'If it sounds hollow, it's done.'

She knocks again, a question on her face, and Tina nods: 'I see – well, I hear.'

Fran puts the bread in the middle of the table and sits down next to Tina. 'Those boys of mine are always late down. Fred will be asleep in the bath. Roddy will be getting his hair just right for you. Shall we do the cross-word while we're waiting?'

It feels strange to Tina to be here as a guest. She's been in before, of course, running errands for Fred or squashed around the table with the rest of the staff for updates or celebration drinks. During the day this is a working kitchen, an Aga with a dog bed in front of it at one end, piles of papers and catalogues on the table, boots in the corner, dust on the dresser, an unruly crowd of mugs and plates ever growing by the sink. But this April evening, with the heavy curtains half drawn against the apricot sky beyond, lamps lit and the smells of bread and meat and the quiet of a day's work done, it feels like a home.

Roddy comes down first, before they are halfway through the across clues. He is wearing jeans and a checked shirt that's buttoned at the cuffs, loose at the neck. He is barefoot. Tina is even more glad she's refused heels: apart from being out of place on her, they would have been out of place here. She looks at Roddy's toes. He lost a couple of toenails after a tussle with a new arrival last summer. The horse had stood on his foot while being unloaded from the horsebox; the nail of the big toe on his left foot is half growing back. Tina remembers Ells saying as much as lascivious proof that she had seen Roddy naked; Tina blushes at the memory. Roddy kisses her on the cheek and ignores her blush, or doesn't notice. Tina isn't sure whether ignoring or not noticing would be preferable. She wishes there was a recipe for starting a relationship, or that everyone had the same set of rules. He says, 'I'm glad you came.'

'Tina brought gingerbread,' Fran says. She's put it on a plate, a long china oval with blowsy roses and a chip on one end. The sticky surfaces of the cake gleam.

'Lovely,' Roddy smiles, 'I didn't know you could cook.'

'My mum helped,' Tina says, then wants to bite off her tongue because it makes her sound twelve, not nineteen.

But again, Roddy either doesn't notice or doesn't comment. He just sits down next to her with a tack catalogue. 'I was hoping you'd help me choose. We need new flysheets and stable blankets for Snowdrop and Foxglove, at least. Bea's and Bob's are getting a bit hard up, too. There's only so long TLC will hold them together.' Tina is sitting on the chesterfield that takes up the wall opposite the dresser. It's cracked from the heat at one end, piled with cushions and Whiskers, the ancient cat, at the other, so she and Roddy sit close together in the middle. Most of the horses at the stable are at livery, and their owners provide all of their kit: it's the Floods' own mounts that Roddy is shopping for. Here's something Tina can get absorbed in, forgetting that she's on a date, let alone a fourth or fifth one, if Sam is right. She and

Roddy are comparing the dimensions of different blankets when Fred walks in. Tina makes to stand, but Fred waves her back into her seat. She realizes as she leans back that Roddy has stretched his arm along the back of the sofa. Of course, that might be to make it more comfortable as they peer at the catalogue together. Her stomach gives a happy churn anyway. He's just a little taller than she is, and the way her shoulder fits against him when she leans back feels just right. Maybe he squeezes her to him, just a little; it's hard to tell, because Fred bends and kisses her cheek at the same time.

'Welcome to chaos,' he says.

'Tina's brought gingerbread, Fred,' Fran says.

'How marvellous. And thoughtful,' Fred says. 'We've got so much wine that we need to start washing the yard down with it if we're ever going to be rid of it.'

Tina laughs. 'My dad built a wine rack under the stairs, but he says it won't seem to stay stocked.'

'My dad's exaggerating,' Roddy says, then, 'Dad, Tina and I are sussing out new blankets for Foxglove and Snowdrop. Maybe Bea and Bob, too. Mr Darcy and Blaze got new kit not long ago, so I think they should be all right.'

'Good. Good. I was thinking the other day that our horses are the worst turned out of any of them. There's only so long TLC will hold these things together.'

Fran catches Tina's glance and they smile at each other. 'Tina will think she's in some sort of repetitive conversation hell,' she says. 'Is your house like this?'

Tina thinks about the meals she shares with her

parents these days, the fourth seat at the table so very empty. She has realized that she thinks most about how much she likes being a twin when Sam isn't there. Being a de facto only child she finds crushing, exhausting, with too much responsibility and so many moments when she turns round to say something to someone who isn't there, and should be.

'Yes and no,' she says, 'it's a bit odd with my brother away at university.'

'Ah yes,' Fred says, 'you're a twin, aren't you?'

'Yes.' She wonders what will come next: already sees herself talking to Sam later, telling him about how she got the are-you-telepathic question or the do-you-like-all-the-same-things question or the observation that it's impossible to answer because they have never known anything else: 'that must be odd' or 'how is it different to having an ordinary sibling'. But Fred just nods, and goes to open a bottle of wine, and Roddy definitely squeezes her shoulder this time, and Fran brings plates and cutlery to the table, and Tina feels something unclench a little as she feels, for the first time, the possibility, the simplicity, in being next to Roddy.

When the meal is ready, and Roddy gets up and reaches out his hands for Tina's to pull her up, he keeps his right hand in her left as he leads her the few steps to the table. He stands behind her with his hands on her shoulders for a minute or two when she sits.

'It's goulash,' Fran says, 'Fred's favourite, so Roddy and I tolerate it, once a fortnight or so. I hope you'll like it. Roddy thought you would. He said you wouldn't want fuss.'

* * *

The next morning, as Tina sits in the kitchen at home, eating toast and idly watching the birds so she can tell her mother what she's seen, the thought of Roddy and Fran discussing what she would like to eat still makes her feel warm. She had promised to tell Katrina all about the meal last night – and Sam had asked for 'the edited highlights' – but she can't really find words for the way she had felt as the evening progressed.

As they'd eaten Tina had felt comfortable, welcome, gradually more relaxed, gradually more at home, so much so that when Fred and Fran had excused them-selves – 'Our bones are a lot older than yours and if they're going to get up at six they need to lie down by ten,' Fred had said – she hadn't felt the need to wonder what would happen next.

Roddy had put on the lamp and switched off the over-head light. He'd leaned over Tina's chair and tilted up her chin and kissed her. Then, in a rewound version of what had happened earlier, he had taken her left hand in his right, led her back to the sofa, sat down with her, put his arm around her shoulder, and kissed her again. They had kissed for a long time, their familiarity as workmates and people-you-see-every-day meeting the newness of this new relationship. Roddy's mouth had been soft but the skin on his hands was like any rider's hands, rough and well worn by leather, sun and wind. As he ran them over her arms, up her neck, into her hair where the dry skin caught on the kinks and then let them go, Tina had felt her body wonder at what was happening to it.

And then Roddy had stood up. Tina thought she knew what was coming next: she knew his reputation for one-night stands and easy-come, easy-go girlfriends. She had thought about what she would say in just this situation, although she hadn't been sure it would come to this at all, and certainly not on an evening that began with a meal with his parents. She had remembered the first part of her planned speech about being someone who didn't really rush into things but she couldn't remember the rest, and anyway her mouth didn't seem very keen on saying any of it. Her body had been very keen, all of a sudden, on the idea of a one-night stand.

But Roddy had smiled and said, 'I'd like to walk you home,' and his voice had sounded deeper than usual so Tina had had to spend a moment replaying the words, understanding them. Wondering what test she had failed that meant he wasn't leading her to his bedroom, hadn't even tried to get under her clothes.

The walk home through the dark streets of Missingham had been friendly and chatty, but Roddy's hands had stayed rammed in his pockets, and so Tina had kept hers in her pockets too, and when they had got to her gate he had kissed her on both cheeks – although the kisses had been gentler, less formal, than the standard peck-peck she saw him use with visitors to the yard – and said, 'Thank you,' and he'd watched her to her door and – well. And what? Tina has no idea.

And then the phone rings. Flora, who has been quietly licking butter from Tina's fingers, looks at her as if to say: that's probably for you. It's before eight. Tina guesses it's the stables calling, as only someone from there would assume that anyone else was up and prepared to have a conversation at this hour.

She's right. It's Roddy.

'I know it's your day off,' he says, and he sounds so formal, his voice so clipped and matter-of-fact, that Tina immediately thinks that she must have read way too much into all that kissing, not enough into the formal walking-home, 'but I wondered if you wanted to come into town with me, to take a look at those blankets?'

'The blankets?' she says. Her voice sounds thin and dry: this was the last thing she was expecting.

'Are you busy today?' His voice still sounds as formal, but of course he will be in the yard, using the phone in the office there. Tina can hear the clatter and shouts of the morning's first round of work coming to an end.

'No,' she says, 'I'd love to come.'

'Oh, I should have said, I thought we could get the train in. We could walk to the station. I can come and pick you up on my way.'

'That would be great. If you don't mind.'

'Of course I don't mind,' she thinks she can hear him smiling, 'I wouldn't have suggested it if I did. Shall we say ten? Once we've looked at the blankets and stuff we can have lunch. I don't really need to be back here until five.'

'That sounds great,' Tina says.

'It's a date,' he says, and puts down the phone.

When he comes to collect her, Roddy introduces himself and shakes hands with her father and kisses her mother, who twitters like a thrush about how even though they aren't horse people they always watch when

93

he's on the TV. He smiles, and explains their plans for the day – Tina's heart does a little pirouette when he says 'Tina and I' – and how much he and his parents had all enjoyed the gingerbread. 'We had some of it for breakfast,' he says, 'with butter. It was just the thing.'

'Oh, my!' Alice says, as though this is the single most exciting thing she had ever heard. Howard catches Tina's eye and smiles too, a smile that says 'everyone your mother meets for the next three weeks will hear about the Floods having gingerbread-and-butter for breakfast'. Tina smiles back. Roddy is talking about birds now, saying that he'd seen a buzzard when he was out riding that morning, and Alice points out the tree in the garden where the wagtail likes to sit.

Roddy takes Tina's hand as they get on to the train, and keeps hold of it until they are sitting down together. Then he puts his arm around her and his feet up on the seat opposite, and Tina surprises herself by saying, 'Other people will be sitting there,' and he grins his funny twisted grin and takes his boots off the worn brown velour, and she adds, because she doesn't want to sound like his mother, or hers, or one of the bossy girls in the yard, not that it would occur to most of them to catch a train, 'I do like your boots, though.'

Roddy turns his ankle this way and that. 'Thanks. My mother says they're a bit much.'

'They are quite a lot of everything,' Tina agrees. The cowboy boots have a long, tapering toe, and there isn't an inch of them that isn't tooled with twirls and scrolls. Above the heel, a band of silver sits. 'I think you're wise to leave the spurs off. But I like them. They are just,' she indicates proximity with her finger and thumb, 'just this side of classy.'

Roddy laughs. 'Tina Randolph, I could get into a lot of trouble with you,' he says.

And he kisses her, on the lips, just like that, and she realizes that being with Roddy is as easy as falling off Bobby Dazzler when he has the wind up his tail; that there might be something else as good as a gallop on winter mornings when the sun is just starting to shiver into the sky. In short, Tina Randolph admits that she is in love. Lost to it. And she hopes that that's what Roddy means when he talks about being in trouble, because if he doesn't love her too, she doesn't know what she'll do.

Part Three: Throckton, 2013

THE MEMORY OF the conversation with Rufus keeps Bettina awake at night. She turns over, rearranges pillows, sits up and sips water, as though finding physical comfort will make her emotions lie smoothly too. But her gut is agitated and her mind goes over and over what she said to him. She hears her own voice, in her head, explaining that the part of her that could really love is missing, and wonders if that is true. At one lonely 2am, Bettina wonders whether it's easier for her to think that the part of her that could love is dead than it is to consider that it might be dormant, and could be coaxed back to life, with all of the risk and heartbreak that that might involve. She doesn't know the answer. But thinking about the question brings tears to her eyes. She's tempted to put on some shoes, step across the street and knock on Rufus's door, but she can't bring herself to do it. Because if she did it she would have to be sure that it was what she wanted, and all that she is really sure of is that she has had enough of heartbreak for one lifetime. Rufus has been into the shop once or twice. He has been friendly, formal, polite. Bettina had been hurt, just a little, her heart as though it had brushed against a nettle, until she realized that Rufus was treating her the way she was treating him.

One night, late/early, giving up on sleep and striving to understand her misery, she takes a shoebox from under her bed and finds the letter from her father that she hasn't read since she settled in Throckton. It was waiting for her when she returned from France after her father's sudden death, three years before.

My dear Bettina,

I hope you never have to read this, because I hope that I will outlive your mother and you will never have to experience her illness at close quarters. I know that you have noticed how strange she is on the phone with you sometimes, when she talks about people we haven't seen since before you and Sam were born, repeats herself, sometimes stops talking mid-sentence and hands the phone to me as though it's a cup of tea she's just made. Forgive me for telling you that her distraction was caused by tiredness, or an unusual bird in the garden.

The doctors say that the fall is what triggered the dementia. How I wish I had been the one who'd gone out to feed the birds that day; such a simple decision, with such monstrous consequences, to start on the washing-up instead, not to insist that your mother put her garden boots on, and to let her go out in those ridiculous slippers. But whatever began it, only you and I know the dark, deep well it drew from. There is so much strength in old misery.

Her decline began slowly. A forgotten message, a

jumbling of speech forgivable in someone tired or depressed. But then she started putting her clothes on in the wrong order – blouses over sweaters, dress back to front – and she would lay the table for the four of us.

I didn't tell you because I have always been sure that your decision to be far away from us was your only way of coping with the tragedy in our lives. I couldn't see how I could justify bringing you back to something that was difficult to cope with in itself. It would have been like asking you to bear two impossibly heavy weights.

And, as I am confessing, I will confess all. Before your mother got to the point at which she is as I write – with most of her sense of herself gone, and only a few memories remaining – in her lucid moments she said some things that were not easy to hear. She talked about Sam as though he had stepped out of the room, and she talked about you as though you were still the hard-working young woman with all of her life waiting. She speculated about your future, and Sam's, and talked about wedding hats and grandchildren as though we still had nothing to worry about. It was unspeakably difficult to hear; worse, somehow, than the moments when she didn't know who I was, or even have much of a clue who she was. It was like watching the person she would rather have been. And so, out of a father's desire to protect, I decided to keep you in ignorance. I have no defence, except my desire to do the right thing, in a situation where there wasn't really a right thing to do. I hope that, in time, you will forgive me, and perhaps also learn to forgive yourself.

And now, some last advice, or perhaps it is a plea. Please, Bettina, don't give up your life to care for your mother. Although it's a difficult, heartbreaking job, that's not the reason why I don't want you to do it. I want you to keep on having the life that you've rebuilt for yourself, and I want you to have the future you deserve. You've always allowed yourself to be outshone, but I have always seen how you shine.

You've suffered enough. We've all suffered enough. There are people who are much better equipped to care for your mother than you are, and there's no shame in that. (They are, doubtless, better equipped to care for her than I was, but you know that I am nothing without your mother, and so I have been selfish in keeping what remains of her close to me.)

There is money, and insurance, and most of all there is my wish. Find a place where your mother will be happy and well cared for, and let her go.

Love

Dad.

Bettina sits on her bedroom floor and cries, softly, as though there is someone she might wake. Her memories of her return from France overwhelm her. When her father described a 'difficult, heartbreaking job' it was an understatement. She found the pain of being close to her confused and diminished mother unbearable. What had made it worse was her own grief for a man that his wife barely remembered. Alice spent a lot of time snoring in front of the television, blissfully unaware that she was a widow. And Bettina watched her and missed France, the easiness of a life that meant being ever-so-slightly disconnected from the world as others experienced it: rising in the dark, working in silence. For a month after her return, Bettina read books about dementia, and talked to the people her father had relied on, and saw the bread she baked while her mother slept become as dull as Alice's skin and as tasteless as her own tears.

She'd taken trouble to find the right care home. She agreed a care plan that involved respect, activity, a room that looked over a garden, and an agreement that her mother's life would not be needlessly prolonged when the time came.

In her heart, Bettina thanked her father for his investment in health insurance, his well-ordered filing cabinet, and for the enduring power of attorney he'd had couriered to her in France to sign. She signed the contract with the care home and then she went immediately to buy a stone bird-bath and a wooden bird-table and had them sited outside her mother's window. She went systematically through her parents' home, getting rid of almost everything. All the photograph albums had moved with her mother, so she was spared looking at those.

Bettina had the bungalow stripped, refitted and painted, and engaged a letting agent to lease her parents' old home. She put her own few things into storage, and she returned to France. A little bronze of a horse and an old grey dressing gown were the only things she took back with her.

Apart from the grief, and the guilt, of course. She knew that her heart, already smashed twice before, was broken three times again, once for each of her parents, once for the way she wasn't the daughter she might have been. And then there was the old space where Sam wasn't, gaping open once more. Her bread began to show her strain. But it wasn't anything like as bad as it was when she had first come to France, all those years before. In the interim, she had learned how to bring her love for her craft to the kitchen, and so there was always something good and honest to knead and roll from her heart to her hands to her dough.

'What is it telling you?' one of her colleagues had said when he came into the kitchen at the end of a shift, to find Bettina standing with a loaf in her hand, breaking it slowly, scrutinizing the crust.

'It's telling me it's time to go home.' As soon as she'd said it, she felt relieved, and could admit that, since her return, she had been bothered by things that had never bothered her before. Suddenly she didn't like the way the language disconnected her, ever so slightly, from her surroundings, although she was now fluent enough to think and dream and count in French. She longed for and missed 6.30pm English television local news programmes, which in her parents' house had been the signal that the evening had begun, her father coming in from the garden and her mother setting the table, she and Sam putting their homework away until after supper. She baked hot cross buns and Eccles cakes and they came from the oven reproachful in their perfection.

After seven months, when the letting agent emailed to ask her instructions now that the initial six-month contract was up and her tenants had moved out, Bettina stopped fighting her fate. She packed up what she needed, gave away what she didn't care about and returned to the dreary suburb of Guildford where her parents had lived when Missingham became unbearable. She travelled to the nursing home and sat with her mother in the mornings, when the light seemed more likely to catch a facet of the woman she remembered. She learned to dissemble and distract when her mother didn't recognize her. She resisted the urge to talk about her father, knowing that her mother would give her nothing more than a puzzled look that would make her feel as lonely and cold as the first snowdrop of January.

On Bettina's thirty-fourth birthday, she made her visit early, taking gingerbread still warm from the oven. Her mother greeted it with a simple delight that made her daughter, shamefully, envy her for a moment. And then Bettina took three trains and got herself to Throckton, and met an estate agent who showed her round a café that seemed as empty and forlorn as she was, a kitchen whose grime made her blanch, and a flat that would do if it wasn't quite so dark. Here was work, and plenty of it. Here was a place that didn't know her. Here was home. Bettina shook hands on a three-year lease that afternoon, and on the day she got the keys and stood in what would be her home and her business, she realized that it had been almost fifteen years since she had spent as long as three years anywhere.

And now here she is, sitting on the floor, crying.

It's almost a relief when morning comes and it's time to go to see Alice. Bettina takes the *Throckton Warbler* article about Adventures in Bread to show her mother, even though she knows it's a redundant exercise. The photoshoot had been horrendous. The photographer, as unpleasant as Verity had been kind, had posed Bettina in the kitchen, where he'd complained about the light, then the shop, where he'd complained about the limited space. In the end she'd stood, struggling to smile, in the street outside, clutching an armful of baguettes while the photographer had knelt on the ground in front of her, trying to get the bread, Bettina and the shop sign into shot. Bettina's only comfort was that the angle made her virtually unrecognizable, all chin and cheeks and little points for eyes. As her eyes were the thing that everyone seemed to recognize first about her, the fact that they were as good as absent from the photograph meant that she was pretty much in disguise.

It takes a while to get to her mother's nursing home, which is only one of the reasons that she makes the journey just once a month. She goes by train, taking the branch line into Marsham, travelling a couple of stops on the main line, and then taking another branch line out again, which is a two-and-a-half-hour door-to-door trip at best. 'I know you get travel-sick,' Rufus had said, when he was still trying to please her, 'but going by car would only take an hour and a half. We could go very gently, and you could try magnetic bracelets – Kate uses them with Daisy—'

'I've tried that,' Bettina had said.

'Ah, but you need one on each wrist . . .'

'Really, Rufus, no,' she'd replied, more sharply than she'd meant to, 'I like the train, it gives me time to think. And anyway I just don't like cars. I get sick, really sick, and it's not worth it. Believe me, three hours on trains makes much more sense than one hour in a car if you're throwing up twice a mile.' Which was true, and he'd nodded, and dropped the subject.

But she does like her time on the train, so long as she keeps her thoughts on the right track. She manages the journey carefully, keeping busy with lists and emails, spreadsheets and planning, so she doesn't focus on where she's going and what she might find when she gets there.

Before she has had time to think about her mother very much at all, Bettina is stepping from the train and starting the walk that will take her twenty minutes, although she often does it in ten when she's coming the other way, because she cannot help but scurry for the safety of life as she now knows it.

On the walk, though, she does think about the mother who brought her and Sam up: the bright heart of their family, their power and their sunshine, not perfect by any means but always fun to be close to, always ready to be roped into an adventure or, more likely, to rope them into one of hers. Bettina remembers being woken before five to hear the first cuckoo, standing blearily in the garden and hearing the sound that made her mother beam, even if she couldn't easily differentiate it from that of a pigeon.

She remembers her family, as it was then, having dinner at their house in Missingham, on the day she announced what she thought her future was going to be.

'I'm going to apply for a job at the stables,' she had said.

'Of course you are, darling,' Alice had said with a smile, then, 'I wanted to be an actress, or a singer. The nuns didn't like it. Secretary or nurse were your options, as far as they were concerned. Until you got married.'

'Those were the days,' Howard had said, bracing for the outrage.

'Oh, you're hilarious,' Alice had said.

'Didn't you have the option to be a nun?' Sam had asked.

'Well, they never asked me about being a nun, darling,' Alice had said. 'I don't suppose they thought I had the . . .' she had searched for the word, 'the knack. And to be fair, they were right.'

Now, hand on the nursing-home door, Bettina wants to step back and tell that Tina to remember, to treasure those memories, because her mother won't always be rushing from work as a school secretary to home for tea to the amateur dramatics rehearsal, via a kiss for them all and a moment to watch the birds at the kitchen door.

Today, Alice won't know who she is, for a start, and will prattle about the young Bettina as though the daughter before her is a stranger. Or she will talk about things that make no sense. Or she will doze in her chair while Bettina watches her and wonders how the mother who was once so bright that being embraced by her was like being tumbled into a rainbow now sits as frail as one of her beloved fuchsias in February.

But none of these is the worst case scenario. The worst case scenario is the one where Alice May Randolph, mother of Bettina May, is enough of herself to ask where

Samuel Randolph is. If that happens, Bettina will make a choice. She will dissemble, lightly, changing the subject or telling what she has heard described as a 'therapeutic fib': she will say something like 'Sam can't come today', and talk about something else. This has the advantage of making for a peaceful afternoon. It has the disadvantage of making Bettina rage at herself for cowardice.

Her other choice, and, in Bettina's mind, the Right Thing if not the easy one, is to tell the truth, which has unpredictable results, none of them pleasant. If she does this, the visit can go many ways. One is the inconsolable sobbing which is not, in essence, any different to the way her mother would have first received the news. Her mother will wail and keen and Bettina will watch her, unable even to hold her mother's hands as they fight free of her own and grasp and pull helplessly against each other. Sometimes, Bettina finds herself wailing too. More often, more painfully, she sits quietly and thinks thoughts that shame her: that this reaction, horrible as it is to watch, shows her that somewhere in there is a mother still. And so the times when Alice responds to the news-that-isn't-news with a blank expression, because she's already forgotten the question that she asked, are easier, but also worse. So Bettina hopes that she won't be asked the question about Sam, because none of the options open to her then lead to a good place, and because once the question is asked she has only choices she doesn't want. And even after sixteen years, the pain isn't that far removed from her mother's when she does choose to tell the truth, and Alice chooses to understand it.

The air in the nursing home is always slightly too hot, and a bit too dry. So Bettina is glad to be told that her mother is in the garden. For all that Alice Randolph has forgotten, she has remembered that she loves wildlife, and flowers, and so she sits quietly on a bench in the feeble sunshine, eyes following the birds as they move from tree to lawn. Bettina almost turns and goes, because her mother looks so happy, so relaxed in her own orbit. She knows that as soon as she goes to talk to her she will move her from a world that is unchanged since the days when she sat in her own garden with her twins asleep in their great unwieldy pram, still young and lovely and blessing her life, to this new world that she knows must seem wrong, where everything – even her own hands, the wedding ring she looks at as though it is part of a puzzle – will be unfamiliar.

Alice seems so much older than her sixty-seven years, but so much younger too. She always seems a little too small for her clothes, and try as Bettina might, she cannot help but think of her mother as she imagines she would think of a child, someone she must coax and praise and be perpetually patient with. Someone who has an endless, although unconscious, ability to make her feel guilty, because there is always more that she can do for her.

But Bettina doesn't go. She approaches. She says, 'Mum, it's me.' By and by, she will wonder whether what happens next is caused by the fact that her mother looks away from bright sunshine to her daughter, who must be silhouetted in the change of light. But in the moment, her heart dances when her mother says, unexpectedly, matter-of-factly, 'Oh, hello, Bettina, I wondered if you would come out to the garden.'

The care home manager does report 'occasional lucidity', but it's been a long time since Bettina has been witness to it. Her mother speaks less, does less, eats less these days. She's shrinking out of existence. The daughter sits down on the bench, afraid to speak, to look, in case in doing so she breaks this crackling line of communication. Her mother reaches out a hand, and clasps Bettina's own. Bettina notices that her mother's nails are short, shaped, clean; remembers how they used always to be painted red or pink or purple. The house would smell of nail varnish and acetone on a Saturday afternoon, and her mother would sit in a dressing gown, hair in a towel, arms and legs outstretched, toes separated by kitchen roll folded into strips and woven in and out of the spaces, and sing out, 'You can fend for yourselves tonight, you two, because your dad is taking me out. I don't know where, and I don't much care, so long as I'm not doing the cooking.' And later, she and Sam would open the fridge and find that their mother had, in fact, left a pizza or a pie to go with the beer that they'd pilfered from the cupboard under the stairs. Bettina wonders whether, next time, she should bring nail varnish with her, or whether seeing the colour she used to love on the hands she didn't recognize might make her mother distressed.

Bettina holds her breath as her mother turns to look at her. But her mother's smile doesn't change; there's no confusion in her eyes. The precarious path between them grows wider. The scent of early lavender is in the air.

'Hello, Mum. How are you today?'

'Me? Oh, I'm fine. I'm just watching the world go by. Are you growing your hair?'

Bettina sometimes has a dream not dissimilar to this one, when she arrives at her mother's care home and is greeted by the mother of old. This was the mother who, when Bettina was awake, she didn't dare think of, but her dreaming self clearly longed for. The dream-mother, always ready to cheer and defend her children, was made of memories: facing down the headmaster when Sam had been up to mischief, then grounding Sam for a week and confiscating his walkie-talkies for a month. Plaiting Bettina's hair before gymkhanas, driving for hours to stand in the rain for more hours, waiting for her little daughter to catch her eye when she came into the ring ready to start her three-minute showjumping round, talking all the way home as though Bettina had won, rather than being unplaced again.

'I'm not sure,' Bettina says, 'I might have it cut shorter for summer.'

Her mother nods. 'Less bother,' she says, 'it will dry in no time.'

'Yes.' Maybe I should go, she thinks, go now, take this small perfect pebble and not worry about the terrible, rocky road.

But then, in the same tone, with the same familiar, conversational lightness, Alice says, 'Roddy was here. It's always good to see Roddy. He's such a nice boy.'

A flash-flood of melancholy rises in Bettina. She's

112

shocked to hear a name she didn't expect to hear. And behind the shock washes the sadness, for all that Roddy was, and could have been, in his own right and with her. For a moment she is with her mother, deep in the past. She's choked by love and want and need, so powerfully felt, unmoderated because she hadn't known, then, how life would hurt less if feelings were tempered with distance and distraction. And the undertow is worse. The moment or two of present-day conversation with her mother has gone, as she harks back nearly two decades to talk affectionately of someone whose name, later, she would refuse to hear spoken in her presence.

Bettina listens to the sound of her body as she breathes deeply. Her mother has turned her face towards the sun and closed her eyes, the way a cat would when the clouds receded. This is why I bring the Sunday newspapers, she reminds herself, this is what the food is for. It's all protection. She opens up her bag and says, 'I brought you some shortbread. I made it this morning, before I got the train. I put some lavender in it, because my friend brought me two lavender bushes in big pewter-coloured pots, and I've put one out the front of the shop and one just outside the kitchen door, with the herb planters. I wonder if the marjoram will attract as many butterflies as it did last year.' The more she says, the less her mother will say, and that's all she can think of as she talks.

'How lovely' is all Alice says, and she takes a piece of shortbread from the opened box that Bettina offers her, crumbles it between her fingers, and starts to throw it to the birds. She is oblivious to her daughter, who, for all Bettina knows, has stopped being a daughter again as far as her mother is concerned. She might be just the other woman on the bench by now. The one with the short-bread and the tears in her eyes. The one who, trying to find a bright side, is glad that at least she hasn't had to decide whether or not to explain why Sam isn't here.

On the way home, Bettina can do nothing but look out of the window on every train she takes. She has no energy for reading and she's too tired for sleep. She tells herself off for wallowing, but it's only a half-felt reprimand, because she's only half wallowing. And with the other half of her mind, that's buzzing like a wasp in an upturned wine glass, she's wondering whether she is just as trapped in the past as her mother is. Bettina thinks about how much of what she does, she does because of what happened all that time ago. Hearing Roddy's name where she had expected Sam's to crop up had made her feel the way she used to when she came off over a jump. She's jarred right through. Although it wasn't really the mention of his name that rattled her, more the tone of her mother's words. Alice had spoken of him the way she had when he was the handsome boy still, when her mother winked at Bettina behind his back and said, you enjoy yourself, my girl, I would if I were you, and Bettina would blush and rush to get Roddy out of the house before Alice could say anything worse. That was when the mention of Roddy had made her heart flutter and fly rather than tear at itself. That was a long time ago.

Rufus is tired after a long meeting with a client. It's a barn conversion – it always seems to be a barn conversion, if it isn't a conservatory. The brief was to create a headquarters building for an up-and-coming company, and Rufus had suggested a central area with skylights above an informal meeting space. The MD thought it was a wasteful idea, because she didn't think it would be used. Rufus had countered that, if the space was there, so was the expectation. He'd reminded his client of her original brief, that the company needed room to grow. She'd agreed, but it was the kind of agreement that Rufus doubted would stick. His plan for the evening is therefore to sketch out an alternative, ready for the email he suspects will come in the morning. But before he begins, he pours himself a glass of wine, puts on the news, and wonders whether he had done the same thing with Bettina the other night. He had tried to create the semblance of the relationship he wanted, in the hope that the relationship itself might follow. If that's the case, perhaps he needs to review this approach. It's not working.

And then the doorbell rings. It's Bettina. She hasn't texted, or called first. This never happens. Suddenly, there's hope, a switch flicked on in a dusky room.

'Hello,' she says, 'can I come in?'

'Of course.' They kiss, both cheeks, their habit; her face is wet.

'Are you crying, Bettina?' He doesn't think he's ever seen her cry.

'Yes, I'm crying. This is me, crying. Even though I never cry.' She's half laughing, as well. For a moment Rufus thinks of something terrible. This is hysteria, reaction to tragedy. He steps back to let her pass, then follows her up the stairs, and notices how her left foot is dragging, just a little, a sure sign that she's tired.

'Could I have a glass of wine?' she asks when they are in his small sitting room.

'Of course.'

Bettina looks exhausted. Her face is a little out of its usual shape, made puffy and pallid by tiredness and tears, her eyes dull and swollen. 'I need to talk to you. I need you to listen,' she says. Her voice is so quiet that he has to lean forward to hear her. He nods, waits. Despite all that he's told himself over the last few days, he knows that Bettina is his best chance of happiness, and of the relationship he would have if he was a better man. He thinks, not for the first time, of how good it is to be with someone who says what they mean, simply, without accusation or pretence, and how it makes him honest in return. He likes the man he is when he is close to Bettina.

'When I went to see my mother today, it made me think about things. You know she has dementia?'

Rufus nods.

'Well, sometimes she doesn't say much, and sometimes she doesn't know who I am, and I can cope with both of those things.' The wine has gone, gulped down: Rufus fetches the bottle.

'It's hard, though,' Rufus says.

'Yes. But today was – today was worse. Because I thought that she knew me, but she was talking to a younger me, and she was so – stuck in the past.' She stops, shakes her head. 'I'm sorry. I'm not explaining very well.'

'Let me be the judge of that,' Rufus says gently.

'She was talking about people who – who if she saw them now she wouldn't want to talk to. She was talking about them as though they were friends. She doesn't remember my father at all. Never talks about him.' Tears are in her voice again, although they don't fall.

Rufus puts his hands over her clenched ones, a roof over a rock. 'That must be horrible, Bettina,' he says quietly.

She looks up at him, quickly, then moves her gaze so that she's looking out of the window. 'It is. It makes me feel – lonelier – than when she doesn't know me at all.'

'Yes,' Rufus says. His thumb strokes the knuckle of her first finger. She goes quiet, still, as though breathing is all that she can do, as though it takes all of her will to sit here. Rufus waits.

'And it made me think about what you said the other night—'

'I wasn't at my best—'

'Please, Rufus, let me talk.'

'Sorry. I'm listening.'

'I was thinking about how my mother has no choice but to live the way she does. This – thing – is rotting her brain and she has no control over it, and I feel sorry for her, and everyone looks after her knowing that she's ill, that she can't help herself.'

She looks at Rufus. He feels as though he is being told something very important. He doesn't know why, yet. He nods, a small nod.

'And she mentioned something – someone – and I realized that I'm as stuck in the past as she is. The difference is, I'm choosing to be. It's not – it's no way to live.' She looks at him again, gauging, waiting. He nods again. 'It was the best I could do, for a while. But I think I can do better now. I think I need to try to do things differently.'

'I see,' says Rufus, hoping that he does. The song thrush so close he can see each feather on its breast.

Bettina pulls a pack of tissues from her bag, takes one out, rubs her eyes then blows her nose. She looks full into his face: her eyes black and bronze in the fading evening light. 'I brought my toothbrush,' she says. 'Please may I stay the night?'

Part Four: Missingham,
1997–1998

TINA AND RODDY first spend the night together in early December, when Fred and Fran are away. Tina has bought new pyjamas for the occasion. She and Katrina had spent most of the previous Saturday afternoon choosing them. Katrina had been delighted with the task; Tina, thoroughly embarrassed, had refused point-blank to contemplate anything lacy, frilly or satin. She had tried to explain that she wasn't looking for what she called 'girlfriend clothes', it was just that the only pyjamas she possessed were either worn out or had some sort of horse theme – the Randolphs have a tradition of new pyjamas on Christmas Eve and Alice prides herself on finding something appropriate. 'But don't you want to look . . .' Katrina had asked with a raised eyebrow, holding up something that Tina couldn't see herself wearing in a million years.

'Honestly, Katrina,' she'd said, 'all I'd look in that is uncomfortable. And Roddy won't care.'

'You don't know anything about what Roddy cares about, in the pyjama department. Yet.'

'No, but I know that he likes people to be themselves. And that's not me.' In the end, she'd bought a pair of short cotton pyjamas that satisfied her because they were plain and kept Katrina happy because they were black. And Tina had tried to explain that, if Roddy cared what his girlfriend looked like, then he wouldn't be going out with her at all. Katrina had taken this as a cue for a motivational talk about self-esteem, but Tina knew what she meant. If you threw a stick in the yard at Flood Farm you'd hit six people more suitable to be Roddy's girl-friend than she was. But somehow, there she was, buying pyjamas and disposable razors and looking forward to the following Friday night, when she and Roddy will put an undisturbed end to two months of panting foreplay. She is still getting used to his glorious frankness. 'What do you want to do about contraception?' he'd asked. 'Are you on the pill?'

'No,' she'd said, 'I've never really liked the idea.'

'Fair enough,' Roddy had nodded. 'Condoms, then?'

At last Friday night comes round – Tina hasn't seen much of Roddy during the week as he's been away at a training event, and so when she walks up to the farm-house with her overnight bag she's all the more ready to see him. She can't believe how easily he's weaving his way into her life. Her heart is on a helter-skelter. Tina can feel that she walks differently. Despite her protest-ations to Katrina, mascara doesn't seem like such a chore any more. Sometimes she wills the afternoons past so that her plans with Roddy for the evening can begin. Roddy, on the other hand, strides the same, and jokes the same, and works in silence with the horses the same. As he talks his way through his working day he laughs and claps backs and never looks twice at Tina, except when he asks for her to come and work with him, which they do in the same near-silence as they always have.

When Tina arrives he greets her with a long kiss, looks her up and down as though he wants to eat her, and says, 'I'm starving. I was going to get fish and chips.'

'Good idea.' Tina's not sure she can eat anything. The December air has made her face and hands cold but her heart is overheating.

'I assume you want to stay here? I thought I'd drive. So nothing gets cold.'

'Yes, thank you.'

'Make yourself at home.' Another kiss, and he's gone. It feels as though Tina has barely had time to make a fuss of the dogs, cautiously pet the uneven-tempered cat, and find plates and cutlery, before Roddy bursts back through the door. He's brought fish and chips, mushy peas, curry sauce, gravy, a pickled onion and a pickled egg. 'It's funny,' he says as they lay out the cartons, unwrap the paper, 'I feel as though I've always known you, but then I got to the front of the queue and realized I don't know what you like with fish and chips. So I thought I'd just bring everything, so I'll know in future.' He stands behind her, circles her waist with his arms, puts his chin on her shoulder.

'I need to think about this, then,' Tina says, laughing.

'Yup. Choose carefully. Whatever you have tonight, that's your fish and chip supper for the next fifty years.' Tina thinks of something Sam says sometimes, about indirections finding directions out, and that's how Tina often feels about Roddy: he doesn't talk about his feelings much, but then he mentions something like feeling as though he has always known her, or says 'in future' like that, and her head lets her be sure of what her heart already knows.

'The thing you'll find with the Flood boys,' Fran had said one weekend, as Fred had dozed behind the newspaper and Roddy had gone upstairs to bring down a jumper for Tina because she was cold, 'is that actions will always speak louder than words. They might not say how they feel but they'll show you.' Stable legend had it that, when a young Fran had badly fractured a wrist taking a tumble on a point-to-point course in Scotland, Fred had driven through the night to collect her, driven her straight back home to Surrey, seen her settled with her mother, had a cup of tea and a cheese sandwich, and then got a train back to Scotland to collect her horsebox and the horse that was being looked after by friends. Seeing how the Floods behaved day-to-day, Tina could well believe the legend.

'Do you want to go to bed?' Roddy asks, later, when they've eaten and had another beer and agreed that neither of them needs to try a pickled egg again, ever, and done the rounds of the stables in the half-dark. The stove is banked up with coal, and the animals are fed, fish for Whiskers and the rest of the leftovers for Dylan and Jenny.

'Yes,' Tina says, 'let's go to bed.' And Roddy smiles and touches the tip of her nose, and takes her hand and leads her up the stairs to his room, which is directly over the kitchen, although it's an up-and-round-and-back route to get there.

She has a moment of nervousness when he closes the door. Her own experience has been more fumble than fire, neither of her previous lovers had managed to make her feel even half as good as she can make herself feel. And – because Roddy's great gift is to be so utterly himself that it's impossible for anyone close to him to be anything other than themselves – she blurts, 'I've only had sex about fifteen times,' as he looks up from her shirt buttons, which he has been undoing, 'with two different people.'

Roddy's hand is resting on her breast now, moving slowly back and forward, the smallest amount. 'So?'

'I might not be as good at it as . . . as some people.'

He puts his hands on her shoulders. Her breast is not impressed. He smiles. 'Surely it's not about how good you are, it's about how good you make each other feel.' He lifts her hair, applies his mouth to the skin underneath her ear, lifts his head again. 'And I don't know about you, but I'm feeling pretty good.'

Tina has another moment where she wishes she's Roddy Flood. She has at least a couple of such moments in an average week. He sees everything so clearly; so simply.

'You're right,' she says, and she raises her hands from where they had been sitting on his hips, pulls his shirt from his jeans, and starts to undo the buttons from the bottom, working up.

With Roddy, she blazes. With Roddy, everything makes sense. All the bits of her body have a purpose, and none of them is embarrassed, or wants to hide. Afterwards, Roddy sleeps, his legs and one arm sprawled over the bed while the other pulls her into his chest.

'You should leave some things here,' he says in the morning, as they eat hot toast with unsalted butter by the Aga. Tina hadn't known that butter could be unsalted. She's never been in a house where tea is always made from loose leaves in a pot. She is careful not to mention these details to her mother, who is both hungry for insight into Flood life and defensive of any suggestion that the way they do things is any better than the way the Randolphs do them. Roddy feeds corners of toast to Dylan, the chocolate Labrador with the sixth sense for scraps. They'd slept until seven, unheard-of for both of them.

'I brought some pyjamas,' Tina says. 'They're in my bag, still.' They had woken in the night, cold where they had kicked blankets off, and Roddy had got up and brought her a checked flannel shirt of his to sleep in, although there hadn't been any more sleep for a while.

'I like you in my shirt. And don't bring a dressing gown. You look just right in that one.'

'Won't your parents mind?'

'It's my dressing gown.'

Tina pulls a face at him. In a funny way it's a bit like spending time with Sam: she acts and speaks before she thinks. 'Very funny. Won't your parents mind about me staying over?'

'Of course they won't. Why should they? You're my girlfriend.'

And Tina decides that it can be that simple. Which it is, really. Until it isn't.

* * *

126

It's a Friday night in early June, and Tina is at the Floods', as usual, although this isn't going to be anything like one of their usual – comfortable, happy, settled – nights. It's goulash night, and she has arrived early to help make the bread with Fran. Tina has grown up with Alice baking cakes, biscuits and scones, and much to her mother's indignation has always considered cakes bought from a shop to be a great treat. But she has never met anyone who baked bread before, and she finds herself fascinated by the whole process. All the more so when she sees what goes into a loaf: flour, water, salt, and something Fran calls 'leaven' which she says is also made of flour and water and 'long ago, a little bit of honeycomb to get it going'.

'I thought you needed yeast for bread,' Tina says, looking at the plump dough and wondering why it's rising.

'Well, leaven is a wild yeast,' Fran replies, 'and why would you go to all the trouble of making your own bread and use someone else's yeast?' Tina agrees. Like the flow of a horse beneath her, the simplicity of bread makes her tingle.

And so they sit around the table: Fred, Fran, Roddy, Tina. The last few weeks have been busy with visitors. Tina is getting better at talking to new people, although she sticks to asking questions and doesn't say a lot about herself.

'It's nice to be back to just the family,' Fred says as he sits.

'Yes,' Roddy says. Tina is more a part of the Flood family than Roddy is yet one of the Randolphs. Howard gets on well with Roddy, treating him as a replacement son in Sam's absence, and Alice is charmed by him, but Roddy's time at Tina's home still has the feeling of a special occasion. So Tina sleeps about half the week in Roddy's bed, and for the other half tries to be the best daughter she can be at home. On her days off, she goes shopping with her mother, buying skirts and camisole tops to humour her and enduring make-up counters for the sake of the pleasure it gives Alice, although mascara and tinted moisturizer are Tina's limits. But she has to admit that she feels herself moving differently these days, looking in the mirror more often, if only to try to see what Roddy sees. Yes, life is good.

Until.

Roddy says to Fred, 'I'm all sorted for July and August with the Fieldens, by the way.' His tone is so casual that Tina almost misses the importance of what he's saying. She replays it, in her mind, in case she has misheard. But she doesn't think she has. She puts down her fork. Her appetite has gone, because her stomach has been replaced by a clenched fist of nervousness and dread.

'What's this?' Tina is glad that Fran asks the question, because her throat feels too tight to speak. Edward and Arabella Fielden are breeders who live in the west country, about four hours' drive away; their eldest daughter Aurora is often mentioned in the same sentence as Roddy. The two have competed against and alongside each other for most of their lives. In fact, Tina knows that if she looks to her left she will see a photo on the dresser, of a twelve-year-old Roddy next to a slightly taller Aurora, both holding trophies and grinning proudly. There had been a photo in *Horse and Hound* earlier in the year that was not dissimilar in spirit, although these days Roddy was the taller and Aurora, who had once been spindly and crooked of tooth, now had a figure and a smile every bit as beautiful as the horse she rode. She wears her dark hair in a pixie crop, which makes her green eyes glow. Beneath them her face narrows to an almost pointed chin, and her lips are full and damask-pink. Wherever she goes she stands out, tall and sleek and confident. She has modelled sunglasses for *Tatler* and been featured in *Cosmopolitan*, talking about competing with men and photographed wearing a bikini. 'Aurora Fielden on Medusa' is a tannoy announcement that has even the most weathered, weary and hungover of grooms rushing to the ring. Aurora had stayed with the Floods the previous summer, bringing Medusa for some training with Fred. Tina, low in the pecking order, hadn't been near the horse – Aurora had brought her own groom – and hadn't seen much of the rider, either. At the welcome drinks, Aurora had spoken briefly to Tina, and moved on as soon as it was decent. Although she tried not to let such things bother her, Tina had felt slighted, all the more so because Roddy was too busy with Aurora to call her name in the stable yard. She had been happy to overhear Fred saying to Fran that you could always tell who the most important person in a room was because Aurora Fielden would be standing next to them. This comes back to her now, along with a nauseous dread. Because surely, at the Fielden stables, Roddy Flood, Olympic hopeful, star in the making, will be the person Aurora will want to be next to?

Roddy says, 'I'm going to stay with them for a couple of months. I want to see if I can bring Foxglove and Bob on a bit. We're all getting too comfortable here. And Foxglove is still unpredictable. I want to get his inside turns sorted out.'

Fred nods. 'Edward will bring you on all right.'

Fran looks at Tina. 'Did you know about this, Tina? No one told me.' Her tone is more quizzical than anything else. Fran's ability to take everything calmly is new to Tina. Her own mother tends towards the histrionic, either excited or appalled by most things. And her father tells people that he is a creature of habit as proudly as if he was telling them he was a Knight of the Garter.

'I didn't know,' Tina says, trying to find the same light intonation for her voice.

'I thought I'd said,' Roddy says. 'Sorry. Weren't you there when Aurora and I were talking about it, at the Three Counties show? When we were waiting for the prize-giving?'

'No, I wasn't. I was cleaning out the horseboxes ready for the trip home.' Roddy reaches for her hand under the table, squeezes it. His fingers are as familiar to Tina as her own. She hates the thought of missing out on such easy contact.

Fred says, 'It's probably a good idea, if you're going to take this seriously.' They all knew what that meant: if you're going to make the British squad. Words like 'high-flying' and 'hopeful' and 'rising star' followed Roddy around the way the Labradors did. The same had been true of Fred, twenty years ago, but a bad fall followed by a bad season meant that he went straight from hopeful

130

to has-been without the honour in between. 'Not like my career. Do not pass go. Do not collect two hundred pounds.'

'Oh, Fred,' Fran says.

'Oh, Dad,' Roddy says, at the same time. Tina has encountered Fred with his dressing gown flapping open and seen Fran's bras drying on the radiator in the bathroom, but she has never felt as sharply as she does now that she is seeing something she shouldn't – a little bit of family business too intimate for outside eyes.

She doesn't want to appear sulky so she makes an effort to join in the conversation, talking about the work that Roddy needs to do with his horses, listening to Fred's anecdotes about Edward Fielden. She thinks she does quite well. She can't help but wonder whether this will seem like a natural point for Roddy to break things off with her. She's been living the last months knowing that this whole thing with him is too good to be true. After all, he took no notice of her last summer, when Aurora was around.

As soon as the door to Roddy's room is shut behind them, Roddy takes her by the hand and leads her to the sofa, sweeping a pile of magazines to the floor so that he can sit sideways on to her and lean against one arm of the sofa. He puts his feet on Tina's lap. He has a hole in his sock and his big toe is poking through. She touches the tip of his toenail.

'If it makes you feel any better,' he says, wiggling his toe, 'Aurora and I had a thing.'

'Last summer? And how would that make me feel better?' Tina is glad that her words haven't come out sharply, because she isn't angry, although part of her brain is waving a flag to alert her to the fact that it would be all right to be angry, if she wanted to be. She's genuinely bemused as to how the idea of Roddy and Aurora having had 'a thing', is supposed to make this any easier.

'No, before last summer,' Roddy says, then adds, 'mostly. It's out of our systems now.'

'Is it?' Tina hears crossness in her voice this time. Roddy sighs.

'I think we were about fifteen when it started. It was just – you know. Fumbling.'

'Fumbling?' Now she puts her mind to it, Tina thinks she does remember some gossip. And of course there had been talk last summer, not that talk had been needed, Aurora arm in arm with Roddy everywhere you looked.

'You know,' Roddy has his eyes closed, as though this conversation is too boring to be fully awake for, 'adolescent stuff. It was more to do with proximity than anything else. And availability. She was always there. I was always horny.' Tina has options here. She could point out that, at the Fielden place, Aurora will once more be close, and available. Or she could shake this off and remind Roddy that he is still always horny, and let the evening go in a much more pleasant direction. She's tempted to. But Roddy speaks again, before she can say anything at all.

'She's lovely, but—'

'But what?' Her voice is getting sharper; she can hear it. Roddy sighs again. And now Tina is thinking, God,

132

we're going to have a row. We've never had a row. She would rather pre-empt an argument with an apology (as she does with her mother) or a measured, reasoned assessment of where there may be difficulty or disagreement looming (as she does with her father). Not that the arguments at home are anything significant: who put the immersion heater on and forgot to turn it off, whether it's feasible to build a rockery.

She and Sam are too closely bound together to bother with arguing, or to have a need to. Another twin-question they are often asked is 'Don't you ever argue?' to which Sam's answer is 'Well, no. Would you argue with your own knees?' which pretty much sums it up. But she and Roddy, who always seem to be either working or with other people or with the horses or having sex or half asleep, have yet to find anything to argue about. Until now. Until Aurora.

She turns her own body sideways, to look at him, and the sight of him only reinforces the truth of what she's going to say. He's the only man she's ever seen who, she thinks, looks good with a five-o'clock shadow. His hair is straight when wet but curls a little as it dries. His eyes are so dark they are almost black, his eyebrows perfect curves above. She's changed her mind about the twisted mouth she used to think less than handsome. He's the best-looking man she can imagine, even when he's chewing his lip and pulling at the hole in his sock, as he is now.

'What happened last summer?'

'Not much,' Roddy says, then, more quietly, 'we were drunk. It was – nothing. We were both single. It just seemed like a good idea, at the time.'

Tina feels defeated, lost, the pit of her stomach a long way below ground. 'Well, she's the person you're supposed to end up with, isn't she? In real life.'

Roddy looks up. 'This is real life.'

'You know what I mean.'

'I don't.' He really looks as though he doesn't. Now that she has said the thing that has been haunting her since this romance began, Tina feels something in her deflate, a tension pricked away. 'I really don't, Tina.'

'I don't even have my own horse. I'm a good enough rider but I'll never – shine – like you and Aurora do. My ambition is to manage a yard. Yours is to win an Olympic gold. So is Aurora's.'

'You're not telling me anything I don't already know.'

'Well, you and Aurora are the right fit, aren't you? You match.'

Roddy stands up and walks towards his bedroom door; for a moment, Tina thinks he's going to walk out and leave her or, worse, open the door and usher her away. But when he gets to the door he stops, breathes, turns.

'I can't believe you're saying these things, Tina. What have I ever done to make you think—'

'You don't need to do anything. I'm not exactly your type, am I?'

'Who says? Aurora's a nice enough girl, but—'

Tina laughs at this, inside, feeling further away from Roddy than she has since before they first groomed a horse together. Aurora Fielden, whose autograph Tina had almost asked for the first time she saw her ride, for heaven's sake. And to Roddy, she's a 'nice enough girl'.

But she realizes that if he doesn't see it now, if he really thinks that Aurora is a nice girl who is, essentially, no different to Tina, then she is on a hiding to nothing. At least she is tonight, when her feelings are jangled and her words are shredding the inside of her throat as she speaks.

'Why didn't you tell me?'

'We only sorted it today.'

'Why didn't you tell me you were thinking about it?'

'I'm sorry. I really thought I had. When we were at that show and I was talking to Aurora while we waited for the presentation. I thought you were there.'

'I told you. I was cleaning out the horseboxes ready for the trip home.' Tina has been pre-empting any possible accusations of favouritism from her colleagues by volunteering for all the least popular jobs, including missing prize-givings in order to keep an eye on the other horses and get the horsebox ready for Foxglove when he returns with his latest rosette.

'Oh. Well. It's really just a work thing. I often go somewhere else to train in the summer. It's two months. I'll come and see you. You can come and see me.'

'That's not the point.'

'What is the point? That I didn't ask your permission? Jeez, Tina, I didn't think you were going to be like that.'

'What did you think I would be like? A pushover?' Tina knows she's taking the wrong course. She wishes she'd said: the point is, this feels like the beginning of the end of us, and although I know that that will come, I'm not ready for it yet. She wishes for the simplicity of the saddle, and the way that pressure of opposite heel and hand gets you back on the right track.

'That's not what I meant.' Roddy isn't shouting, but it would be better if he were. His voice is weary, as though this is an old argument, as though she is being tiresome.

'Tell me what you did mean.' She makes it a demand, and is half expecting him to refuse to answer her.

'I thought you understood. How I felt about you.'

'You never say.'

'That's rubbish. I do say. I say you're my girlfriend. I say you're part of the family. I say you're the best thing that ever happened to me, Tina Randolph.'

You don't say you love me. Tina says these words so loudly in her heart that she can't believe he doesn't hear them. But Roddy doesn't. He just keeps looking straight ahead. Tina could say that she loves him, of course. But she doesn't. Because Roddy's words are making themselves at home in her. Girlfriend. Family. Best thing that ever happened to me, Tina Randolph.

'Thanks,' she says, and she reaches out and runs her finger the wrong way up the bristles on his cheek. He turns his head, kisses her fingertip.

'You can come with me, if you want. I'd love you to come.'

The west country, where she's never been. Two months with Roddy, waking up every morning with him, going to bed every night with him. Staying at the famous Fielden stables. Having the chance to see how another yard works. Seeing breeding as well as training.

A lot of new people to meet and explain to them that she doesn't have her own horse. The looks on their faces as they work out where she fits in the hierarchy, and decide she doesn't much matter. An hour-long ride in a Land Rover to get there. Watching Roddy ease himself into a new group as readily as he can saddle up a horse, while it will take her a month before she can really start to make friends. Watching how Aurora pulls everyone to her without even noticing, because her world has always been that way. Missing Sam when he comes down for the summer. Handing over her responsibilities to someone else when she's just starting to get somewhere. Abandoning her job to be with Roddy, when she has been so determined to have a career of her own.

'I thought we would go on like this,' she says.

Roddy's face goes from puzzled to 'is that all'. 'We will go on like this. You'll see.' For him, the key has fitted, turned, opened the door, and that's the end of it. It's 'Aurora's a nice enough girl' all over again. Tina thinks about trying to explain. She thinks about how, now, they are not exactly equal, but close enough. How, as Roddy's career grows, she will have the choice that he's just offered her, writ larger: become part of his entourage, or forge her own career and be left behind. Even if she's only left behind in the literal sense to begin with, how long can it be until she's someone from Roddy's old world, no longer relevant? These few months are both beginning and end. She looks at Roddy, who is studying her again, waiting, and thinks about trying to explain it all to him. She can't see that he will ever understand it. And she prefers his version; she can't share it, but she wants him to enjoy it.

'Duty calls, Tina,' Roddy says, 'that's all. I promise.'

'Yes,' she says. She closes her eyes as he strokes her

hair. She doesn't remember falling asleep, but she must have done, because she does remember Roddy coaxing her out of her clothes, over to the bed, as though she's a toddler who dropped off in the car on the way home.

She wakes folded into his arms as usual, and not at all as usual, sadness and sourness in her heart. It's before six, but she knows she won't get back to sleep. So she untangles herself from Roddy's arms and the bedding, puts on the grey dressing gown and, leaving him sleeping, makes her way down to the kitchen for tea in the quiet.

But Fran is already up and dressed and busy with papers at the kitchen table. 'Habit,' she says when she sees the surprise on Tina's face. 'I don't think I ever sleep past half past five. And I want to get this lot cleared so I can hack Mr Darcy out today.' Mr Darcy is Fran's horse. Although he's ridden in competitions by Ells, Fran and he are devoted to each other. 'There's tea in the pot.'

'Thanks.' Tina helps herself, slowly, thinking that Fran will go back to what she's doing.

But when she turns round, Fran is watching her. She says, carefully, 'Are you all right, Tina?'

'I think so,' Tina replies, testing the place where she hurts to see if there is anything broken. It's just bruised, she decides.

'Don't worry about Aurora,' Fran says. 'Roddy sees her as – I don't know. A sister. The competition. Not a girl-friend. He has one of those.'

'Yes,' Tina says. And this, too, is part of the problem. Any situation in which she puts herself next to Aurora Fielden is disastrous. Pick the best horsewoman of the two: no question, it's Aurora. Who's better educated? Aurora. Who's nicer? Aurora, probably; at least in the sense that she's unlikely, at this moment (or indeed any other), to be feeling annoyed with her boyfriend for something that hasn't yet happened. Richer? Aurora. Prettier? Aurora. Better suited to being the girlfriend of Roddy Flood? Aurora, Aurora, Aurora. Tina takes a big breath and makes a big effort and tells herself to stop being so silly.

'Thanks, Fran.'

'Seriously, darling girl. The Flood men are all loyal to a fault. You'll come second to their careers, but you won't come second to anything else. And this is all about Roddy's career, to him.'

'Yes, I know.' And she almost does. Almost. The difficulty is in keeping on knowing.

Tina does her best, and it works, a lot of the time. Roddy is the same to her as he has always been – well, the same as he has been since she has been his girlfriend – which helps, because it reminds Tina that his trip to the Fieldens' is a career move, nothing more, and, as far as he is concerned, isn't relevant to his relationship with her.

She has been given responsibility for settling a new horse in to the livery. Perry is a high-spirited, fussy grey thoroughbred who doesn't like anything new, so instead of being looked after by whoever is available he has a small team of grooms led by Tina. She spends a lot of time with him, starting early and working late.

She knows that the only way to calm a horse is to be calm yourself, and that you can't fool a horse, least of all

139

one as tuned into his surroundings as Perry. So every morning she starts by taking Snowdrop out for a hack, and she lets him make her steady and calm, as he always does. Then she can go to Perry with the right sort of soul. By the time her day's work is done she is so in the habit of feeling at peace that it would be an effort to stop.

For the rest of June, without discussing or agreeing that they want to make the most of this time, Tina's nights with Roddy go from being three or four to five or six a week. It feels easier for work – often, now, she and Roddy are first in and last out of the yard, Roddy preparing for his trip and Tina working with Perry. But also, despite the agreement that two months apart is just something to be taken in their stride, the threat of parting is drawing them closer together.

They work long and sleep long and find themselves moving from the hope to the certainty that the other is close by. 'There's no place like you,' Roddy says one night as they drift off to sleep, and Tina knows exactly what he means.

The day before the day of departure comes. Foxglove and Bobby Dazzler are prepared, and there have been drinks after work. Now Tina is sitting cross-legged on Roddy's bed, in his grey dressing gown, watching him pack. He is wearing only boxer shorts. When he and Tina had left the party, to a chorus line of winks and raised eyebrows and 'aye-aye's, he'd pulled her into his room and said, well, it would be rude to disappoint them all.

She'd agreed, and because she'd showered and changed after work, undressing had been as simple as stepping out of her knickers and pulling her dress over her head. She had watched Roddy from the bed as he struggled with the buttons on his shirt, his fly. She'd wanted to see everything, and remember. Naked at last, he'd walked towards her, then stopped. Looked. Kept looking. Said: 'God, Tina, you've no idea how I'm going to miss you.'

'I think I do,' she'd said.

Afterwards, they'd dozed in the fading evening light, and were woken by the sounds of the last party guests leaving. Now, Roddy is putting piles of shirts and trousers, jodhpurs and T-shirts on the sofa, and balling underwear into a rucksack. He grins at Tina: 'I've spent the last two weeks getting two horses ready for two months away. I'm doing my own packing in ten minutes. Is that the wrong way round?'

'You know it isn't.'

'Yes, I do.'

When his piles of clothes, toiletries, books seemed to satisfy him, Roddy pulled his jeans back on.

'You need to get dressed,' he says.

'Why? I thought I'd stay.' It comes out a little wounded. Roddy laughs.

'Of course you're staying. I told Dad we'd do the last round of the yard tonight.'

'Really?' Fred is famous for never letting anyone else do the last check if he is on the farm.

'Special treat,' Roddy says. 'Now, put your clothes on. I'll be taking them off again later, but it's getting a bit cool out there.'

So they make their way down through the house, out via the kitchen where Fred and Fran are tidying up and drying glasses.

'Just going to do the rounds,' Roddy says.

'All right,' Fred answers, and it looks as though he winks.

The yard is the not-quite-quiet quiet that Tina loves. It's made by twenty-six horses breathing, shifting their weight, one of the stable cats jumping from a roof to come and see what they are doing. Roddy walks to where Snowdrop is stabled. The horse looks around, whickers, and then goes back to his half-sleep. Tina puts her head on Roddy's shoulder.

'You know the night we talked about me going away?'

'Yes, I do remember that, oddly enough.' She moves closer, just to let him know that she's teasing.

'Well, what I remember,' Roddy says, 'is what you said about how you don't even have a horse.'

'Oh, that.' Tina had been ashamed of that, afterwards.

'Well,' Roddy says, 'now you do. Snowdrop is yours.' His face had been solemn, but at the sight of Tina's he starts to laugh.

'You can't do that,' Tina says, her voice a squeak, her eyes astonished.

'I can. We can. Mum and Dad agree. We're transferring ownership to you.'

'But – I can't afford him.' Tina has seen enough invoices for food, farriers, vets and tack to know. She cannot accept this gift. And yet she cannot take her gaze away from Snowdrop, glowing like a peach where he has absorbed the last of the day's light.

'Everything will be the same. He'll still be on the yard's books for everything. But he's yours.'

'Roddy,' she says, 'Roddy.'

'It was the best present I could think of, to say, don't worry,' Roddy says. He unlatches the door; Tina walks into the stall, leans hand then forehead against the horse's neck. Roddy watches from the doorway. Tina can feel his smile. She lets herself believe that she is safe, and all is well.

She remembers the feeling, in the morning, during the clatter and bustle of his departure. Roddy does nothing more than kiss her forehead and squeeze her arm before he climbs into his car and follows the horsebox, driven by Fred, down the drive. They had said a real goodbye in Roddy's room, earlier. Fred will spend a few days with the Fieldens before driving the empty horsebox back.

Fran and Tina watch the vehicles until they are out of sight. It takes a while because Missingham sits in a small valley, and so from the gate it's possible to see them wind down through the town, disappear briefly behind the church, then wend across to the sharp turn on the opposite hill that takes them out of sight.

They walk back to the farmhouse in silence, skirt the edge of the yard and go into the kitchen. Tina knows that she needs to go back to work, but she isn't quite ready. She looks at the cereal bowls in the sink as though she's never seen cereal bowls before.

Fran says, 'You can still stay here, you know. Whenever

you want. It will save me from dying of boredom watching Fred snore all evening.'

'I don't know,' Tina says. Roddy had said the same – stay whenever you like – but she can't decide whether it would be better to be in the single bed at home, where Roddy has never been, or the too-big bed without him in it.

'Well, you know where we are. Why don't we say that you'll come on a Friday night? If you haven't got anything else on. I won't hold you to it. And why not bring Sam when he's around? I think Sam is the only non-horsey person that Fred has ever bothered to talk to for more than ten minutes.'

'He'll love that.' Sam's passion for history means that he and Fred always have something to talk about, chewing over old invasions and discussing the politics of the Second World War as intently as Tina and Roddy would analyse a showjumping course.

'And Roddy wanted me to give you this.' Fran's voice has changed, from matter-of-fact cheerful to something softer. Tina turns away from the sink and sees that Fran is holding a cardboard box.

'He's already given me a horse.' Tina is still amazed at the wonder of this gift. Her own family is consultative when it comes to gift-giving. Birthdays and Christmasses mean new riding boots, new jodhpurs, leather riding gloves for Tina, things she needs and is always glad of. She and Sam have a 'pick your own' system, whereby at any point in the year they can buy something they like the look of and reclaim the money from the other. Sam buys obscure records, baggy pastel shirts and books from

144

second-hand shops. Tina chooses what she calls 'best jeans' although her mother shakes her head at such an idea. So a surprising present of any sort – let alone a horse, and her favourite horse, and a horse who is so, so far out of her league – is something that takes some thinking about.

'Are you pleased?'

'Yes.' Fred and Fran had been in bed when Tina and Roddy came in from the yard last night. Breakfast had been an affair of last-minute practicalities, without any chance to talk about Snowdrop, although Fred had asked, 'Pleased?' and smiled when he saw her, and she had said 'Yes,' and squeezed his arm, and it had felt as though they had understood each other.

'Fran, I'd never dreamed of such a thing. I can't – I don't think I've absorbed it.'

'It's a silly question. You've still got stars in your eyes.' Fran moves closer. 'Are you crying?'

'No,' Tina says, 'I'm not crying.' But she puts her fingertips to her cheeks to check, because nothing is normal right now.

Fran smiles and hands over the box. 'Well, this comes with Snowdrop. So it's yours, too. Roddy says to take it home with you.'

As Tina takes it, she knows from the weight what's in it. The Floods have a small bronze statue made of each of their horses. They are exquisite creations that live in the yard office, in a cabinet, along with the trophies. She lifts the perfect metal Snowdrop from the scrunch of newspaper that it's been wrapped in. It's beautiful. Heavy and true.

'I can't.'

'You must. Roddy will be upset if you don't. And so will we.'

'Well – thank you.' Tina wishes there were more words: for thank you, for this is too much, for I'm over-whelmed, for I feel as though this is all too good to be true. 'I don't know how to thank you.'

'Thank *you*,' Fran says. 'It's so good that Roddy's picked a girl who's so—' Tina cannot imagine how Fran will complete the sentence. She braces herself: a girl who's so pleasant? so practical? so ordinary? so unlikely to give any trouble? She wraps the bronze back up, carefully, puts it in the box, while she waits. 'A girl who we know will take care of him.'

'Yes,' Tina says. It's a better ending than she could have imagined. At the end of work that day, she takes the bronze, the flannel shirt she sleeps in at the Floods' and Roddy's dressing gown home with her. Watching Roddy drive away had wrenched at her; standing next to Snowdrop had comforted her. She had thought she might cry when she went to bed, after saying goodnight to Roddy down a faint phone line with what sounded like a party going on in the background at his end. But she's worn out and she goes to sleep quickly. When she wakes, although she can't remember them, she can tell that she's had bad dreams.

Part Five: Throckton, May 2013

BETTINA IS PLEASED with the prototypes of her sweet lavender loaf, and now she is wondering at the possibility of using roses, violets, delicate flavours in soft rolls and crusty rounds. Hold your horses, she says to herself as she looks at her to-do list, which is long enough as it is and has nothing about new ranges on it. Let's get the lavender loaf right. And before we even do that, let's get the wretched fête out of the way. Let's take it a day at a time. We know that that's what gets us through. Even though she's busy, Bettina is starting to think about a chain of bakeries, more staff. She reminds herself, sometimes, of the Tina that her father saw, the one who shone. She's starting to want more, and expect more. It's frightening. She feels exposed. Which is the opposite of what she's been for the last fifteen years. But – the quietest of voices suggests, in the early hours – maybe it's time.

'Are you sure I can't help with anything?' Rufus, who has just finished loading Bettina's dishwasher, looks at her sitting at the table with baskets, a roll of red-and-white gingham, pinking shears and brown paper luggage tags. Her laptop is open at a spreadsheet; there are small blackboards at her feet.

The Throckton Spring Fête has made a lot of work for Bettina, and although Rufus keeps on offering to help, she keeps on turning him down. She's seen the precision with which he makes a bed, and puts cups in a cupboard. She knows that she couldn't ask Rufus to fold a napkin or chalk up a price list without it taking longer to discuss with him than it would have taken her to do.

'You made supper,' she says, 'and you've cleared up. That helps. I'll only be another half an hour, and you won't disturb me if you put the TV on.' She glances up; he looks uncertain. 'And anyway, if you were busy at work, I wouldn't assume I could help,' she adds, with a smile. Bettina is thinking of all the people who come into Adventures in Bread, look around, smile benignly at her and say how much they would like to have a baker's shop, as though it's a charming little hobby, something anyone could do. She smiles back and resists the temptation to ask them to come and move some drums of flour, or drop in at 4.30 tomorrow morning to see how it all works behind the scenes.

'I suppose not,' Rufus says, considering, then smiling at her. Bettina likes that he doesn't take offence at things she doesn't realize sound prickly until they come out of her mouth. She's intent on cutting out her gingham squares, but she glances up. Her eyes catch him unawares, each time; his memory can't seem to hold quite how lovely they are, and so every time he sees them he's jolted.

Rufus sits down on the sofa and picks up yesterday's newspaper. He likes to read them in order: it's something that used to annoy Richenda, and that Kate still teases him about. Bettina, on the other hand, says that she can see the sense of not coming in halfway through a story.

It's an hour until she says, 'I think that's enough for tonight,' and gets up. She stretches each leg out to the side, in turn, something that Rufus associates with tiredness in her. 'I was thinking. Why don't I book a weekend off, after the fête,' she says, 'and we can go away?'

'Really?' He is still trying to come to terms with the New Bettina. The one who stays over and treats him like – well, like a partner. Almost. She won't hear the L-word and she won't discuss much of her past. But Rufus thinks there's time for both of these things. And the more time they spend together, the closer that time comes.

Bettina is smiling at the look on his face. 'Well, I'll definitely deserve it. Let me check things out with Angie and find a few days when she, Simon and Josh can cover for me.' As an afterthought, she adds, 'We should set up a joint diary. So we know what we're doing.'

'That's an excellent idea,' Rufus says. 'Well, two excellent ideas.' He's beaming. Bettina likes making him happy. It's so much easier than trying to get him to dress and leave at midnight, and she likes the sound of someone else's breathing nearby as she works or sleeps. She can't feel much, but she can do this, and that's something – and something more than she thought. She feels pleased with herself, and along with that there's another feeling which it takes her a moment to identify: a positive sort of anticipation, something she hasn't experienced in a long time. Looking forward, she supposes, further than the next step.

It's been a long time since she's had a holiday. In fact she doesn't think she has had a holiday, as an adult. When she first went to France, her mother had talked as though her life was one long holiday, but Bettina had worked herself hard, and her breaks had been spent visiting her parents, weeks that left her exhausted and ready for the peace and quiet of a 4am shift, and the sleep that comes after ten hours on your feet in a hot, steamy kitchen. When she and Sam were small there had been caravan holidays, with Sam and Howard fishing and playing tennis, Bettina finding a place where she could go riding, and Alice making friends with the other mothers and pleading that, every other day, her family humour her with a visit to a stately home where she could wonder at the china, the silver and the por- traits, and buy bookmarks and recipe books in the shop. When Bettina had cleared her parents' house she'd found a box with all of the books in the loft. There were chintzy afternoon-tea books, tomes with pictures of roasts on the covers, a pamphlet about scones. Just the sight of that one had made her think of the ginger scones, both bitter and sweet, loved by her and hated by Sam, so they became a treat for her and her mother when they were on their own. 'Let's have proper butter,' her mother would whisper, even though there was no one else to hear and no one would begrudge them butter anyway. But she did make the scones even more of an occasion, not so much by the butter-instead-of-margarine as the conspiracy.

Rufus, his heart in his mouth, the thrush on his hand, asks, 'Shall I book something for us? When we have the dates, I mean?'

'If you don't mind.' She almost says: nothing too romantic, but stops herself. Rufus isn't stupid. There have never been flowers since the peonies: there were the lavender plants in pots, then a herb planter for her kitchen windowsill. Lately he's brought French wine, and a new edition of a falling-apart recipe book that she loves. He will know how to do this.

'Shall we do a train trip? Or would you like to fly somewhere?'

'Planes are OK, but I think I need to be able to get back. Just in case.' In the month since Bettina had taken a deep breath and knocked on Rufus's door with her toothbrush in her handbag, she has twice had to make her way over to her mother's care home in response to phone calls that began with the words 'This isn't an emergency, but . . .' Once was after her mother had had a minor fall and once because of a high temperature which turned out to be no more than a high temperature, but Bettina is more aware than ever of the fragility of her mother's life. And so, now, the thought of getting on a plane – or, more to the point, not being able to get on a plane home if she needed to – is too much of a risk.

'Of course,' Rufus says, 'leave it to me.'

Bettina smiles and says she's going to bed now, and would Rufus like to come? And they go. Though neither says it out loud, each is privately wondering if it can really be this easy.

There's a local legend that the weather is always good for the Throckton Spring Fête, and it seems to be holding true again today. The green next to the churchyard is bright with sunshine and good spirits, people nodding at each other and the sky, as if to say, look, how clever of us, we did it again. Bettina and Angie have been making trips back and forth since 9am to arrange their trestle table, weighted tablecloth and basket after basket full of loaves. Last year, Bettina had left Angie in charge of the shop and run the stall on her own. By lunchtime, she had sold out and Angie had taken less than twenty pounds, so this year Adventures in Bread is not so much closing as decamping in its entirety, a cheerful sign on the door redirecting regular customers to the green, although Angie had laughed and said that the chances of anyone needing directions to the fête were slim to none.

It certainly seems as though everyone Bettina has ever met in Throckton is here. From the moment the event was declared open at 10.30 until Verity arrived at the stall at 12.45 to remind Bettina that the Heart of Throckton New Business Award was going to be presented in fifteen minutes, she and Angie have worked non-stop, seeing familiar face after familiar face arrive, and being introduced to visiting nieces, friends from nearby Marsham, and husbands with face-painted children, tigers and already-smudging sheep, hoisted on to their shoulders. The croissants sell out first, followed by the Scarborough Fair cob loaves: gingerbread, shortbread and coffee cake are soon gone. Simon, who is working an extra shift in the kitchen, arrives with warm baguettes, focaccia and walnut loaves just as the stall is starting to look desolate. 'I've put some more in,' he says, grinning when he sees the look of relief on her face, 'don't panic. Back in an hour.'

So Bettina has no time to worry about the presentation until it happens and she steps up the three steps, solid but slightly too deep for comfort, and stands on the stage with her fellow nominees. Rufus is standing at the front of the small crowd, holding Daisy in his arms: Kate is next to him. Bettina isn't sure whether to look at them or not. She risks a glance and sees that they are talking to each other, not yet looking her way. Verity is bouncing a finger off the top of a microphone. Bettina's fellow nominees are the man who owns the bookshop, who is sweating in the sun, and a woman who runs a bed-and-breakfast that has already won awards. She smiles at Bettina, who smiles back but can't then think of anything to say.

Rufus glances at the stage. Bettina looks uncomfortable and a little stern, but he knows that when she starts talking her face will light up and her words, coming straight from her heart, will win over everyone who hears her.

'You like her, don't you?' Kate says.

'Yes, I do,' Rufus says. Any discussion of life-after-divorce has been off-limits between him and Kate. He decides to make the most of this opening. 'I'm not sure whether she likes me, though.'

'The great thing about you, Dad,' Kate says, 'is that all your faults are on the outside. So if she's got past that she probably does like you. Because you're all right, really.' She puts her head on his shoulder for a second. Daisy reaches for her hair.

'Well,' Rufus says, 'I think that's the nicest back-handed compliment I've ever had.' His tone is light but he's touched.

'I mean it, Dad,' Kate says. 'I've been thinking about this stuff a lot lately.' They are both looking towards the stage, which might be why they're having the conversation at all. Rufus has noticed that Kate often chooses to talk to him about things that are serious, or personal, when he's driving her somewhere and they can't look at each other easily. 'I think you and Mum should be happy. I would have liked it if you were happy together but that was never going to happen. And I think you brought out the worst in each other and you're nicer people separate than you ever looked when you were together.'

'Thanks, Kate,' Rufus says, 'I appreciate that. I really do.'

'Well,' Kate says, 'things aren't simple, are they? Even when you want them to be, they aren't. I thought things were simple, with Mike. I thought that he must love me and because of that he mustn't love his wife, but I was so wrong.' Elizabeth, Mike's widow, has made the effort to become an aunt to Daisy and a careful, at-a-distance support to Kate, something that no one would have predicted and that all of the Micklethwaites, in their different ways, feel shamed by.

Rufus puts his hand on the small of his daughter's back. 'I'm proud of you,' he says.

'Thanks, Dad,' Kate says, 'I'm trying. To grow up.'

'Me too,' Rufus replies.

More people are gathering. The crowd is making Bettina feel uncomfortable, way out of proportion to their holiday faces and cheerful chatter as they wait for the presentation to begin. She looks away, beyond the people, to the horseshoe of stalls. There's her own, the bookstall, then a table of jewellery made with bright beads and leather. Further along Bettina sees picture frames and mirrors that catch the sun and throw it in circles, slabs and shards on to the bodies of the passers-by, T-shirts with slogans printed by an enterprising sixth-former, more jewellery, patterned scarves, leather handbags. Then there's candyfloss, a hog roast, hot doughnuts, and a tombola and stall of bric-a-brac run by the local hospice. Behind the stage, heard but not seen, is the children's area. Younger visitors to her stall during the morning have reported a bouncy castle, pony-riding, duck-hooking, coconut shies. The churchyard with its higgle-piggle of gravestones lies to her right. Beyond it is Throckton proper, built around the long triangle of a marketplace where Adventures in Bread lives. The town spreads up the hill, a gentle slope, and new houses are starting to expand its edges even further.

And then Verity begins to talk. She introduces herself and the three finalists, and then works her way along the line. When it's Bettina's turn, she finds Rufus's face in the crowd and he looks straight into her eyes. He gives a little nod that says: I know you don't like this but you can do it.

'So,' Verity says with an encouraging smile, 'Bettina. How did you come to be in Throckton?' The real answer to this question is so vast and complicated that Bettina almost laughs. She's so glad that she did find a way for Rufus to help with the preparations. They'd thought of the questions that she might be asked and she'd written out answers, learned them, practised.

157

One of the practice questions had been 'How did you come to set up the bakery?' and so she plumps for that one. 'I had spent a lot of time working in other people's bakeries and had decided that it was time to set up on my own. I had a really clear idea of how I wanted Adventures in Bread to be, so really it was a question of finding the place that was already in my imagination. When I came to Throckton, I found that potential.' Verity is smiling, nodding, and still holding the microphone angled towards Bettina, so although she was about to stop talking she casts about for something else. 'And the day I saw the shop here also happened to be my birthday . . .'

'A good time for new beginnings,' Verity says, nodding. The crowd hums an assent. Rufus smiles an I-told-you-so smile: he'd said that people liked that sort of thing. 'And how do you like Throckton life?'

Another one from the list. 'I'm very happy here. In the past I've moved around a lot so it's unusual for me to be in one place for this long. It's a very welcoming place. And everyone seems to appreciate good bread.'

'Yes!' says Verity. 'Any future plans?'

'Well,' Bettina says, 'I'm always trying out new recipes, so there are always plans. One of my younger customers this morning pointed out that I don't have any chocolate bread, so I might have to think about that.'

'Sounds delicious,' Verity says, and then it's over, and Bettina listens to the woman who owns the bed-and-breakfast and is by far the most articulate of them all. She speaks eloquently about how important Throckton is to her and to the visitors who rebook for next year before they leave.

So Bettina is quite taken aback when her name is called as the winner, and all the more so when she hears whoops and cheers from the audience. She picks out Rufus's 'Bravo!' of course; she spots Elizabeth, her contact at the hotel, applauding with her hands above her head. Angie is jumping up and down and waving. She sees three, four, five regular customers waving and grinning. Her heart, which she half expects to shrink away, swells instead. Bettina is proud of herself, her little bakery, and the fact that she is standing up on a stage and smiling.

Rufus is waiting at the bottom of the steps. Bettina can feel how widely she's grinning. Perhaps, she thinks, this is what it's like to be normal. Maybe I am rejoining the world. Maybe I'm ready. She hugs Rufus. He looks shocked. She laughs. She realizes Daisy is next to him.

'Kate's gone to talk to her friend with the jewellery stall,' Rufus says, 'but Daisy wanted to stay with me.'

'Hello, Daisy,' Bettina says, 'I'm Bettina.' She never feels she's very good with children, because she's never had much to do with them. Daisy regards her with a stern stare. Her eyes are a pale blue-grey, the colour barely there at all in the bright sunlight.

'She's not usually shy,' Rufus says.

'What beautiful eyes,' Bettina says, then wishes she hasn't, thinking how often people have said the same to her, how impossible it is to know what to say in return.

'Everyone says that,' and Rufus adds, 'shall we take Bettina with us, Daisy?'

'Angie—' Bettina begins.

'Angie says it's fine. We checked, didn't we?' Daisy nods. 'This is the lady who makes the croissants for you,' Rufus says, and Daisy stretches up a hand to Bettina, who takes it, a little skinny starfish of a hand warm on her palm.

'Where are we going?' Bettina asks.

They're going for a pony ride. Bettina's heart goes from high to low in the time it takes for the three of them to turn round and head off. She hasn't been near a horse in fifteen years. Just the thought of horses, with their honest eyes and their perfect smell, makes her want to curl up and sob for all that she's lost.

There's a queue, and as they wait, Bettina half listens to Rufus prattling to his granddaughter, a slightly self-conscious question-and-answer about butterflies and ducks and trampolines. She wishes she felt more for Rufus than she does, which is something most accurately described as an appreciative tolerance, although she is hoping for something more, and sometimes it seems almost close enough to touch her, although it hasn't, yet. But then, it's always possible that she feels more than she admits to herself. Or maybe part of the reason that their relationship feels odd is because it's been such a long time since Roddy. With him, it was that first young flush and rush. With Rufus, she has something more measured, considered, but she has had none of the increments in between that might make what she's in now feel more natural.

The queue is moving forward, making a sudden jump as one little boy loses his nerve when he gets within touching distance of his waiting mount. Bettina is afraid that she might do the same. She wonders when she last got as close to a horse as she's about to get. Psychologists, physiotherapists, her father had all tried to persuade her that it would be a good thing if she could ride again, but she had refused. She knew that she couldn't put so much as a foot in the world that she had lost and maintain her fragile healing. And when she left the stables, she did leave a whole world. She missed so many things: the feel of a muzzle, soft skin and sharp whiskers, in the palm, the moment when you give a horse the cue to gallop and he takes it, the way that clean, warm leather feels in your hand. Fred saying, if you don't know how you are feeling, take a look at your horse's ears and they will tell you. For most of her first twenty years horses had defined her. Now, feeling her body thrum with fear, she realizes that the latter part of her life has been just as defined, but this time by the avoiding of them.

As soon as she was able, Tina had stripped the walls of her bedroom of horse posters, and put all her horse books in one box, all her riding and work clothes in another. Photos, rosettes, tickets, passes all went into a bin bag. The bronze statue of Snowdrop was the only thing that she kept, knowing it was too valuable to be thrown away, and that she couldn't bear to part with it.

Bettina is brought back to the now as Rufus nudges her, and says quietly, 'Look,' indicating Daisy with his glance. She is almost shivering with excitement. Two ponies are making slow progress round a circuit marked with hay bales. One, a grey, looks too good for such pedestrian pursuits and knows it, tossing his head during the breaks between riders, although safe enough when someone is on his back and he is very firmly held by his handler. The other pony is a little bay, solid and round, well groomed and clear-eyed, and when it's Daisy's turn to be lifted up on its back, the look of sweet excitement on her face makes Bettina want to cry, which is not what she was expecting. She's been steeling herself for panic, or for memories terrible in their happiness.

But a gentle comfort takes her unawares. Some long-undisturbed part of her remembers, stretches, wakes as it sees Daisy's face, full of delighted awe.

Bettina has taken the camera from Rufus – it's heavy and looks complicated, but he assures her that it will do all the work for her, and so she presses the shutter button once, twice, three times as Daisy and her steed make their stately lap, Daisy as intent as a nun at her prayers. Then Rufus poses next to her, while she's still mounted. He gestures to Bettina to join him.

'It's OK, Rufus,' Bettina says, 'people are waiting.'

'Here,' the mother behind Bettina smiles and reaches for the camera, 'let me.'

And so Bettina finds herself standing next to Rufus next to Daisy on a pony. She smells the mixture of hay and heat and earth and apples and manure that her mother used to despair of getting out of her clothes. She's so overwhelmed that the next thing she knows is Rufus guiding her away, saying something about ice cream, while Daisy bounces in his arms.

* * *

At first, Bettina thinks she imagines the voice calling her old name.

But it isn't her imagination. 'Tina! Tina!' hurtles through the air. Rufus ignores it, of course, because he doesn't know a Tina. Not this one, anyway. The call is getting louder, closer. Bettina thinks she won't be able to avoid answering it. She turns.

The sun is in her eyes, but there's definitely someone striding towards her, waving. She can't see who it is. She tells Rufus she will catch him up, and takes a couple of steps towards the stranger.

And she gets close enough and the sun goes behind a cloud and she's looking at Aurora Fielden, who engulfs and embraces her, smelling of hairspray and something floral, not CK One any more. Her body is soft and her grip is firm.

'Tina Randolph! You haven't changed a bit!'

'Aurora.' Bettina can't manage to get the exclamation mark on the end, although she can't imagine that Aurora is any more surprised than she is. They stand back and look at each other.

Aurora is dressed with the same careless expense as ever. She wears navy linen trousers, a white linen shirt and a long silk scarf with what might be a horse print on it. She's heavier but not overweight, and looks better for it, her angles softening. Her jewellery is gold, heavier too than the delicate chains and bangles she used to wear. Sunglasses pull her hair, which is longer now, back out of her face on to the top of her head. Her skin is smooth, smoother than Bettina's, who doesn't think of herself as vain but nevertheless despairs at the sight of her face in the mirror in the mornings.

Bettina doesn't know what to think. One of the words she only ever heard her father use comes back to her: 'poleaxed', as in, your mother was absolutely poleaxed when she found out that Roddy Flood had given you a horse.

The thing she has dreaded for all these years is happening, right this minute, and she's in it. She doesn't know what to do, even though she's been braced for someone who knew her as Tina Randolph to crash through the undergrowth and into the quiet shelter of Bettina's life now.

So, here's the moment. Bettina's brain is an empty barn, nothing in it but cold air and waiting. Aurora hasn't noticed.

'It's so good to see you!'

'Yes,' Bettina gets out.

'My ma-in-law told me about meeting you, and your little horse bronze, and of course that put me in mind of the Floods, but she said "Bettina" and I didn't make the connection. We never called you Bettina, did we? Roddy didn't, I'm sure.'

'Your mother-in-law?' Bettina's brain has chosen those words to repeat, but she knows it could have been any of them. Little horse bronze? In mind of the Floods? Never called me Bettina?

'Verity Ross. She works for the *Throckton Warbler*. She's been there thirty years and we can't get her to stop,' Aurora explains, then adds, 'I'm married to her Patrick. Didn't you know? I thought everyone knew.' She looks perplexed. Bettina, who knows she ought to be annoyed

164

by such assumptions, wants to laugh. Or perhaps cry, if she were more of a crier. She remembers how Aurora can draw the world to her and in doing so make the ground under everyone else's feet unsteady.

'I was in France for a while,' Bettina says. 'I didn't really keep up with things.' She could add: just the mention of your name, Roddy's name, was enough to make me sick.

'Ah. Well,' Aurora says, with the kindly expression of one explaining the homework to someone who's missed a lesson, 'I met him when I bought my little cottage. After the Olympics, you know, when I decided it was time to stop. And I settled a little way away from Missingham, because then I knew I could stable Medusa with the Floods, and I'd always loved that part of the world, and I knew that my folks would find a way of keeping me at it, with the horses, if I stuck around their place. So, I bought the cottage, and I wanted the garden done but I didn't really have the time, and it all takes so long, not just the digging and whatnot but waiting for the wretched stuff to grow, and so I picked a landscape gardener out of the Yellow Pages and it was Patrick!'

She pauses to look at Bettina, who arranges her face into something approximating delight at the way the universe had delivered Aurora's husband to her.

'And we were married within a year, and then we had our children – Patrick said that we should stop at four, but then along came Tilly,' she makes a 'what can you do' face, as though her endless fecundity, another whole human being brought to life, is just one of those things, 'and so we stopped at five, and here we are.'

'Well,' says Bettina, 'good.' She tries to think of more to say. Her brain won't supply anything. Her tongue won't move in her mouth. Her feet have grown weights.

'It's a bit of a trek for us to get over here, a good couple of hours, but we like to support Verity,' Aurora says, then, as though it's a continuation of the same thought, 'Who was that you were with?'

'Ah, that's Rufus,' Bettina says, then in desperation to keep the conversation away from her own life, now or then, adds, as though continuing the story of the years since she saw Aurora last, 'My father died a few years ago, and I came back. My mother has dementia. She's in a nursing home.' It's a small truth, offered up as a way of avoiding other, bigger ones.

'Ohhhh,' Aurora says, 'how awful for you. My folks aren't slowing down any. Still, they have eleven grand-children to keep them busy!'

'Well,' Bettina says, 'that's a lot.' She has, occasionally, wondered whether her own bolted-together pelvis could really have carried a child if she had ever tried to have one – her surgeon had reassured her that it would – but by and large children are something that belong in other people's lives.

And then Rufus's hand is on her back, making her jump. She finds the words to deflect the conversation before she can be drawn into introductions, explanations, 'And these are your ponies? You're still involved?'

'Yes, well,' Aurora says, 'they are two of ours, but we only keep them as a hobby, really, for the sprogs to ride. Horses to hormones to horticulture, that's me. Now we have some garden centres. Patrick's thing, really, but you know, stand by your man and all that.'

Her smile takes in Rufus now, and Daisy, who looks curiously at Aurora, then at Bettina, as though she can feel that there's something new in the air. Cautiously, Bettina puts out her arms; if she is holding Daisy and then she walks away, Rufus will have to follow. Daisy responds by stretching hers out, and now Bettina is holding Daisy against her hip, raising her free arm to shield her eyes from the sun so she can see Aurora properly.

'Well, it's lovely to see you, but we've promised this little one a toffee apple. Then maybe an ice cream.'

Daisy, in a move that guarantees her a batch of mini-croissants just the right size to fit in her hand every time Bettina makes them, claps and nods and chants: ice cream! ice cream!

'Isn't it just? Let's keep in touch.'

'It's amazing to bump into you, Aurora!' Bettina says, finding an exclamation mark now that the end of this encounter is in sight, and it's starting to feel like an unfortunate incident rather than a disaster. It's a broken rein rather than a broken clavicle.

And then, in another cloud of perfume, it's over. Aurora turns away. Bettina breathes, breathes, makes herself breathe. Daisy stretches her arms out to Rufus again. 'You can walk, Daisy,' Rufus says. 'You know your mummy will tell me off if I carry you everywhere.'

'I need to check in on Angie,' Bettina says. 'I'll meet you at the ice-cream van.' She watches them go; turns the other way to check that Aurora has gone. And is horrified to see her coming back.

Aurora's face has a quieter look now. She might even have a tear in her eye. 'I don't want to rake over the past . . .' she says.

'No,' Bettina replies. It's a hope, a plea, that Aurora will stop talking. But Aurora doesn't stop talking.

'And I'm not going to hold you up,' she says, 'but I just wanted to say that I've often thought about you – well, about the whole thing, really. We were all so sad about – what happened. Your handsome brother. And Roddy, of course. Poor Roddy.'

'Yes,' Bettina says. The sun is out again. She raises a hand to protect her eyes. She never thinks to take sunglasses anywhere. She imagines that Aurora sleeps in hers. Maybe that's it, she thinks, and gets ready to walk away. But then Aurora puts her hand on her arm. Bettina turns towards her. She's moved away from the sharpness of the sun and there's nothing to protect her from the seriousness, the genuineness, shining out at her from Aurora's eyes.

'I just want to say. All of that silly business with me teasing Roddy all the time. We were all silly then, weren't we? We didn't really know how lucky we were.'

'I suppose not.' Bettina is beyond uncomfortable now: even Aurora looks as though she doesn't quite know what to say, or how to say it. But she ploughs on.

'You probably don't remember what I was like,' Aurora says, 'but I was an awful flirt, really. Roddy never took the blindest bit of notice, of course.' She laughs, as though she's about to share a slightly amusing memory, which Bettina, afterwards, supposes that it is, to her: 'I

168

remember one morning at my parents' place. I knocked at his bedroom door in nothing but my knickers. Roddy looked me straight in the eyes and said, "I can't wait to see Tina."'

'Oh.' Aurora releases Bettina's arm, and nudges her sunglasses down to cover her eyes. Bettina closes her eyes: tries to find a place of balance, of calm.

'I suppose I was jealous of you,' Aurora shrugs, 'because I wasn't used to taking no for an answer. But he was never interested in me, you know.'

'I know,' Bettina says. And she thinks of how she wishes that she had.

Part Six: Missingham, July 1998

THERE'S NOTHING QUITE like being away from home, Roddy thinks, to make you want to be back there. He likes Missingham, his parents and their set-up. He always has. That's not to say he won't do things differently, when it's his turn. But he has no doubt as to which corner of the world fits all of his corners.

Still, Roddy has learned a lot with the Fieldens. They run a tight, commercial operation – not that the Floods are exactly sentimental – and they treat their horses, their competitors and their clients all with the same businesslike affability. Edward and Arabella were both products of the boarding school system that Roddy managed to avoid, by virtue of there being a good private school close enough to Missingham for him to attend as a day boy. Edward and Arabella, though, seem to have enjoyed boarding school so much that their home is run along similar lines. They are fond of timetables and order, and impervious to noise.

The dining table seats twelve and is usually full to capacity, with two parents and four daughters, at least two of whom would have a boyfriend in tow, and the others likely to have at least one giggling friend, any visitors to the yard, plus Roddy. (It had taken a while for Roddy to understand that he was the cause of much of the giggling: in fact, Arabella calling 'will you girls please stop talking about poor Roddy like that, he does have ears, you know' had made it all much worse for him, although the girls had only giggled more.) If the table looks as though it will run out of elbow room, Arabella will call the names or catch the eyes of her younger daughters and, with a jerk of her head, dismiss them, chattering and laughing, to eat in the living room, where they are allowed to sprawl and watch television as they eat.

'I bet it's not often that you can't get a word in edge-ways!' Aurora says one morning as they walk across from the house to the stables. Foxglove and Bob will already have been groomed and tacked up – something Roddy can't get used to. Riding without the preparation feels like cheating.

'True,' he says.

'I bet you can't wait to get back.'

'No, not at all.' Roddy hates the idea that he might be showing his occasional annoyance, his tiredness, his wish for Tina's quiet hands working next to his. 'It's just different.'

'You must miss Tina, though.'

'Yes,' he says firmly. Because all the rules seem to be different here – especially the ones about manners and personal space – it has taken Roddy a while to get wise to Aurora's attempts at – well, seduction is too sophisti-cated a word for it, really. He often finds Aurora wandering around the kitchen in the morning in only knickers and a T-shirt that barely covers her midriff. She knocks on his door when wearing nothing but a towel, looking to borrow a magazine, or something else that she could easily ask for when fully dressed. And as if Aurora's advances weren't enough to contend with, there's Anastasia, Aurora's next sister down. (He thinks she's next anyway; they all begin with A, all have dark hair and green eyes, all smell of peach soap and heavy perfume and illicit cigarettes, so although he's sorted out the names, he isn't completely clear on ages.) It had begun with friendly questions about Flood Farm, but ended with a hand on his thigh and an inept reference to loneliness. There had been a time when Roddy would have taken up such offers – although only from one of the sisters, he wasn't an idiot. Or rather, there had been a time when the memory of a girl he liked a hundred and fifty miles away would have faded with the distance, and left him free when he arrived at his new destination. Roddy has never cheated on a girl, never would; instead, he's remained uncommitted, un-promised, and no one has ever been surprised when he's moved on.

The frustrating thing is that now he can't manage to have a decent conversation with Tina. The distance has confirmed the way he feels about her, even though she seems to have absolutely no idea of how special she is – to him, and in her own right, someone who is self-possessed and steady, who knows how to work and who is thoughtful and honest and direct. He has a mobile phone but the Fieldens' place is too far away from anywhere to get reception. Tina doesn't have a mobile – she says she has more important things to spend her money on, and she sees everyone she needs to talk to most days – and the phone at her house is in the corner of the living room, so there's no privacy for her. He calls home to Flood Farm on a Friday night, when he knows that she will be there, and she carries the phone to sit on the stairs and talk to him, and he sits on the stairs at the Fielden place, but all they can manage to discuss is their horses. Tina's tongue is loosened by the mention of Snowdrop, and so Roddy questions her about him, asks about progress with Perry, and laughs at things that aren't really very funny, just for the relief of talking to her.

Of course he would never have given her Snowdrop – and his parents would never have agreed to it – if he hadn't known that Tina Randolph was The One. What he hadn't understood, until now, sitting on the stairs with a Siamese cat yowling round his ankles and the sound of at least seven conversations coming through the wall at him from the dining room, was how deeply love would affect him. He'd thought he would miss Tina, but 'missing' had been an abstract concept, something that he didn't think would get in the way. He hadn't thought he would lie awake thinking about her, hadn't imagined that saying goodbye to her on the phone would mean that he would need to step outside the back door and breathe the warm evening air until his heart had steadied and he could go back into the house and play his part: Roddy Flood, rising star, down-to-earth sort, practically one of the family.

One night, he'd attempted to tell Tina that he missed her; but as soon as the words were out of his mouth, there was a fit of giggling from below, and Antonia and Amber, Fieldens three and four (Roddy thinks), clattered out from under the stairs where they had been listening in. So Roddy didn't even hear Tina's reply.

Still. It's only a week until his trip home for the Flood Ball, which falls in the middle of his time away. He'd hoped that Tina would come down to see him, or he would come up, some time before, but his show schedule is heavy and the Floods' stable yard staffing is stretched, partly by his absence and partly because it's the summer holiday season so they are at least one groom down every day. After the ball, it's only four weeks until he goes home for good. Or, if not for good, home for the last time before he makes things with Tina more permanent. He, Fred and Fran had always talked, in a one-of-these-days way, about converting one of the out-buildings for Roddy when he wanted to have his own place, but given the easy relationship he had with his parents, and the fact that they didn't mind his girlfriends staying over and didn't comment about who those girl-friends were, there has never been much of a need. Now, it feels like time for him and Tina to have their own place. He thinks Tina will agree. He thinks that she loves him. But he thinks, too, about the things she said about the two of them, that strange night when she'd cried.

He wishes he'd managed to tell her, better than he did, that he felt as though he was the lucky one, saved from the Auroras and Fudges of the world by her simple, quiet way of being. He's arrived at the place where he wants to be, and found it as solid and calm as a steady canter. He gets all the excitement that he needs in his life by jumping a clear round, and anyway life with Tina near him is quietly, viscerally thrilling, because he just cannot believe that she would want to put up with him and all that comes with him, the weight of expectation, the crazy years of competition coming up, the fact that he didn't even think about what effect his being away would have on her. He had been amazed to find that Tina would think any differently about the two of them, let alone see herself as a second-best option. He was glad that she was so moved by his gift of Snowdrop. There had been a moment, as they made their way down to the yard, when he doubted his wisdom. He had wondered whether she would turn to him and say, but don't you see, this just goes to show how different we are. You live in a world where you can give a horse away. But she had got it, and he had headed for the Fieldens' place as sure as he could be that all was well.

'Still, not long to the ball!' Aurora says, as they walk the course that's set up for them today. The turns are tight.

'Yes.'

'Anastasia's agitating to come this year, but I've told her there won't be enough room in the car.'

'You're coming?' He hopes he doesn't sound disappointed.

'Yes, of course, we always come! Don't you remember our little . . . escapade?'

Ah, yes, he does. Well, barely. He remembers getting drunk and being pulled into a – what was it, a cupboard, a cloakroom? – by Aurora, who had tried to take his trousers off. She had been as drunk as he was, and she gave up on his cummerbund in giggles, and undid his zip instead. Her bracelet had caught in it, so they had to be rescued by – he can't remember who. He remembers a lot of whispering, though, and how the story expanded and expanded until it was a legend nothing like the tawdry, disorienting fumble Roddy can only half recall.

'Anastasia might enjoy herself,' he says.

Aurora pulls a face. 'Yes, but we'll have to listen to her jabbering all the way, and all the way back, and with Ma and Pa and you and me and Anastasia and all the dresses and everything squashed into the car, it will be a nightmare.'

Roddy laughs, enjoying Aurora's cheerful ignorance of her own non-stop talking. 'Yes, it would be,' he says, 'but I'll take the Cosworth, and then you can all travel in a bit more comfort.'

'Oh, good,' Aurora says, 'that sounds like fun! I'll come with you.'

Roddy's mother is rarely uncharitable, but she has been heard to say that when Aurora Fielden dies her epitaph will be 'you couldn't knock her back with a stick'. This comes back to Roddy more than once as he tries to dissuade Aurora from travelling with him. He tells her that he has to take a detour to collect something for his father. She doesn't mind a bit. He says that he drives too fast. She says she likes speed. He had half planned to meet up with some old friends. That's all right: Aurora might know them, and if she doesn't, he can just leave her somewhere to do a bit of shopping, or she can join in the fun and he'll hardly know she's there.

He might stay on an extra day or two to spend some time with Tina. Well, Aurora can make herself useful around the yard, see what else she can pick up from the Floods, and she's sure Fran won't mind a bit of girl-talk around the place for a change. Roddy laughs when Aurora says this. Aurora takes this as assent. And so the plan is in place.

Even though the Flood Ball has been the main topic of conversation between the Fielden women for what feels like weeks, on the night before the ball it seems that none of them has yet decided what they are going to wear.

Arabella is torn between three dresses that she already owns, trying to decide which will best set off the diamonds she has inherited from her mother-in-law since last year's event. Aurora has a new ice-blue strapless dress that she keeps taking off and putting on, and something that's the colour of blood with a full skirt, and wondering whether she shouldn't have had it altered. And Anastasia, who has never been to the Flood Ball before, seems to have a never-ending supply of things to try on, although some of them are Aurora's cast-offs. Sometimes when Aurora sees her sister in them she wonders about reclaiming them, and Anastasia pouts and shrieks about looking better in them than Aurora does, and Roddy thanks the moon and stars that he doesn't have sisters.

Aurora is able to remember not only what she's worn over the last several years, but what her mother, Fran, and almost anyone else the others could name had worn, too. Edward and Roddy are asked their opinion on several dresses, but soon ignored, as Roddy tactfully says that everyone looks lovely in everything, and Edward says that all dresses look the same to him.

Roddy manages to slope off to phone Tina.

'What are you wearing to the ball?' he asks, hoping that there will be a simple answer.

'Oh. Black,' Tina says as though that is all the description a dress needs and deserves, 'and a choker and earrings of Katrina's. Quite nice shoes but I don't know if I can walk in them. My mother's been making me practise.' Her voice says everything about how she feels about this. 'In fact, I'm wearing them now. With your shirt, to try to break them in a bit.'

'God, Tina.' Roddy is practically growling with lust, not so much at the shoes as at the idea of Tina in the shirt that he's peeled off her so many times. 'Let's just get the bloody ball over with. I can't wait to have you to myself.'

'Me too,' Tina says, then, in fear of sounding ungrateful, or unsupportive, she adds, 'I'm sure the ball will be fun, but I really don't see what all the fuss is about.' She tells Roddy about her mother and father bickering that afternoon, her mother having been climbing a ladder in a pair of high black slingbacks to try to persuade Flora down from the apple tree. Alice had thought that her behaviour was entirely reasonable: if I'm going to be dancing in them, she'd said, I have to be used to them, and so I'm wearing them all day. I'd forgotten I even had them on, which just goes to show that I was perfectly safe. She'd rolled her eyes at Tina, who was spending her

181

day off in the kitchen, trying to replicate Fran's walnut and honey loaf, but without the walnuts as Sam didn't like them. ('Look like brains, taste like dust,' he would say as he picked them off the top of coffee cakes.) Her father's talk of broken ankles and cats who can go up being able to come down had been ignored, even when Flora strolled in having got down from the tree unaided. And Tina had kneaded and watched and counted down the hours, not until the ball but to the time when the ball was over, when it would be just her and Roddy and they could be, she hoped, as they were. She tells Roddy about her mother, the slingbacks, the ladder, and then she hears herself saying, 'I've missed you.'

Roddy says, 'Yes. Me too.'

'I can't wait to see you,' she says, her voice low. 'I've missed you so much.' It's as though he can feel her heart pulsing its beat down the line.

'Me too. Me too.'

The first and worst part of the separation is almost over – the ball sits just after the midpoint of Roddy's stay with the Fieldens – and that, coupled with the fact that this time tomorrow – tomorrow! – they will be together, is making a telephone line an easier thing to negotiate.

'This has been harder than I thought,' Tina says.

'I know.'

'Still. Tomorrow.'

'Yes.' He can't bring himself to tell her that he's got stuck with Aurora for the journey; there's such a calm accord between them now, he doesn't want even the thought of Aurora to get in the way. 'I'll be glad when the ball is over and it's just us.' He knows there's something he's supposed to ask Tina – his mother had recited his duties to him down the phone earlier, and although it was mostly the usual meet-and-greet and making sure no one did anything really stupid, he thinks there was something to do with Tina, too.

'Me too.' It's as though he can hear her smiling. Anastasia, in a satin dressing gown now and carrying four shoeboxes balanced with the point of her chin, comes past. Roddy reaches out from his perch on the third step up the stairs to kick the door open for her. She winks at him.

'We can talk about what we do next, too.'

'What we do next?' Tina sounds puzzled, a little bit frightened. A burst of laughter comes from the Fielden kitchen. At Tina's end of the line, a steady beep begins.

'It'll wait,' Roddy says, 'but it's all good.'

'I need to go,' Tina says. 'My bread's done.'

'See you tomorrow, love,' he says. But she's gone. He wonders if she is as sure of him as he is of her. He's never known anyone who has made him think like this before.

The day of the Flood Ball is a short day at the Flood stables. All afternoon lessons are cancelled, and anyone who's not going to the ball takes on the bulk of the afternoon work so that those who are can go and get ready. Tina, who plans to shower, shave her legs and armpits, dress, and let Katrina do her make-up, cannot see how even in slow motion getting ready will take more than an hour and a half. So she stays at the stables until it's time for the hairdressing appointment that her mother has insisted on, and hopes that Roddy will get back before she has to go.

She hacks out on Snowdrop and then drinks tea with Fran, who is finalizing the table plan and swearing blind that they won't be doing this next year, which Roddy says happens every year. But the Flood Ball has been a tradition for twenty years, the Coach and Horses at Coltswell booked out for the night, dinner and dancing for two hundred, with a Flood guest list of staff and friends and the rest of the great and good scrambling over each other to pay fifty pounds per ticket, all proceeds to charity.

'I don't know whether to pray for rain or hope that this weather holds until tomorrow,' she says, as Tina opens a window and props the back door open. After a fortnight of relentless sun, horses and people alike are getting tetchy. Every other conversation around the stable yard has been about how hairspray and make-up will behave in the heat at the ball. Tina has been sleeping with the window open, on top of her bedclothes, and still waking in a sweat, her hair damp.

'Do you think your parents will mind sitting with us tonight, Tina?'

'Not at all. Quite the opposite.' Alice is fascinated by the Floods. She can't quite get over the fact that her daughter is going out with someone whose photo has been in the papers. Tina has often heard her mother joke about how both of her children have ideas above their station. She hopes she has the sense not to say so tonight.

'Good.' Tick. 'I've put Aurora and Anastasia on a

separate table to you and Roddy – I think he's fairly desperate for a break from them – but whether they'll stay there is another matter. Those girls are a law unto themselves. I'm sure Roddy's told you.'

'He doesn't say a lot about them, to be honest.' And Tina can't help but wonder why. If Roddy really didn't care about Aurora, surely he would talk about her more – the two of them are spending most of every day together, after all. If there's nothing to hide, why hide it? The nearer their reunion gets, the more knotted up Tina is becoming; everything that's been lying buried is coming to the surface.

'What about Sam? I've put him with you and Roddy and a few of Roddy's old crowd, is that all right?'

'Of course.' Tick.

'I loathed my brother and sister,' Fran says, looking up. 'You and Sam are a revelation to me.' She goes back to her list. 'And we're still picking up your parents, is that right? And Sam can come with us? I'll put his name down for the coach home, in case he wants to stay longer than we do. I assume you'll come with Roddy in his car?'

'I think that's the plan.' Tick.

'And you're staying over at the Coach and Horses?' Fran is working through her list, her questions not really questions, and so Tina hates to interrupt.

'I don't know anything about that.'

'Oh. Well. We always get a couple of complimentary rooms. Fred and I used to stay over, but I'm going to drive this year. Edward and Arabella are having the other room. I asked Roddy if the two of you would want it.'

'He hasn't mentioned it to me.' Why wouldn't he want her to spend the night with him? Was he keeping his options open? Has he changed his mind about her? He would want to tell her that he was ending their relationship in person: he would consider doing it on the phone dishonourable. Tina takes a deep breath, tells herself to stop. She knows she's being ridiculous.

Fran is continuing as though Tina hasn't said a word. 'Last year there were a couple of things that didn't go very well, and so I need to make sure there's at least one clear head among us. So it makes sense for us to drive back. Do you remember last year?'

Tina remembers the yard tales of a joker lacing the non-alcoholic punch with something very definitely not non-alcoholic, and an argument that ended in, depending on who you listened to, either a broken earring or a torn earlobe, with or without an accompanying fistful of bloodied hair. 'I wasn't there last year,' she says.

'Oh, of course not,' Fran says, matter-of-factly. She is very unlike Tina's own mother, who can imagine nothing better than a party, people and noise and dressing-up. 'The bits I'll like most tonight will be talking to the people I haven't seen in a while, our former staff who have grown up and moved on, and I could do that just as happily in my jeans in this kitchen. And for you young ones, if you're not part of the in-crowd, well . . .'

'I know,' Tina says. She had never been to a Flood Ball because she knew she'd stand on the sidelines there as much as she did in the yard. Even though, as one of the staff, she was always invited, the thought of spending her wages on a dress that made her feel awkward and shoes that would hurt her feet hadn't appealed. But this year she would be with Roddy, and because Roddy was there she thought she might enjoy it. So long as there's not too much Aurora; so long as her worst fears aren't realized. She breathes deeply again.

To turn her thoughts away from the Roddy/Flood Ball stories that had filled the yard on the morning after, over the years, she asks, 'What are you wearing?'

'God knows,' Fran says. 'I'll probably be going in my jeans at this rate.'

And then there's a familiar sound in the driveway. Tina never thought she would be able to identify the sound of one particular car, but the rumble of Roddy's Cosworth is unmistakable. She and Fran look at each other, jump to their feet, as though they are children who just heard sleighbells on the roof.

The first thing Tina notices is how tanned Roddy is. He gets out of the car and stretches his arms above his head, and where the arms of his T-shirt fall back, there's a line where his skin goes from pale roan to cream. He might be a bit more solid than he was. Those cowboy boots, the hair that kinks. He winks. Tina's thighs tingle; her stomach lurches; her mouth is warming, waiting. She and Fran start to walk down the path towards him. Instead of him coming towards them, though, he walks to the passenger door and opens it.

'It's Aurora,' Fran says. 'I assumed she'd be coming with the rest of the Fieldens.'

'Of course it's Aurora,' Tina mutters uncharitably. Fran gives no sign of hearing. Tina's stomach ties itself in a knot and her heart says, I told you so. Roddy hadn't mentioned that he was bringing Aurora. And why would she come with him when she could travel with her family? Anyone would think she and Roddy would be sick of the sight of each other by now. Tina had resolved, on the walk from the farmhouse to the drive, that she would stop letting Aurora bring out the worst in her. Which is so much easier, it turns out, when Aurora isn't there.

Fran goes first to Aurora, embraces her and steers her away, round the back of the car while Tina goes round the front to where Roddy is waiting, hands by his sides, until she's close enough to touch and then he grabs her round the waist, spins her, spins her, spins her. Kisses her. Kisses her again. She's smelling aftershave and shampoo. She's tasting coffee and apples and bacon and feeling the roughness of his fingertips on her throat. Her whole body is an aching, hungry thing. She's laughing at herself, at the impulses in her own fingers and limbs.

Roddy isn't laughing. 'You, you, you,' he says. 'You, you, you. God, Tina.'

'I know,' Tina says. 'Me too.' They kiss again; parts of her melt, other parts beg.

'Do you think anyone would notice if we disappeared upstairs for a bit?' Roddy asks.

Tina laughs. 'Yes, they would notice,' she says, her hand running up his spine under his T-shirt.

There's a growl, the sound of the Range Rover pulling off the main road, bringing the rest of the Fieldens.

'Do you think anyone would mind, then? We haven't seen each other for weeks.'

'I wouldn't mind,' Tina says.

'That's the spirit.' He takes her hand; her fingers shiver. She stops.

'Oh, hell, Roddy—'

'What?'

'Hairdresser. I have to go to the hairdresser.'

'I'll do your hair. I'll do it sort of – mussy.' He runs his fingers up her skull, base to crown. Tina's scalp dances. Her mouth waters.

'My mother's taking me. I'm under orders. Sorry. It will have to be later.' Being wanted makes Tina taller, makes her smile, makes her wonder whether this feeling, this glow in the cradle of her stomach, this sense of light bending towards her, is what it feels like to be Aurora Fielden all the time. It probably is. Aurora probably doesn't notice. The Range Rover is coming up the drive. Before Roddy and Tina can get away, Tina is engulfed in Aurora, who hugs her and then steps back. Tina is no expert but she thinks Aurora's earrings are real diamonds. She smells of CK One.

'Hello, Tina! This boy of yours nearly killed me in his rush to get back here to see you,' she lowers her voice, 'although you need to watch him. He could tell you which knickers I'm wearing, right now!'

Roddy rolls his eyes and shakes his head. Aurora laughs and shoves his arm. Tina reminds herself that she's not going to let Aurora get the better of her, but her stomach shrivels and her heart cries out.

'I have to go,' Tina says, 'hairdresser. My mum will kill me if I'm late. She says it's the busiest day of the year and it took a Bakewell slice and a parkin to get us in. I'll see you all later.'

189

'Tell your parents and Sam we'll collect them at seven, Tina,' Fran calls.

'Will do,' Tina calls back. She eases herself away from the hubbub of the Fieldens' tumultuous disembarking. Roddy follows.

'I thought I'd drive you tonight,' Roddy says as they walk down to the gate, where Alice is waiting, looking at her watch as though trying to slow down the passage of time with her glare.

'I made her late, Mrs Randolph,' he says, kissing Alice on the cheek. 'It's my fault.'

'Oh, don't be silly, Roddy, it's only the hairdresser,' Alice says, while Tina tries not to catch Roddy's eye, feeling the laughter waiting in them both. 'It's good to have you home. She's been pining for you.'

'Not as much as I've been pining for her.' Roddy kisses Tina, gently, on the cheek, squeezes her, hard, on the bottom, which her mother can't see. When Alice has turned away she slides her fingers down the front of his jeans. He growls. She laughs. She loves the person Roddy makes her.

'He's a lovely boy, is Roddy. Lovely manners,' her mother says as they race down the road, Tina in her trainers struggling to keep up with her mother's fierce tip-tapping.

Katrina has assured Tina that her hair is long enough to go up in a chignon, although when Katrina had tried it the result had been painful and only briefly successful, her curls springing free before enough hairspray could be added to keep them in place. The hairdresser does better, and even Tina has to admit that she looks sophisticated. Alice's hair plans are more ambitious –

she has a picture torn from a magazine, of Bette Midler on a red carpet, her hair in ringlets.

The hairdresser manages it to Alice's satisfaction, and Tina and her mother return home, where Katrina and Sam are sitting chatting on the sofa. Tina couldn't swear to it but she thinks Sam might have his hand on her knee when they walk in. Katrina's make-up box and brushes are at her feet. 'Right!' she says when she sees her friend. 'Let's get started.'

At six, everyone is called to the kitchen. Howard is in his dressing gown and has just shaved, as evidenced by the neatly folded squares of toilet roll to the right of his chin and the left of his ear. He is pouring tea into mugs and buttering toast. Alice, sitting next to him, is fully made up, wrapped in a kimono and sipping her tea through a straw. 'Smaller,' she says as her husband offers her a square of toast, 'I've just spent twenty minutes setting my lipstick and I don't want to do it again.'

Obediently, as though he's doing the most normal thing in the world, Howard cuts the toast again, and pops it into his wife's mouth piece by piece, while she opens and closes her lips like a hungry chick. Tina, in Roddy's dressing gown, is being guided to her place by a solicitous Katrina, who has wadded Tina's toenails apart with foam separators.

'You lot are a sight for sore eyes,' Sam says as he comes downstairs, a towel round his waist. University, where he rows and runs for his college, has made him longer and stronger. He's shaved too, and pulled back his hair into a ponytail. Even Tina can see that he's heart-stoppingly handsome, although she usually regards her twin in much the same way as she regards her own face – barely worth considering, as she's stuck with it. She glances at Katrina, who is cherry pink to the earlobes at the sight of this nearly naked vision.

'Hey, Katrina,' Sam says, with a grin so flirtatious it would make a stripper blush, 'how are you doing with trying to make my sister presentable?'

'Sam, behave,' Tina says, at the same moment her mother says, 'Sam, go and put something on.'

'I don't want to get butter on my shirt,' Sam says, 'which, also, I need to iron. Unless someone would like to iron it for me.'

'I think your watch stopped sixty years ago, darling,' Alice says. The rest of them laugh.

'Well said, Mum,' Tina says.

'The Floods will be here for us in an hour,' Alice says, 'and you need to be ready.'

'It won't take him an hour to iron his shirt, Alice,' Howard says, 'he's just teasing you.'

'Well, he should know better than to tease his poor old mother.' They all laugh, at the thought of anyone considering Alice either poor or old. Alice beams and adds, 'Anyway, you've always said that boy would be late for his own funeral.'

'I'm getting better,' Sam says, 'I've hardly been late for anything.'

'You did miss your train yesterday,' Tina says mildly. Katrina laughs.

'Trains are different,' Sam says, making Katrina laugh again. He takes another slice of toast. 'Aren't they feeding us?' he asks.

'Yes,' Howard says, 'but we won't sit down until eight, or more likely half past. The starter won't be much of anything, so that means nine before we get something decent to eat.'

'What your father means,' Alice says, 'is that he wants to weigh me down a bit so I don't get over-excited with the wine and the high heels and run off with a steeplechaser.'

Tina's father holds his hands up.

Sam adds marmalade. He's the only one who's eating toast in any quantity; Tina is all nerves, her mother all tiny bites, her father, if the crumbs caught in the lapels of his navy towelling dressing gown are anything to go by, had his as he was waiting for everyone else to answer his call.

Sam asks, 'Is this bread one of yours, Tina?' Flora is curled on his lap, and the weight of her is pulling the knot of his towel apart at the waist. No one has noticed except Katrina, who can't look away.

'Yes,' Tina says, 'it's not very good. That's why we're toasting it.'

'Waste not, want not,' Howard says.

'It's still better than shop bread,' Alice says, 'and it fills Tina's evenings when she's missing Roddy.'

'She's not missing him any more,' Katrina says, daring a glance at Sam, rewarded with a smile. And this time Tina blushes. She doesn't dare wiggle her toes, for fear of spoiling Katrina's handiwork. She wonders whether the ball will be anything like as much fun as things are now, with her family, round this table. The thoughts of Roddy all to herself later, of Snowdrop bedded down, sleek and

193

happy, make her warm. Though Roddy didn't mention them staying over. She gets a little cooler, worry and goosebumps over her heart.

As sudden as tripping on a pavement, there's the sound of summer rain against the window. Alice wails, and Howard goes to hunt out golf umbrellas from the cupboard under the stairs, and Sam smiles a broad smile at Katrina and Tina and they smile broad smiles back, and the preparations are on again.

Although Tina doesn't care for dressing up, she's pleased with how she looks. Her hair is so solid that the hairdresser gave her special instructions for how to disassemble it. It's not too fussy, and the tendrils that the hairdresser has pulled down either side of her face have been straightened, so she almost doesn't recognize herself without a curl somewhere. Katrina's choker and earrings are made of black beads, round and tearshaped, and the choker sits nicely at Tina's throat. She's not used to the sight of herself with anything more than mascara on, and had told Katrina that if there was too much make-up she would wait until her friend had left, wash it all off and go to the ball barefaced. But Katrina has done well, using mascara, eyeliner and a smudge of turquoise eyeshadow, a shimmer of blusher and lipgloss.

Tina's dress is crushed black velvet, with a neckline that scoops from shoulder-tip to shoulder-tip, just under her clavicle. It fits her body neatly, and ends at her knee. Her tights and shoes are black and her fingernails are newly painted the pale, frosted pink of candyfloss. She looks at herself in the mirror, up and down, thinks of the Fielden girls with their choice of ball dresses, with fish-tails and trains and bows on the shoulders or at the top of perky backsides, and makes up her mind that if ever there was a time to be happy in her skin, it's tonight. She might not look fancy compared to the others, but she feels fancy enough. She just hopes that she's fancy enough for Roddy.

'Thanks, Katrina,' she says.

'Don't hug me, you'll smudge!' her friend says, and calls, 'Here she comes!' from the bedroom door.

Katrina ushers her downstairs. Tina wonders whether this is what being a bride is like, even the most ordinary of activities managed as though they are tricky fences, and applauded and wondered at accordingly. 'Goodness!' says Alice, with delight and an undertow of reproach. 'You see how lovely you look?' Her father nods and smiles.

This is ridiculous, Tina thinks, being congratulated for looking like a girl for once. But actually, they all look different. Special. Her mother is in the cerise that makes her skin come alive, and is as thrilled as a three-year-old by her new shoes, which she keeps pulling back her dress to admire. 'I can climb a ladder in these, you know, Katrina,' she says, and Katrina laughs.

Howard tuts and says, 'Katrina, you have no idea what I have to put up with.'

Katrina isn't listening because she's straightening Sam's tie. 'I can get it ninety-five per cent there,' he says, 'but the other five per cent always eludes me.' Katrina steps back to admire – ostensibly, the tie, but her eyes stray up, down.

'It seems a shame that you're not coming with us,' Sam says to her.

'It's fifty pounds,' Katrina says, a shrug in her shoulders, 'and I'm saving for a car.'

'Well, next year,' Sam says, 'will you come with us? With me?'

'Of course I will,' Katrina says. She looks at Tina, as if to say, did you hear this?

'Photos!' Alice says, but before she can line them up, arrange them, there's the sound of a knock, only just louder than the hammering rain.

Howard opens the door and Fran steps over their threshold. There's a flurry of greetings, and then she says, 'Fred's just turning the car round.' Her hair is twisted up on the top of her head, and she wears tiny sapphire studs, no other jewellery apart from her wedding ring. Her dress is deep blue satin, and she holds the skirt scooped in her arms as though it's a cat she's just found in the washing basket.

'Well, you all look lovely,' Fran says, surveying. 'Tina, Roddy won't be able to take his eyes off you. You're all he's talked about since he got back.'

'Really?' Tina says. She doesn't think she's spoken a word about Roddy. But she's thought about him. And Aurora.

'You'd better watch out, Tina,' Sam says, 'they're doing the mother-in-law look.' And Alice and Fran are smiling at each other in a way that seems all conspiracy.

'No time for this,' Howard says matter-of-factly, 'let's get this show on the road.'

'I'm afraid we've got Anastasia in the car with us,'

Fran says, 'because she couldn't make up her mind which dress to wear, and then the dress she chose means that she doesn't think she'll be able to get up the coach steps. It's sort of a – oh, I don't know. Mermaid? Fish-tail? Very tight around the knees anyway.'

'Oh, I know the sort of thing,' Alice says. 'Lovely if you have the figure for it.'

Sam has whispered something to Katrina, who is giggling.

'Anyway,' Fran says, 'we were hoping we'd have room for Sam, but now there's Anastasia, which means there are five of us. Edward and Arabella went ahead with the place cards and seating plan so that the restaurant can have them set up when people start arriving. These things never go to plan, do they – so . . . Sam, I'm sorry, would you mind going on the coach? Or Roddy says if you don't mind squashing into the back of the Cosworth you can get a lift with him and Tina. He says he'll be here at half past.'

'I'm easy,' Sam says.

'Well, Aurora says she'll save you a seat if you do want to go on the coach. I think Roddy well and truly put her off the Cosworth this afternoon.'

'You can come with us,' Tina says to her brother.

'Are you sure? I don't want to be a gooseberry.'

'You won't be.'

Katrina dashes back home under a borrowed umbrella when Fred, Fran, Howard, Alice and Anastasia drive away. Sam and Tina stand in the porch, waving them off. The rain stutters, then stops. The air smells good after it, full of roses and hedges and a comforting warmth.

'This is weird. Like being an adult,' Sam says.

'I suppose it is,' Tina says, although she's not feeling much like one. 'Oh, and don't tease Katrina.'

'I wasn't teasing her.'

'About the ball next year.'

'I wasn't teasing.'

'What about—' Tina struggles to remember Sam's girlfriend's name, 'Debbie?'

Sam looks blank. 'Oh, you mean Dana. Oh, that crashed and burned. Not literally.'

'I thought you liked her.' There had been photos, at Easter, and talk of summer plans together.

'The thing is, for all the attractions of Oxford, I haven't seen a girl in the world I like as much as Katrina.'

'You never liked her before.'

'Well, university opens your eyes to a lot of things. Including how lovely Katrina is.'

'Are you teasing me?' All of her instincts – twinstincts, Katrina calls them – say that he isn't, but this is such an unexpected idea. When Sam had gone to Oxford Tina thought it would be the start of his great adventure, and that he'd never look back.

'No, I'm not teasing. I need to know where I'm going to be, though, so I can persuade her to come with me. You and Roddy can keep the Missingham fires burning. Double wedding, then Katrina and I will be off somewhere exciting, and you and Roddy can stay here. We'll come back and be prodigal once a year; you can come to us for holidays. Happy ever after. Job done.'

'You are teasing me,' Tina says. But if he is, it's the best sort of teasing, a tease with a little bit of truth to it.

Because Tina would marry Roddy right now if he asked her, although if he didn't she would happily sleep in his shirt, with him at her side, for ever.

Part Seven: Throckton and
Missingham, 2013

Since the Throckton Spring Fête Bettina and Rufus have managed only a quiet dinner and a couple of nights together. On one of the nights Bettina had been quieter than ever, and had been asleep – or appeared asleep – when he came out of the bathroom to join her in bed. The next morning, a Monday, they had had gentle, half-asleep sex; Rufus had gone to work leaving Bettina already at her laptop. Throughout the other night Bettina had tossed and turned in her sleep, waking Rufus with muttered gibberish spiked with the occasional clear word: bob, perry, snowdrop. He has put her unsettled night down to her being in his bed rather than him in hers and it gets him thinking, about how the future might be easier.

When she leaves him, Bettina kisses him on the mouth and says, I'm sorry to be always rushing, but there's a lot going on at the moment. And she's gone, before Rufus can formulate the thought that, if the fête was taking up all of her time and the fête is now over, then surely there should be more time for them, not less. He has noticed that her limp seems more pronounced. He's just done a barn conversion for an orthopaedic surgeon, who says that surgery has come on a great deal in fifteen years, and he would be happy to meet Rufus's paramour – the surgeon's word, although Rufus rather likes it – and see if he can fix her up. ('Fix her up' Rufus likes less.)

But when he had asked Bettina about the limp, she'd smiled a sad smile and said, I don't think it's fixable because I don't think there's a medical reason for it. I think I limp because of what I lost. It makes him think that, if surgery can't solve the problem, then perhaps love can. So he loves.

It's just over two weeks since the fête, a few minutes after eight on a warm Monday evening, when Rufus comes home to find Bettina waiting at his door. She's pale and determined-looking, her skin pinching at the corners of her eyes. 'I was watching for your car,' she says. 'It's my mother.'

Rufus assumes that Alice has died. He puts a hand to Bettina's waist as he reaches to unlock the door. 'I'm so sorry,' he says, and steps back so that she can go into the flat. But she stands outside. 'No, not that,' she says, 'but I have to go. She's getting worse. Her chest. It's getting worse.'

'I see,' Rufus says. He doesn't quite. Unless, 'You want me to drive you there?'

'Yes,' Bettina says, 'no. I mean, I don't really want to go in a car. But I think the trains might take too long. They rang at four but I didn't hear the phone. I've taken my anti-sickness tablets.' Her eyes are darker than usual in her paler than usual face. Her lips are the same colour as her skin. She's shaking. There's a piece of paper in her hand; she holds it out and it vibrates in the evening air.

It's the letterhead of the care home, with the address.

'Are you ready to go?'

'Yes.' She's holding her usual handbag, a woven brown leather satchel that doesn't look as though it will hold very much.

'You don't want to take anything?'

'I just want to go.' Her voice is steady but her eyes plead. So Rufus closes his front door again and walks her to the car; opens the passenger door for her, and then gets in the driver's side. He's in, seat-belted, and has set up the sat-nav before Bettina has got in and closed the door.

He turns the key in the ignition and the engine starts. He feels how her body reacts, a jolt of tension running through it.

'Would you like the radio on, or some music?'

'Music, please. Nothing with words. You choose.'

Rufus does. He wonders whether the shaking is actually shivering. It's cooler now that the sun is going down. Although Bettina is wearing a cardigan, it doesn't look warm.

'Are you cold?' he asks.

'I don't know,' she half smiles, as if to say, fancy not knowing whether I'm cold or not.

'I'll put your heated seat on. Tell me if you get too hot.'

'Heated seat?'

'Yes. It'll take a minute or two, but then you'll feel it.'

The other half of the smile comes along. 'It's my first time in a heated seat.'

Rufus reverses out of his parking space. A glance tells

him that Bettina has, somehow, got paler still, the tone of her skin moving from ricepaper to tracing paper. He stops the car and touches her knee, and asks: 'Do you need anything else?'

'I've taken my tablets. I won't be sick,' she says. 'They make me drowsy, though. I might go to sleep.'

'That seems like a good way to spend the time,' Rufus says, thinking that she might not get a lot of sleep tonight. 'Are you ready?'

She nods, closes her eyes.

Bettina doesn't recognize the classical music but it's just right. Complicated and intense, neither sad nor ecstatic, it holds her in a place between panic and peace that isn't comfortable, but it's bearable. Her hands pick at each other but the rest of her is still. She breathes in leather and Rufus's aftershave, which is musky, almost sweet. She keeps her eyes closed and waits for the journey to be over, although she doesn't really want to arrive. Somewhere, she dozes, but she doesn't know how long for.

It's after half past nine and moving from dusk to darkness when they pull into the car park, which is emptier than Bettina has ever seen it. Rufus parks by the door, switches off the engine, gets out, opens her door for her, leans over to unbuckle her seat belt. He says, 'Take your time,' although she clearly can't, with someone already holding the care-home door open for her.

Bettina gets out of the car, turns round, puts both hands on the roof, closes her eyes, opens them, closes them. Tries a deep breath. Decides that she isn't going to be sick. Rufus touches her shoulder. She takes her hands off the roof and feels her weight square above her feet again.

'I'll park, then I'll wait in reception for you. Don't worry about me. Just let me know if you want me.'

'Ms May,' says the woman at the door, by way of greeting. Bettina recognizes her as one of the managers, and someone who has always seemed calm and capable. She's glad to see a face she knows. She nods a greeting and walks into the squat, nondescript building that she likes to think of as her mother's home, and would like to think that her mother thinks of as home too, although there's no telling. She can't for the life of her remember the manager's name, although she's sure it's something biblical. Ruth, maybe, or Naomi. Sarah. No – Rebecca.

Too soon, they are at the door, and Bettina finds that her mother is sleeping, but it seems to be a shallow sleep; her hands under the blanket are twitching, and there's no snoring, a sure sign that Alice is either drifting down to slumber, or up from it. The nurse stands and greets Bettina with a small smile. She shakes her head when the manager asks if there's been any change.

Bettina rarely sees her mother in bed. Her visits usually involve sitting in the garden or, in poor weather, settling down by the window in the main room where they can still see the flowers and trees. Although Alice has never articulated it, she has never seemed to want to spend a lot of time in her room, and Bettina has assumed that she associates it with being alone, never her mother's favourite way to spend time. On her last couple of visits, with Alice incapacitated by bruising or by her cough, Bettina had found it strange to see her mother in a single bed. She looks displaced, wrong, without the allowance of space for her husband beside her. The feeling is made worse because the room has recently been redecorated. The paint is bright, the bedding new, and against it her mother looks frail and shabby, an old rug put on top of a new carpet. Bettina sits in the chair near the head of the bed. She touches her mother's forehead, which is hot, and reaches under the duvet for her hand, which is cold. She moves her mother's arm, as biddable as a doll's, and puts it on top of the bedclothes, so that she can hold her hand between both of her own. Alice's hand takes Bettina's and grips it, tightly. Bettina knows that the need to hold a hand is a reflex common to all dementia patients, but she appreciates it, anyway. She thinks about nail varnish. She looks at the pattern on the bedding. When she had realized after her last visit that her mother was likely to be spending more time in bed, she'd ordered it online and had it sent straight to the care home. It's as pretty as she'd hoped, a pattern of entwined leaves and bright magenta flowers, humming-birds hovering here and there.

Her mother had a kimono once, with humming-birds on it. She'd worn it until it wore out, and then put it away to make cushion covers with, although she never had, and Bettina hadn't come across it when she'd cleared what her parents euphemistically called their 'retirement bungalow'. They'd gone, every week, to stand by Sam's grave. Bettina hadn't visited it again, after the first time, until or since her father died.

After Sam died she can't remember her mother willingly making anything, ever again. Toast, tea; that had been it, everything else they ate coming from a packet or a jar, once the casseroles and bakes brought by their neighbours and her mother's many drama-group friends had stopped coming.

The friends had stopped coming too, for no other reason, Bettina thinks, than that they knew they weren't wanted, and they couldn't be a friend to someone who did not so much reject friendship as ignore it, or fail to notice it.

Bettina, who had once been protected from having to see anyone by the nurses at the hospital then her parents – I'm afraid she's not seeing anyone, she would hear her father say, she's not really up to it, and then there'd be a little bit of hushed conversation, the clang of a gate and the sound of a car pulling away – had watched and learned and used this strategy herself when she had moved away. Run away.

'Does she need anything?' Bettina asks, and the nurse shakes her head. 'She's comfortable?' Bettina persists.

'Yes,' the nurse says.

The manager asks, 'Are you happy that we follow our agreed care plan? Some people change their minds. It's an important decision, and sometimes it looks different when we get to this point.'

Bettina thinks of the other option for Alice, which is a late dash to the hospital, then her mother being treated in a room she doesn't recognize, drip-fed and dragged back into a world that she hasn't known how to exist in for a long time. Of course not. All her instincts tell her that this would be the wrong thing to do for her mother, whose body is at last catching up with her threadbare mind.

She pushes away the temptation to save her mother for herself, for the sake of having a mother of sorts, still, of not being alone in the world just yet. But, she reminds herself, this moment, now, is exactly why she made the right decisions in advance. No resuscitations from heart attacks, no antibiotics for serious infections. No prolonging the agony.

'Yes,' Bettina says, 'I'm sure.' Her voice twitches, cracks, in the dry air. She holds her mother's hand and thinks of the quiet, dignified death that is all she can give Alice now.

The manager nods. 'Do you want me to bring your friend along?'

'No, no thank you.'

'Shall I put him in the family bedroom?'

'That would be lovely.' Although Bettina hasn't been thinking about Rufus, doomed to reading and re-reading his *Telegraph* and whatever magazines are in the reception hall, she's glad to have the problem solved. She can imagine her mother's horror at the thought of being introduced to someone when she is in bed. The mother Bettina once had, anyway.

The first part of getting dressed, for Alice, had always been her make-up. Bettina gently puts down her mother's hand and goes into her bathroom, where she finds a little pouch of cosmetics. There is foundation, powder, mascara, lipstick like a robin's breast, eyeshadow the teal of a pigeon's throat. She takes the lipstick back to the bedside and tries to apply it to her mother's mouth, but her lips are dry and slack so the lipstick drags the mouth with it. Bettina rubs her fingertip against the colour and smudges it on that way. Her mother looks at once both more ill, her lips too bright for her pale face, and more like herself.

Sitting in the quiet room, watching her mother sleep, Bettina loses all sense of time and place. The world is shrunk to the ascent and fall of Alice's ribcage, the occasional pauses in her breathing which have Bettina holding her breath, the nurse leaning forward, only to sit back again when Alice inhales.

Somewhere around three, the nurse checks her mother's pulse and nods to Bettina, saying, 'It won't be long now. Her pulse is very faint.'

Bettina nods.

'She can still hear you.'

Bettina nods again. She understands this is her chance to say a last thing, but cannot imagine how to choose such significant words. The last thing she'd said to Sam was, you should be so lucky. The last conversation with her father was about fougasse, a bread where the dough is cut and stretched into a leaf shape, and which she's never been able to look at, let alone bake, since.

She wants to say that she's sorry. She wants to say thank you. But these are words that she uses every day as she gets in Angie's way or takes money or is too tired to stay up beyond nine or as a response to someone who says how much they like her focaccia: and they won't do. Perhaps she should choose a memory to talk about.

But her memories too seem unsuitable, either too grim or too trite.

It's her mother who has the last word. Somewhere around the time that the dawn coughs and shufflings are starting in the rooms around them, Alice opens her eyes.

'Bettina?'

'I'm here, Mum.' Her voice sounds rusty, raw, as though unused for years.

'Bettina. Is that you?'

'Yes.' Please, please, don't ask about Sam, Bettina thinks. Because if you do, I will lie to you and say that he's just gone to get a cup of tea, and I don't want the last thing that you can hear to be a lie.

But Alice's mind, it seems, is wandering another world.

'Roddy was here,' she says, 'lovely boy, Roddy. You could do a lot worse than Roddy, Bettina.'

'Yes,' Bettina says, 'yes.' As the tears come the nurse touches her on the shoulder, but it's a comfort that means nothing against a pain that twists everything. There is almost no one left in the world who would understand exactly how much these words hurt Bettina, pointing as they do to a life that she might have had once, and, if she's honest with herself, must admit that she has never stopped wanting. She weeps in a ferocious near-silence as the day breaks.

At seven, the nurses change shift, the doctor comes in and goes out again, and still Alice's breath is here, tissue-thin, cotton-soft, as she fades the way a winter's day fades into a winter's night. Finally, shortly after nine, the last breath is breathed. Before she leaves the room, Bettina smudges the colour off her mother's lips: without life in her skin it looks horrible.

'Are you all right?' the nurse asks. She has kind eyes, Bettina notices, and her words sound as though she means them, understanding that these moments immediately after a death will never be forgotten.

'Yes,' Bettina says, automatically. But then she realizes that it's true, because she's been grieving for her mother for a long time. And since her father's death – maybe even since Sam's – Alice has been ticking off the remaining days of her own life without much care or interest. She goes to sit in the relatives' room while she waits for Rufus to collect her. He had left early to go home, shower and go to work: he'd left instructions that he would come to fetch her as soon as she sent word. Rebecca brings her a sandwich, and tea, and Bettina understands that she must be hungry and thirsty and so she eats and drinks: soft, spongy bread that she would normally rather starve than eat, ham that tastes of salt and water, just-too-strong tea.

'Did she say anything?' Rebecca asks. 'People sometimes do.'

'No. Yes,' Bettina shakes her head, 'well, nothing real. She woke up at about five and talked about Roddy coming to see her. We knew Roddy a long time ago. She was still wandering. But she knew who I was.' At this, Bettina's throat seizes.

'Roddy?' Rebecca asks. 'Roddy, the gentleman in the wheelchair?'

'Yes—' Bettina can feel herself staring, the already

tired muscles in the back of her eyes stretched with unbelief.

'He was here yesterday. David mentioned it at our handover.'

'I think you must be mistaken. Roddy wouldn't – Roddy didn't know she was here.'

'One moment,' Rebecca says. Bettina, left alone, feels as though she has been pulled into the space her mother has left, a world where nothing makes sense, where time slides and folds, and things that should be separate are combined.

Rebecca is back, with the register. She sits down next to Bettina and puts the file on to her lap.

'Yes, he was here, with his mother, I think. They both seemed to think a great deal of Alice.'

And there it is. Roddy's signature, the tall spines of the R and F, the tail of the final 'd' stretching back to underline his surname. Beneath it, the letters of 'F. Flood' curl as precisely as hair just released from the tongs. Just the sight of their writing is a shock, a hand coming out of a coffin and making everyone in the cinema jump.

'They were here?' Bettina looks from the page to Rebecca and back to the page. She checks her watch, as though knowing what time it is will make a difference to the confusion. Her mother's last words were not a delusion, then, but an unexpected truth. Bettina starts from her chair, her first thought to go and ask Alice what she meant. Grief stronger than gravity pushes her to sitting again as she remembers that her mother has really gone. It feels as though someone is kneading her guts.

'I wasn't on duty,' Rebecca says, 'but I remember my

colleague saying that they were very emotional. They said they had lost touch when your father died and they didn't know what had happened to your mother.'

Bettina nods. Or perhaps she shakes her head. It's hard to know quite what she's doing. She knows that she's shocked because her brain is telling her that she is; but shocked, calm, grieving are all just words to her at this point. A disconnected part of her is wondering why Roddy and Fran came to find her mother, rather than her, after hearing from Aurora, which they must have done. That same place is wondering what Roddy looks like now. She's remembering his round fingernails, straight nose, the hair at his navel, all things she hasn't thought of – she thinks – in years. Things that she should have forgotten. Things she will think about more, later.

But for now her heart is shocked, still, the heart of a motherless daughter that must feel nothing until it's ready to feel the first part of the something that's waiting. She looks out of the window. It's almost noon already on this lost day, measured out and marked by her mother's breathing and then the lack of it. Clouds dull the sky. A V of geese unskeins and Bettina watches them as they move across the rectangle of her view.

In the aftermath of Alice's death, Rufus finds that his new position in Bettina's affections is not as secure as he had hoped. The day he had driven her back home, she had said nothing, but had twisted her mother's wedding ring round and round the third finger of her left hand, looking out of the window rather than closing her eyes and holding her hands in her lap. Rufus had

215

asked, music or not, and she'd said, not, if that's OK, and he'd said, of course it is, and that had been the extent of their conversation. Bettina twists, twists, twists the ring and looks, mostly, to the sky out of the passenger window. The hair on the right side of her head is mussed from where, he imagines, she must have slept a little, against the back of a chair, or with her head propped on her hand, although he'd like to think someone would have woken her, made her comfortable, offered her a pillow or the chance to lie down for half an hour, with a promise of being woken when she was needed. But it wasn't the time to ask for details.

When they had pulled up back at their homes – the restaurant starting to bustle, the bakery blank-eyed with the blinds down – Rufus had said, let me make you an omelette or order some food, and Bettina had put her hand on his for a second and said, I think I have to sleep. Of course, he'd said. He liked himself in this role of supporter and supplier of quiet, reliable strength. He is the man who, later, Bettina will come to see that she is unable to do without. He had helped her out of the car, stood next to her as she stood with her hands on the roof, steadying, a sailor returned to the shore.

She'd turned to look at him. 'You hadn't booked anything for our weekend away, Rufus, had you?'

'No, I hadn't.' He hadn't, though he had found a hotel, a restaurant, and an artisan bakery of considerable reputation that he'd thought Bettina wouldn't have been able to resist looking in on. He'd been planning to confirm the dates with her and book the hotel this week. Never mind. It would have to wait, for happier times.

'Good,' she had said, and he'd waited for her to say more, but instead she'd stood on the pavement, one hand still on the roof of the car. He'd pushed the button to lock the car, and when the noise hadn't roused her, he'd put his hands on her shoulders and turned her so that she faced the alleyway that led to the door of her flat on one side and his on the other, and had walked her gently forward. She'd moved along with him.

When they reached their doors, Rufus had said, 'Let me know if you need anything.'

'I won't,' she'd said firmly, then: 'I mean, I won't need anything, but thank you. Thank you for taking me. And bringing me back.' She'd looked him in the face, then, her eyes dull and her skin a wretched grey, and she'd nodded, and then she'd unlocked the door of her flat and gone in.

A week had passed and since then Rufus has spent only two nights with her, both at his own instigation. The sum total of conversations they have had, if compressed into one evening, would barely have filled a quarter of it. He goes into the shop, most days, on the pretext of sandwiches or with invitations. Bettina has always smiled; she's stopped, and talked a little – the home was being very helpful, the funeral was organized, her mother's possessions packed up and waiting to be collected; she thinks she will have them put into storage for a while, until she's ready; there wasn't really anything for her to do now except – except – and Rufus had put his hand on her arm and said, yes. Bettina had nodded, smiled, gone out to the kitchen and come back with a dozen tiny croissants. Daisy-sized, she'd explained, tell her hello. There had been dismissal on her face. I can drive you to the funeral, Rufus had said, just let me know when.

It's all right, she'd said, I'm going by train. It's only going to be the family.

And it wasn't really a lie. Bettina's first impulse had been to make the funeral a family-only event. When her father had died, she had insisted on this. The thought of returning to Missingham had been bad enough, without the possibility of unexpected or unwanted additions from the Randolph family past coming along. Alice, subdued by illness, loss and medication, hadn't objected. She had been serene until they reached the graveside, when she had started to sob and wail and cling. Bettina had let herself be clung to, and watched her father's coffin join her brother's and thought: when it's me, what will I do? Where will I go? Pragmatically, she didn't much care, or at least that's what she told herself. She had thought about her choices: here, in a place that made her heart hurt, that she dreaded even the name of, with her family: or somewhere else – where? – alone.

Earth thrown, they had turned away, and as they did so Bettina had thought she heard her name called, and that she could see someone waving. But it couldn't be anyone she wanted to see, and so she had kept on walking. When she thought about it later, she became sure that the wave and the shout were imagined, and the person she had seen was just another mourning pilgrim, laying flowers in the sun.

But now, for Alice's funeral, there isn't a lot of family

to call upon. The thought of standing by the grave as the sole mourner, the orphan outnumbered by the three dead members of her family, had struck Bettina as being needlessly melodramatic, and exactly the sort of thing that her mother wouldn't have wanted. So she had extended a general invitation to the care home for anyone who wanted to be present. 'Staff and residents,' she carefully added to the email, 'but otherwise this is a private affair.'

She goes by train to Missingham, a messy journey south with changes at Reading and Guildford. She's carrying a basket full of bread, which she takes to the Green Dragon before making her way to the church. She checks the cheese and wine, and makes sure that there are turning circles for wheelchairs, straight-backed, high-seated chairs for those who struggle to sit down and get up, as well as sofas for the more sprightly. Cups and saucers stand ready next to wine glasses on the table at one end of the function room. There's nothing for Bettina to do. So she makes her way up the hill to the church. She goes to the graveside first, just to test how she will feel at the sight of her brother's and father's names, and thinks of how the three of them will soon be lying side by side, her the odd one out. Her mother's grave, freshly dug, waits with an unseemly hunger.

The service is brief. Most of the small congregation trills valiantly through 'All Things Bright And Beautiful', although Bettina's vocal cords will not loosen and allow her to join in. The wake is cheerful. Most of the guests are old women. They line up to tell Bettina how much her mother liked to watch everything that was going on, whether she remembered it or not; how she liked her food; oh, how that woman snored! The staff who came with them have similar stories, but add, carefully, that they believe that Alice was happy. Bettina nods. She believes them, knowing she could choose not to but not seeing the point.

Once everyone has said what they need to her, she finds a sofa, takes Brie and grapes and baguette, and watches as her guests chirrup and smile about her mother, happy to have known her, unsurprised by the way – and the fact – that her life has ended. She supposes that everyone here is used to death, and sees it as natural, inevitable, and maybe even welcome.

For Bettina, deaths have been, for the most part, shocks, wrenches. She thinks she might be able to manage this one better, and twists Alice's ring, which still sits on her own wedding finger. Every time she thinks of putting it away, she can't decide where to put it. She doesn't have enough jewellery to justify a jewellery box and nowhere else feels safe enough. She wonders whether it's too late to be happy, and, if it isn't, where she will find her happiness. When she isn't with Rufus, it feels as though he would be just right for her. When they are together, she feels as though she is wearing the wrong shoes all the time, although he does nothing to make her feel that way. It's probably her, with her unrealistic expectations, her shrivelled heart. 'Are you all right?' Rufus asks, often, in the evenings that they spend together.

'No,' she will say, then, 'Yes,' and she will remind herself that she is not herself, and that she can't be easy to be around right now, and she will smile and reach out to him, and he will smile and touch her hair. She suspects that they both, separately, remind themselves that these are not easy times, and that making a relationship work, like working through grief, is a job that needs to be done. She can see how much effort he is putting in, and she hopes that he can see hers. She's noticed that he has photographs on his fridge now. There's one of Rufus, Bettina and Daisy and the horse, and one of Kate and Daisy, looking not at the camera but at each other, Daisy's finger on Kate's nose, the two of them laughing. There's one of her and Rufus smiling for a stranger they had asked to take their photograph on a Sunday walk, although she doesn't think either of them look very happy in it. When she'd said so to Rufus, he'd said, well, we will just have to pose for more photographs, until we get better at it. They seem to have gone from not-even-dating to settled with very little in between. Bettina thinks perhaps that's best. She doesn't want to be swept off her feet. She likes the ground, which she trusts. And this is the closest she's had to a relationship for a very long time.

The door to the function room opens. Bettina glances up, wondering whether there's a latecomer that she'll need to go and talk to.

And there is Roddy Flood, as real as this morning, as smart as an extended trot, looking around the room. She's not sure whether she gasps aloud but her whole body seems to grab for breath, for purchase. It's been fifteen years. Since the moment she'd discovered that Roddy had been to see Alice, Bettina has turned over the possibility of him coming to find her, too; but she hasn't been able to get past her memories of Roddy, striding, swinging a leg over a horse as he dismounts, wrapping his legs around hers to stop her from getting out of his bed. Whether she has thought about Roddy or deliberately not thought about him, for the last fifteen years he has been the background to everything, becoming more myth or dream than man.

As soon as he sees her he starts to cross the room towards her, and she's glad that she thought about wheelchairs, although anyone from the nursing home who needs help to get around is using walking sticks or wheeled frames. As he makes his way, with a series of 'excuse me's and 'thank you's, Bettina gets to hear his voice before he reaches her: remembers how soft it is, a dark-brown voice, her mother used to say. 'Roddy's on the phone,' she'd call, and then, as she handed over the receiver, 'lovely voice, that boy.' He still has the same physical confidence, moving his wheelchair the way he could make a horse move, tight inside turns and perfect aerodynamics. But then again, he has had fifteen years to get used to it. His hair is as dark as it always was, but cut close to his head now. He's almost upon her before he looks full into her face.

Bettina knows she should have got up and gone to greet him, but she has no feeling anywhere except in her heart, which is a fish on a hook, and her eyes, which are taking in every last bit of him, soaking him up. His broad shoulders, his solid body, his still legs, his feet in cowboy boots. His eyes. His smile, that twists, and twists a smile from her in answer.

'Tina.'

'Yes.' She starts to nod and can't stop. Her mouth is dry. Her hands are hot. Her heart – oh, there are no words for all that's happening in her heart.

'I know I wasn't invited. I wanted to—' He holds up his hands, a gesture that says, I'm just going to say it. 'I wanted to see you.'

Bettina nods. She knows that she can see him, hear him, but she's waiting for it to feel real.

'I'm sorry about your mother,' he says.

'Yes.' Bettina can't seem to find another word. Her hands have found some feeling now, though, want to move; to touch his face, hair, hand, mouth. She makes them go to her lap instead, where they worry at each other.

'It was good to see her still enjoying her birds.'

'Yes.' Roddy's ten words disrupt a fragile heap of memories. Her mother's excitement at the yellow-hammer's occasional visits, the elaborate seed-and-lard concoctions she used to make, slice and put out on the lawn on frosty mornings. Roddy's face as he struggled to hold a conversation about sparrows and tits. She smiles, and tears come to her eyes for the first time today. She feels her head nodding. She can feel that Roddy is watching her, although she has turned her face away.

'Aurora told us your mother was in a home, and we called everywhere until we found her,' Roddy says. 'I hope you don't mind.'

'Of course not,' Bettina says. He nods. There's the smile. There's Bettina's own smile, reflecting back, like an old dance step never forgotten.

223

'It's just that—' Now Roddy looks away, quiet.

'What?' She wants to touch his hand. Even after all this time, even with his chair and her limp and the fifteen years and the room full of elderly ladies, it seems wrong to sit this close to Roddy and not to touch him. He still looks good in a five-o'clock shadow.

'I didn't know that I'd be welcome,' Roddy says. 'I know she thought it was all my fault.'

'She thought it was my fault too. And my father's, and her own.'

Roddy shrugs. It's a gesture that says, I know I'm right, but I'm not going to argue with you. 'She seemed pleased to see me. I don't think she knew who my mother was. I felt as though we had gone,' he thinks about his words, 'a long way back.'

'The last thing she said was that you'd been, and that you're a lovely boy.' Bettina's left hand reaches for his hand, squeezes it.

'Really?' Bettina had been hoping to comfort, but Roddy looks stricken. He closes his eyes, opens them, and using his left hand moves his chair, just a fraction, so that she has to let go. She sits her hand back in her lap, her fingertips and palm slighted.

The wake, excited for a moment by the new arrival, has gone back to talking among itself.

'My mum still bakes her own bread.'

'Does she?' Bettina isn't good at conversational gear changes.

'They live in the main house, still. I live in the grounds. A converted barn, but converted to a bungalow,' he gestures towards his wheels, 'obviously.'

He laughs. Bettina doesn't. She has a sensation of watching herself from above: sees her shoulders tight, the pulse of her breathing at her breasts instead of her stomach, her hands holding each other.

Roddy looks around. He indicates the table, where a few baguettes, breadsticks, small plaited rolls and half a soft sage loaf sit. 'Did you bake those?'

'Yes.' Her first plan had been to provide cheese and baguettes. Then, last night, she'd thought of false teeth and old, tired jaws, and gone back down to the shop kitchen in her pyjamas to mix up some plump, white dough to bake plump, white bread from. It had sat, still warm, next to her on the train, and she'd pulled the basket on to her lap and felt it comfort her. She thinks, after all this time, we are talking about bread. She still wakes from dreams where all she can remember is that she was dreaming of Roddy and her body is hot and longing.

'Is your leg all right? Your pelvis?'

'Yes.' Somehow, on this more dangerous ground Bettina is more free to speak. Perhaps it's because this is closer to the conversation she thought they might have. 'It hurts sometimes, I limp sometimes, when I'm tired. It's – it's the place where my stress goes.' Roddy is looking down at his hands in his lap. Or maybe at his own legs. 'I have no right to complain,' she adds, shamed.

He looks up. 'Because you're alive? Because you're not in a wheelchair?'

Bettina can't read his face. His face was never unreadable to her, before. Even when she woke up before him, in the farmhouse, she could tell whether he was

225

dreaming. When he rode back into the stable yard, she could see whether he was pleased with the way he'd ridden and whether he thought he had done justice to himself, his mount, his father. But now, there's nothing she can make sense of in his almost-smile, his eyes looking down at her hands. She wonders whether she is unreadable to him, or if he can see what she's feeling. Is this what happens, her heart is asking, when the thing you've been dreading finally comes to pass, and it turns out to be like this? Unleavened. Changing nothing. When you admit that what you say you have been dreading might really have been what you were hoping for, and it turns out that it was just a stupid waste of hope.

'We trained two horses that went to the Olympics, and two to the Paralympics,' Roddy says. His tone is light, conversational, but Bettina hears: you gave up. People worse off than you, people who have been through worse than you, are riding still.

'That's good,' she says.

'Yes,' he says. She wants to touch him again; doesn't dare.

Rebecca is standing behind Roddy. When she sees that Bettina has noticed her, she explains that the minibus is here, and they need to be getting back.

Bettina stands and smiles, bracing for the last round of her duties today. Her legs are steady enough but her heart is shaking in her chest.

'I'm sorry to interrupt,' Rebecca says.

Roddy looks up at her, and says, 'You're not interrupting anything.' He shifts his glance, and seems to look worlds at Bettina, but 'Goodbye, Tina' is all he says before he turns more or less on the spot and starts to head back to the door.

Bettina is only just starting to understand how much she has been waiting to see Roddy again. She panics, flails.

'Roddy,' she says, and he turns back to her, 'you know where I am now. The shop.' It's not what she wants to say. She wants to say, maybe enough time has passed for us to see each other without unhealing the healing that we've managed to do. She wants to say, I'm looking at you and I feel exactly like I did when I was nineteen, before it all went wrong, and I know that it wasn't calf-love, now. I should have had the courage to come to you. And I've missed you. And I can't believe I ever thought Aurora was a threat.

He looks at her, a hubbub of putting-on of coats behind him but his own self, and hers, completely still.

'Tina,' he says, 'you always knew where I was.'

The train connections are not on Bettina's side on the journey back. She doesn't mind, because the three hours of journeying is three hours she would have spent doing not much wherever she was. At least no one tries to talk to you on a train. No one can ambush you, call you Tina and break your heart when you're not expecting it. She thinks she might drink, when she gets home. Not a gentle wine-with-dinner drink but solitary, focused, brandy-on-an-empty-stomach drinking that will give her – what? Distance, maybe, and sleep, for sure, and the distraction of a banging headache tomorrow. Even as

227

she's planning it, she knows she won't do it. There's nothing to be done, now, but getting on with life as she knows it, because it's the only life she's ever going to have.

Her key is barely in the lock when Rufus emerges from his flat. 'I was watching for you,' he says. 'I brought dinner.'

Objections leap to the ready. She's had a hard day, she's tired, she needs to be alone. 'Rufus—'

'You don't have to eat with me,' he says, 'I just wanted you to have something to eat. I know you haven't had a lot of' – he hesitates between 'time' and 'appetite', realizes that he's seen so little of her that he can't really make any assertions, 'even you can't live on toast.'

He proffers a carrier bag. Rufus might only cook omelettes and risotto, but he knows about food. Suddenly, Bettina realizes she is ravenous, not only for food but for someone else's company, and news of things that are outside her little world of grief and disappointment. 'Come up,' she says, 'I need to have a shower and change, and then I'm all yours.'

Rufus persuades her that the food won't spoil and he can keep himself occupied if she would rather take a bath, which she does. Meanwhile he puts out the collection of olives, salads and meats he's brought, and opens some wine. After they've eaten, they talk. Bettina's hair is frizzing as it dries, although Rufus knows that as soon as she pulls a comb through it it will wave and curl. She tells him about the funeral. She hadn't planned to, but once she starts, it feels like a point of honour to describe everything exactly, from the flowers in the church to the words the vicar had used to the hats of her mother's old friends and the unbearable slowness of the walk to the graveside along the unfriendly gravel path.

She stops before she gets to the Roddy part. Already it seems too bad to be true, and she doesn't want to have to explain it all just yet, if ever. The thought had occurred to her, when she was in the bath, that if she was really going to have a relationship with Rufus she should stop doing it by half-measures, and that that probably meant she had to tell him about her past. He's already asked about Aurora a couple of times. But she can't bring herself to do it now. She doesn't know where she would begin. 'Anyway,' she says, 'that was it. All done.'

'Yes,' Rufus says, 'it sounds as though it went well. As well as these things do.'

'Yes,' Bettina says, 'and now it's time to look forward.'

'I'd like that,' Rufus says. He thinks about the plot of land he's acquiring, below the town, beside the river, where he could build the house that he's always wanted to build, all light and space and curves and grace. And he thinks about how much Bettina would enjoy looking at his plans, making suggestions for the best way for a kitchen to work or thinking about the kind of environment that she would like to wake up in. Maybe, he thinks, the reason that he hasn't got around to building his perfect house is because it needs this woman to make it perfect with him.

'Rufus.' Bettina looks tired but she's smiling, a little bit. 'You look as though you're thinking serious thoughts.'

'I am,' he says.

'Penny for them?'

'I'm not sure you'd want to know.' When Bettina proposed that they spend a few days away together, they had both known it was a big step beyond their usual, not-quite-casual-but-in-no-way-committed way of doing things. He doesn't think she's ready to hear that he is building a house for them, in his mind, and that he has put an offer in on the land.

'Really?'

'I'm planning ahead,' Rufus says, 'but I know it's early days. I'm saying nothing.'

'You have the patience of a saint,' she says.

'Thank you.' He's not sure that she's complimented him before. She's thanked him, often, for things that he's done, and she's been complimentary about things that he owns – his ties, his butter dish, his mattress, so much more comfortable than her own. But this is new ground. 'I try.'

'I know you do. And I'm going to try too.'

'I'm glad to hear it.' He smiles. Perhaps they should have two kitchens, one purely for Bettina's baking and the other kitted out for their life together, with a separate fridge for wine and a marble larder for cheeses.

But Bettina isn't smiling. She's looking more serious than he's seen her since he drove her to the nursing home the night her mother died. She takes a deep breath. Another.

'Rufus, I need to tell you something, if we're going to take things any further.'

He shifts in his seat, leaning forward, ready. 'I'm listening,' he says.

'My full name is Bettina May Randolph. When I was a teenager, I called myself Tina. Tina Randolph. I worked at the Flood stable in Missingham. And – something happened, and I've never really got over it.'

Part Eight: Missingham, 1998

Tina and Sam could hear the Cosworth before it came into view. And then it's there, and Roddy is handsome, and Tina feels as though she's in a film, where her brother and her boyfriend are James Bond lookalikes, and she herself is someone who can make her boyfriend do a double take. The rain has stopped, though it doesn't feel as though it's stopped for long.

'Tina,' he says, 'beautiful Tina.'

'Handsome Roddy,' she says.

'Gorgeous car,' Sam says.

And they are on their way. Sam clambers in past the folded-forward passenger seat and sprawls in the back. Tina sits neatly in the front, breathing in the hairspray and CK One perfume left behind by Aurora on her headrest. The smell at least takes the edge off the leather smell, which is different on a car from how it is on a saddle. Tina thinks it's because on a horse the leather has so much air to breathe. Enclosed, the smell is of nothing so much as a slow dying. She hasn't taken her motion sickness tablets because they don't go well with alcohol.

'All right?' Roddy says, and Tina nods and closes her eyes.

'How long?' she asks.

'Twenty minutes, max. Ten if I floor it.' Her eyes jump open, like a doll moved suddenly to upright. Roddy touches her cheek with the back of his fingers, a promise. 'I won't. I'm just showing off because Sam's here.'

'Katrina will kill you if you make me sick,' she says. She winds down the window. Fresh air helps, especially this air, so new and living after the rain.

Sam says, 'We could drop Tina off, and then you could take me for a quick show-off, if you like.'

Roddy pulls a face. 'Another time. Duty calls. Not Tina, but all the glad-handing. Flood of Flood Ball.' He turns the key in the ignition. Tina risks a look to the side, a smile: she loves that he does the right thing. Of course he wouldn't do anything with Aurora. She's been ridiculous. He smiles at her. 'I'll be glad when it's over.'

'Me too.' Tina closes her eyes. The car moves away.

'Here comes the rain again,' says Sam.

And it is sudden and heavy, plump drops hurtling towards the earth. 'I'm glad the weather's broken at last,' Roddy says, 'but it could have waited until we got there.' Tina knows exactly what he means. For the last two weeks there's been dust everywhere in the yard, dry air in the fields, stinging in your eyes from the grit the horse in front kicks up. The tack has taken so much more cleaning, the manes so much more brushing. A little rain will make tomorrow in the yard much easier. The windscreen wipers are going faster and faster. The rain on the roof is a staccato fall; the water is bouncing in through the window. Tina winds it up. Although it's early on the summer's evening, it's dark. The rainclouds

236

have brought a November light with them. Roddy puts the headlights on.

'This is one crazy amount of rain,' Sam says.

'I'm glad I'm not driving the coach,' Roddy says. The route to the Coach and Horses takes a sweep around the hill, on the way out of Missingham, where there's a rocky outcrop which forces the road into a deep curve, with a lot of adverse camber. Most locals who fail driving tests fail it here, missing the sweet spot between going too slowly and having the tilt throw them into the wrong side of the road. Fred claims that when you drive a horsebox out of Missingham you can feel the horses hold their breath on this corner.

'We're all glad you're not driving the coach,' Sam says, 'especially if you drove it like you drive a horse.'

'You don't drive a horse,' Tina and Roddy say in unison.

Sam laughs. 'You two,' he says, 'works every time.'

Tina laughs. She can't help herself. She sees Roddy looking at her, laughing too.

'Roddy, you and I need a word. My sister tells me that you've been looking at another woman,' Sam says. Tina hadn't meant to say anything, telling herself that Aurora was just Aurora and Roddy had made his choice. But then at the hairdresser's, she'd picked up an old *Tatler* with photos of Aurora in it – she'd been at the wedding of someone Tina had never heard of, bare-headed and wearing a slim lilac dress, no jewellery, while everyone else was hatted and jewelled almost to the point of caricature. In the photos Aurora stood out like a beacon of beauty – and Tina, despite herself, had got a bit

237

wobbly. So while Katrina was unpacking her make-up case and fussing about the light in Tina's bedroom, she'd told Sam about Aurora's jokes and what Roddy had told her about the Fielden place. 'Don't worry,' Sam had said, 'I'll sort him out for you.' She'd resolved to put the whole thing out of her mind, although she knew that as soon as she laid eyes on Aurora that might change.

'God, Aurora, she's a bloody handful,' Roddy says. 'You're not really bothered, are you, Tina? You know what she's like.'

'No, of course not,' Tina says, but her voice comes out sadder, thinner, than she had thought it would.

'Look at me, Tina,' Roddy says, 'look at me.'

'Actually, look at the road,' Sam says, 'you two can sort this out later.'

'Tina?' She moves her head to look at him although it makes the sickness worse. He's looking at her, willing her to understand. She wants to smile. She tries, but when she moves her mouth she blurts, 'Why didn't you ask me to stay over at the hotel? Are you staying with her?'

'What? Who?'

'Roddy,' Sam says, his voice reasonable, 'why don't you have this conversation later?' Roddy ignores him. He puts his hand out to reach for Tina's. She flails it away. All the worry and jealousy that she has tried to ignore has actually, it seems, been growing in the dark, and now it's coming out, unstoppable.

'Aurora,' Tina says, 'is she staying with you? Tonight?'

'I hadn't even thought—'

'You haven't decided?' Tina says. She looks ahead

again, although she sees nothing but the rain. Her heart is not so much breaking as dying. Her head says: you knew this would happen.

'Tina, that's not what I was going to say—' Roddy says.

'For fuck's sake, watch the road,' Sam says, his voice stricken and sharp.

There's a sound, a sound that's bigger than the rain, bigger than the sound of the engine of Roddy's car and the water it's crushing as it moves up the hill. And although Tina wants to close her eyes – when she thinks of it afterwards she feels the tiny muscles at the outer corners of her eyelids start to spasm – she sees everything.

She can see the windscreen wipers working, back-forth back-forth back-forth, but raindrops endlessly gathering at the top of the glass and rolling down, warping the view before being caught and hurled aside by the rubber blades.

She can see Roddy's face, all determination now, his knuckles tight and his eyes wide, his mouth fixed and taut.

And she can see something coming towards them, something that manages to be terrifying although it makes no sense. Perhaps that's why it's terrifying. There's noise, but it's the wrong sort of noise. There are lights, but they're in the wrong place. The cab of an articulated lorry, side on to them, headlights glowing across the verges and the hillside, the side of it almost black, making a dark, solid wall that both blocks and brings the sound of screeching. Roddy's voice: There's a lorry in a skid but we can dodge it. We've got time.

And the driver does straighten his cab, and Tina hears the tension in the car release, for a second, feels Sam's arm, which has been braced against the back of her seat, relax, his elbow bending as her own lungs unbrace too, letting her breathe in again.

'That was close,' Roddy says, his voice twitching with tension releasing.

'This is going to be a story that the ladies at the ball will love,' Sam says, his voice striving for lightness.

'You should be so lucky,' Tina says. And for a second, it's all right. And it's going to be all right.

But then, Roddy says 'Shit!' and Sam shouts 'Fuck!' and Tina says nothing because she can make no sense of what she's seeing, lights slewing into her vision at the bottom-left corner of the windscreen, coming towards them.

'He's jackknifed,' Sam shouts, 'he's jackknifed,' and suddenly it makes sense, that what is coming their way is the back of the lorry, pivoting around the place where it's attached to the cab, slow but gaining in speed, in inevitability. It's overtaking the cab, which is turning away from them now, the driver's face a set contrast to his thrashing arms, which are turning the wheel as though – well, as though his life depended on it.

Tina hears a new sound. She doesn't know what it is. It might be her. It might be crying. It might be inside her, or outside. She thinks of their parents, champagne already in their hands; their father, watching out of the window, waiting for them to arrive. Not both of us, she thinks as she sees the corner of the truck's rear approaching them, not both of us.

'I'm going to try to get around it,' Roddy says, his voice a grim hard calm, 'hold tight.'

'Yes,' Sam shouts, as Tina hears her own voice scream, 'No!'

She can't move anything, not a lash, not a follicle, not a single muscle cell. Her body is locked, trapped, as the dislocated arm of the lorry's load flaps towards them.

And it looks as though they are going to make it; as though the sheer will of the three people in the car, the total of their youth and their love for each other and their smart clothes and their parents waiting and the whole and happy endlessness of possibilities for their lives, not so much added together but multiplied and multiplied again, squared and cubed and quadrupled, over and over, potential times love times need times devotion times cheerful sex times heedless loving times the girl from down the street times the quirk of the uterus that made Sam and Tina two where they could have been one times the how-did-it-go-so-wrong-so-fast birth of Roddy that made him a precious only, and lucky to have a mother who lived to tell the tale, although no one ever told the tale.

Yes, it looks as though they are going to make it.

The body of the Cosworth is low and the bottom of the lorry's load is high; and for just a slow, beautiful moment it looks as though the complex mathematics of the universe, of god and fate and good deeds done and future gold medals and honours degrees and plump new grandchildren like catkins on a spring branch, of Roddy's driving and the lorry driver's determination that this shall not happen, not today – it looks as though it

241

might just work out. Tina can see them, telling the tale, the imaginings of their listeners not coming anywhere near this – this – this thing that there are no words for. She can almost see the three of them, looking round at their listeners' horrified faces, bonded even more closely together by the terror of the moment.

But.

Just the very outside corner of the back of the lorry catches the door post on the driver's side as Roddy swings the car left. They are on the tip of the outside bend of the road; beyond the back of the lorry the thick hedge, gloaming wet, is swinging back in, showing them a sweeping way to safety, the place they would have been if things had been a fraction of a centimetre different.

But the car is going the other way, and it's going fast. It's through something and over something else – Tina has her eyes closed again now, willed or maybe burned shut by the noise and the sparks – and one minute she's being shaken and the next she's weightless, and then there's the sound of a crumple and then there's the feel of it, concertina-ing her up, and blackness and a smell that's metal and heat and the tang of blood, and then nothing. Nothing for a long time.

The coach is coming up from the Flood farmhouse. Aurora Fielden is enjoying the space of two seats to herself – she can make sure the hem of her dress doesn't touch the floor, and take off her shoes and tuck her feet underneath her. It looks as though Roddy is not so much off-limits as unreachable these days. During his stay she'd knocked on his door on a variety of pretexts in

242

everything from a towel to a ball gown and there was no getting so much as a rise out of him – he'd been wearing a towel himself, one day, she'd checked. Even her black lace knickers hadn't got a flicker of interest, and they never failed. Maybe she's played it wrong. Maybe Tina wears something cotton, and practical, and that's what gets him going.

She's heard good things about Tina's brother, though, and she thinks she could do with a change from her usual crowd. She's worked hard all summer, and practically been a nun this year. She deserves a fling. She might rearrange some place cards, if they get there in time for her to do it without anyone noticing.

The bus is full of excited chatter and the smells of too much perfume and aftershave expanding in the warm, enclosed space. After the endless talk about what to wear, within five minutes of meeting at the stables the ball-goers had forgotten their finery and were the same relaxed, friendly crowd that they usually were: Aurora was saving her energy, though, and so she'd made for the back of the coach and feigned sleep to save her voice for later. She hears Roddy's name mentioned once or twice, usually with Tina's close by, but otherwise there's nothing much of interest. Perhaps she does doze a little bit; certainly when the coach stops she feels as though she's jolted back to life from a very long way away.

The coach has stopped too suddenly and too soon. The driver gets out, and Aurora becomes aware of a swell of panicky chatter moving from the front of the bus to the back. She dreads a flat tyre, or a roadblock, or anything that might mean she has to walk anywhere in her heels. The clouds are still heavy and close, making the light an eerie dark grey-blue: all she sees when she looks out of the window is rain, sheets and sheets of it coming down.

And then the crying starts, and before the news makes its way back to her, she hears and senses the forward movement of everyone leaving the coach, and knows that it's more than a minor hitch. So she puts on her shoes and goes down to the front to investigate. And, faster than she knows how, but in memory ever after with a horrible slowness, as though the realization of what lies before her must be given piece by piece, lest the whole is too much, she sees it all.

The headlights of the stopped coach, on full beam, are lighting the place where the hedge is ragged and broken. There's a crowd of people standing next to the gap and a tattered line of onlookers spreading out each way.

Some of them are crying, some silent. Aurora walks back up the bus steps so she can get a clear view into the field below, and she sees the car that made the hole in the hedge. There's a steep, rocky drop between the road and the field where it's now lying, upside down.

The headlamps of the car are still working, still shining, but everything else about it screams 'broken'. It seems to have bounced, and spun, so in the line of light spilling out from it there's a gouge of fresh earth that shows where it has been.

One of its wheels, the one closest to Aurora, is spinning still, faltering to a halt, a dropped coin on a tiled floor. The other tyres seem to be still. Aurora realizes that she's watching the wheel because it's the only thing moving.

She can't remember when she understands that it's Roddy's car. She can't remember anyone saying it. Maybe the noise that sounds like summer rain, falling still but unnoticed now, is actually the sound of names being breathed, just below the breath-line, over and over: Roddy, Tina, Roddy, Tina, Roddy, Tina, Roddy. Tina, Roddy.

The lorry driver is standing on the road, to the right of the group by the hedge.

Aurora can see him shaking from where she is standing on the step, which must be ten feet away. 'I've called for help on the radio,' he says, to no one and everyone, to himself, to his hand, which he is examining in amazement, as though he has never seen such a miracle of life before. 'They're coming.' Aurora is just thinking that someone should help him – that whatever has happened, and they don't know what that is, he's shocked and hurt – when one of the stable girls goes to him, touches him, and examines the blood on his head and face. Aurora thinks it's Fudge, although everyone looks different in their dressed-up clothes and hair, with expressions she's never seen on their faces before.

'You need to sit down,' Fudge says, gently, to the driver. She touches his upper arm, cautiously. When he doesn't react, she takes a firmer hold.

'The road was wet,' he says, 'I couldn't stop it.'

'Come and sit down,' Fudge says, and she steers him to the side of the road, out of the light from the head-lights of his cab, and Aurora can't see them any more, although his voice – nothing I could do, nothing I could do – beats quietly on.

Aurora pulls her phone from her bag. There's no reception. She wonders about walking up to the Coach and Horses to get help. But there are enough people here to do whatever first aid is necessary. They need ambulances and the fire brigade, and they need them soon.

She can feel her agitation rising. She looks around the field, to see where the help is – there must be help, surely, coming – and sees the coach driver scrambling down the embankment with a first-aid kit slung over his shoulder. She recognizes the Floods' farrier and a couple of the grooms who work in the yard following him. Some of the girls have moved from shock to shocked action. Ells scrambles past Aurora and into the coach, and comes back holding the trainers that she'd brought with her for the walk home from the stables, later. She sits on the bottom step, shoves her feet into them, and then uses her teeth to tear at the hem of her dress. Once she's made a rip she grabs and pulls the fabric of the skirt. She stands and moves her legs, making sure she can move freely. She sees Aurora watching her.

'First aid,' she says, 'I'm trained. I don't know what I'll be able to do, but – I'm trained. I can try.' She looks at Aurora with eyes that say: I doubt I can make things any worse. She rubs the rain from her face, only for new rain to replace it.

'Laces,' Aurora hears herself say, 'tie the laces. You'll be no help if you fall.'

Ells bends, knots, nods, and pushes her way through the crowd and down the embankment. There's a slow trail now, a scramble of makeshift rescuers pushing wet

246

hair from their faces and carrying blankets, coats, anything they have that they hope might help.

Two cars have pulled up behind the coach, and trained their headlights over the scene as well. The rain is starting to ease and the clouds to pull away, so it's as though a new day is dawning, and the headlights only serve to make the scene below stand out even more brightly.

Somewhere there's the sound of a siren. It doesn't seem very close. Not close enough, anyway. Aurora wonders whether news has reached the Floods and her parents and Anastasia yet, or whether they are still waiting at the Coach and Horses, chatting about traffic and rain and looking out of the window and wondering where everyone has got to.

When Aurora looks back down to the scene in the field, there are people grouped at either side of the car. And there's a shout, suddenly, that passes up the line, as strange and true as a new foal: Roddy's talking. Roddy's talking. Tina's breathing and bloody Roddy Flood is still talking! People start to laugh, too loudly, and Aurora feels her own relief start to bubble and gather between heart and throat.

But she doesn't dare let it out, because something's not right. She doesn't know what it is, but she feels like the person standing at the city walls watching the comet come out of the sky while the rest of the citizens sleep.

And then she sees it. There's another group in the field. They're standing away from the lights of the Cosworth, and they aren't talking, or listening, or doing anything. One of them is kneeling while the others stand. Someone in the group shifts – turns away, towards

247

one of the others, who puts an arm around them in a gesture that's neither comfort nor despair, so perfectly is it poised between. Aurora sees what is at the centre of that pocket of silence.

She sees the foot first, the wet leather shining against the light. She struggles to make out the leg, because it's in black trousers made matt by water, dark against the mud and the grass, and anyway all wrong, thrusting as though it's trying to escape the body it's attached to.

Then she makes out the torso, follows the line of the body up, her eye caught by the white of a cuff and the gold of a borrowed cufflink and the grey of a hand. She knows she shouldn't be glad that the body is face-down, but she is.

And then someone standing next to the body finds their voice, cries out: and all of the watchers look, away from the car, away from the pulse of relief that there is life, talking, breathing life, and they see what Aurora is seeing.

There's a rush of inward breath, as though everyone must do something, anything, in this second, to protect their own life.

'Who is it?' someone asks, although her voice barely scratches the air. The talk is already coming up the line: no one knows. No one wants to put a hand under that shoulder and haul a dead weight on to its dead back.

But Aurora knows. She thinks of the empty seat beside her on the coach, and her plans for who would be next to her in it on the way home.

'It's Sam,' she says, 'Tina's brother. It's Sam Randolph.'

* * *

Roddy's world doesn't extend to the noise outside the car. He feels very little. There's a pain on the side of his face which is cut and, later, will bruise to black. No one will say it to him, but it's likely that his cheek has been caught by the buckle on the side of Sam's shoe as Sam's body went through the windscreen, the skin scraped and cut from back to front rather than from front to back, the opposite of all the tiny nicks and scrapes from the shattered windscreen. There's warm wind blowing through the hole where the windscreen used to be; his headrest is in the wrong place; it's hard to breathe because his body is wedged sideways between the seat and the bottom of the steering wheel.

He remembers the impact, and the sideways shunt. He's twisted so he can see Tina, whose eyes are closed, whose face is bloody, whose hair is perfect. The part of his brain that's calm and knows what to do tells him that it's a better sign if she's conscious, if she's talking.

'Tina,' he says, 'it's Roddy. Tina, I need you to talk to me.'

He thinks she says something, but at that moment there's a rushing of chatter from outside the car, and he misses her words, if they are words.

He sees one of the girls from the stable, beyond Tina; she's reaching in through the broken glass of the passenger window, finding Tina's wrist.

'Hey, Roddy,' she says, her voice a controlled, unnatural evenness, 'I know this is going to be tough for you, but try not to talk.'

'Tina,' he says.

'She's breathing,' the girl says – her face won't stay in focus long enough for him to understand who he's looking at. 'Roddy, don't worry.'

'Tina,' he says, 'Tina, I need you to open your eyes if you can hear me. I'm here. We're all right, Tina.' In his head, his voice has all of its usual clearness, but he realizes that his words aren't leaving him. His mouth isn't working. He's cold. His eyes want to close.

People are saying his name, over and over, Roddy Roddy Roddy. Not long now, someone says. There's light shining in his eyes, there's a siren, there are more voices, but none of them is Tina's. And so he closes his eyes. She'll be there when he wakes up. When he wakes up, this will all be over.

Howard and Alice and Fred and Fran get the news from a police officer, who comes to the ball. 'Roddy's been done for speeding, d'you reckon?' Fred says to Howard, when he sees the officer walking towards them, but Alice takes Fran's hand.

Aurora gets herself a lift back to the Flood place. She changes, checks the yard, and sweeps the water that's lying everywhere towards the drains. Only then does she let herself into a stall and sit herself down on the hay, her back against the side of a sleeping horse – a bay, she doesn't know which one, it doesn't matter, she just needs the smell and the warmth and the solid beating heart.

She sits and listens as she hears cars arrive, the phone ring, ring, ring again. She thinks about Sam, about Roddy and Tina. They couldn't all be dead. They couldn't all three die. It wasn't possible.

But then, three hours ago, when she was all high heels and lipstick and the hope of a bit of a fling before the evening waned, she would never have said that what has happened was possible.

That dislocated body. That face in the wet earth.

She sits quietly as someone else walks round the yard, quietly, as she has done.

'Is that you, Aurora?'

'Yes.'

'Are you coming in?'

'Not yet.'

'OK. There's no news.'

'OK.'

And this is what it's like; they all get on with things, they all let each other be. The Fieldens stay for a fortnight, while the Floods come and go at odd hours, tear-stained Fran and granite-faced Fred.

And then Edward, Arabella and Anastasia go home, although Edward comes back with Bob and Foxglove. It's as though he's hoping the horses being at the stables will make Roddy fit to ride them. Aurora stays and tries to do what Roddy would do. She wants to make sure that the Floods aren't short-handed, on top of everything else. She works hard, and she puts the higher-spirited horses through their paces. She does everything that Charlie asks her to do, as though she is a groom herself. Aurora isn't often given to reflecting on her own behaviour, but she wishes she had been nicer to Tina. Not that it would have made any difference to the outcome, of course.

Everyone who works at Flood Farm seems lost in their

own worlds. It isn't unusual to look over the door of a silent stall and see a groom standing perfectly still next to the horse, a hand or a forehead resting on the animal's neck.

Sam's funeral happens before July ends. No one apart from the family is invited, but everyone at the yard knows when it is. When the church bells ring, they walk down to the gate of the farm, where they can see Missingham laid out below. They watch the procession come from the church, two parents then a taggle of uncles, aunts, nieces, nephews, and what feels like a very little time before the earth is filled in. Tina isn't there. She's regained consciousness, Fran says, but she can't be moved.

Fred and Fran stand there longest, making their way up to the farmhouse only when the light starts to fade and the graveyard is quiet, when it's hard to pick out the patch of black earth where Sam is invisible under swathes of summer flowers.

When Roddy looks back he'll remember that time in the car as a curious oasis of peace and calm. He drifts between unconsciousness and lucidity, although in his lucid moments he's aware that he might be in a bit of trouble. It's not until he comes to in the hospital that he realizes how serious this could be.

He can't move anything. His head is in a brace, his trunk secured, his legs – he has no idea what's going on with his legs. Everything hurts. Even blinking hurts. He can hear crying. He works out that he isn't in his car any more. He tries to speak but nothing like a word comes out of his mouth. He must manage something, though, because a face he doesn't know looms over him, a shadow between him and the bright strip light above. The sensation of nothingness in his lower body is so closely related to painlessness, such a contrast to the ache of every ribboned nerve in his torso, head, neck, arms, face, that it is almost a relief.

Then everything goes dark again. The next time he wakes, there's daylight. He comes to with memories of being in strange rooms, of lights and sounds and the sense of motion. He can't move his head. He can flex his hands, though. As soon as he does, there's a cry.

Fran's face moves into the space above Roddy's face.

'Don't try to move,' she says. 'You were in an accident. You're wearing a neck brace until the doctors have checked everything.'

'Tina?' he says.

'Tina is in surgery but she's going to be OK,' Fran says. Her voice is sadder than her words. Roddy closes his eyes again.

He remembers, always, the careful words that his parents later use to tell him that Tina has had an operation to repair her shattered pelvis and broken leg, and that she should make a full recovery; but that Sam, unseatbelted, has not fared so well, his neck snapping as his body hit the window, dead before he hit the ground. It was somewhere in that first ten days, because he was still in the hospital, rather than the rehabilitation unit. He wasn't wearing the collar, so it must have been after the first couple of days, once he had been X-rayed to look at his bones and MRI-scanned to examine his soft tissue. He knows he was lying down, but that might have been tiredness, or it might have been that he hadn't been shown how to use the trapeze to pull himself, briefly, upright yet. He remembers the feeling of slight over-stimulation that came with the steroids to keep the swelling down, but he took those for a month.

He knows it must have been after the doctors told him that his spinal cord was sheared right through, twisted and snapped by the impact, although his bones were intact. He remembers exactly when that was: day three, at four o'clock, because his father was growling about them being late, and how he wondered what they could be doing that was more important than this. His mother was red-eyed and quiet. The consultant had brought a model backbone so he could show them where the injury was, in the thoracic spine at T11, and gave them a leaflet listing what was possible for Roddy now, and what was not. Roddy had looked at his legs and tried to understand that they would never do any-thing for him again. From now on, their only option was to hang off the end of his body, dead weights. Both of his parents had cried. He had listened to the doctor, talking about normal bowel and bladder and sexual function as though he was telling Roddy he could fly. And he had felt sorry for himself, a huge miserable wash of despair. He would be moved, the doctor explained, to the rehabilitation unit in Birmingham as soon as he was deemed stable enough to start on the occupational therapy and psychological support which would, apparently, make all the difference. His mother had taken his hand and he had shaken it off. He'd thought about the way it felt to walk down from the farmhouse to the yard, the judder up the spine with every step, a pleasure he has never once thought of as a privilege.

But once he finds out what's happened to Tina, to Sam, the loss of the use of his own legs seems like a meagre punishment, death commuted to life imprisonment in a moment of misplaced clemency. Roddy would rather the rope. He determines to get better, and to be better, and to work out a way to comfort Tina even though he is the one who brought this situation upon them. It was an accident, people say over and over, accidents happen; as though Sam was a mug smashed on the kitchen floor. You weren't there, Roddy says. He knows that it's his fault, and that if he had taken less for granted then there would have been no need for the crash. If he hadn't taken Tina for granted he would have asked her, properly, about staying over with him. He would have thought about how it looked, Aurora getting out of his car when she could have travelled with her family, or when he could have driven Anastasia too and given the Fieldens a bit of peace and Tina some reassurance. He had known that Aurora would make mischief. He knew that she liked to get what she wanted, and if she didn't, there were always repercussions.

It's normal to feel guilty, people say. Roddy nods and knows that that's because he is guilty. He wasn't concentrating on the road, and he should have been. It was as simple as that. Sam even tried to tell him to watch the road, for Christ's sake. In that last moment, when the lorry hit, it caught them only by a fraction, so if Roddy had seen it sooner, slowed down earlier, then they would have had a near miss, instead of a hit.

Every day, the first thing he asks is how Tina is. He recites messages which his mother repeats back to him until she is word-perfect. He asks her to take flowers, chocolates, other inadequate things that cannot even start the conversation that he needs to have with her, but that he hopes say: I am here. I am waiting. I am ready to say the things we need to say. 'Get better,' he says to Tina-via-his-mother over and over, and 'I'm sorry. I'm so sorry.'

And then, the day before he leaves for rehab, Howard comes to see him. Roddy has been lifted into a wheel-chair so he can 'start to get a feel for it'. He'd asked his parents to leave, so he would have a chance to get used to the idea before he had to see them being brave about it. He finds that he's clinging to the arms, feeling unstable and panicky without the familiar ballast and balance of his legs. The muscles in his back ache. A nurse is sitting with him 'just to make sure you're OK'. He supposes this is what his new world is going to be like, unable to sit in a chair without supervision. He pushes the thought away. He can feel himself sweating. And then Howard comes in. There's a blink of shock as they look at each other. You are so different to the last time I saw you, their eyes say to each other, how terrible to meet in this wretched new place.

Howard shakes Roddy's hand. Roddy feels unstable as he lets go of the side of the chair to do it, but he cannot refuse such a generous gesture. He wonders if he will cry.

'It's good to see you, Roddy.'

Roddy nods, then shakes his head, although the movements are increments, made cautious by pain. There's no way he can respond to that.

'Tina,' he says, 'how's Tina?' Talking is a struggle, sometimes, his lungs still learning how to work in a new body that doesn't behave the way the old one did.

'Tina's not great. She's pale. She sleeps a lot, and cries. Her pelvis should heal. She will walk. There's a plate, and some pins, and they've mended her bowel. Her leg's in plaster. She might be home in a month, depending how she does. They keep explaining it to us, but . . .' he shakes his head, 'it doesn't seem to go in, not properly. Alice can explain it better – but she should be all right. Well. You know.'

'Yes. As well as she can be, without Sam.' Roddy is not sure he is even allowed to say Sam's name. The sound of it makes him want to cry, but if Sam's father is dry-eyed, then he can't be allowed to weep.

'Yes. That's true of all of us.' Howard speaks calmly but looks uncomfortable. If he'd had a cap, he'd be turning it round and round in his hands. Instead, his knee starts to bob up and down. He watches it. Puts his hand on it, to still it.

'I'm so sorry,' Roddy says.

'I know you are, son,' Howard says, 'but that's what I came to say. No one blames you—' He pauses, stops, starts again. 'You're not to blame. You didn't have a hope. We all know what that road is like.'

'But—' Roddy can see it now, see it always. A little more conviction in the hands that threw the steering wheel to the left. A little more attention to the rain, the lights, the road so familiar that he had made the mistake of thinking it was a friend to him. A little less trying to look at Tina, sitting next to him, hoping that she would smile at him, the smile that lit him up in a way that he couldn't explain. Explaining about the room at the Coach and Horses, telling her how ridiculous Aurora was so she didn't have to talk to Sam, didn't have to ask. This is where his mind goes most often, the most inconsequential but also the most easily fixed thing: he should have realized how much Aurora's stupid jokes could hurt Tina, even if she had complete faith in him.

All he had to do was pull over for a minute, explain. But no. He had been thinking that he really was Roddy Flood, the man the road rises to meet. And he shouldn't have been. And if he hadn't been thinking that way, Sam might be alive. Tina might be tacking up Snowdrop, or lying in his bed with her hand on his stomach and her head on his shoulder. He might be wiggling his toes into his boot without a thought for what a miracle such movement was.

'Roddy, listen to me.' Howard has waited until Roddy opens his eyes again. 'The lorry driver said he skidded on the road. He said there was nothing he or you could do. It was wet. He put his hands up, straight away, and no one's arguing. He said he thought you were going to be able to get out of the way, but then he felt the back clip you. There was only a hair in it.'

Roddy cannot think of a single word to say. He looks at Howard, mute.

'It was an accident, Roddy. Blaming each other, blaming ourselves, isn't going to bring Sam back.'

'No.'

'And Sam liked you a lot. He liked the way you were with Tina.'

'I was going to ask Tina to move in with me,' Roddy says. It seems like another world. Howard doesn't seem to hear. Maybe Roddy didn't speak aloud. He has so many conversations, with Tina, with Sam, in his head that it's quite possible.

'Your mother and I have been talking a lot.'

'Yes.'

Roddy has heard them, not their words but their voices, in corridors and round corners, although the way he is at the moment, as good as static and numbed by painkillers and shock where he isn't actually paralysed, means that almost every word that comes his way seems indirect, overheard.

'The thing is – Alice isn't doing so well.'

'No.' Roddy remembers his own mother, usually so calm, so steady, so wise and so straightforward, at his bedside, thinking he slept, and making a noise that he barely recognized as human, let alone as a sound made by his mother: a low, aching, discordant strain of sorrow.

'Alice is—' Howard is fumbling for words, but every time he finds a set that seem to say what he needs to without causing any hurt, he turns them over to discover a barb or a jag.

'Just say it, whatever it is,' Roddy says. The tiredness that he can't control is coming again. That, and the feeling he had when he saw the dislocated elbow of the lorry coming towards them, a panic that can't be stopped, unpredictable, unbidden.

'Alice gets upset when she hears anything about you. She's glad you're all right, of course – not all right, but . . .' 'Enraged' would have been a better word than 'upset', but Howard decided not to use it. Every day is like this: picking the least painful from thousands of painful paths.

Roddy would wave his hand, if he had the energy, if the pain would let him. 'I know. Not dead.'

Howard nods, a small nod that Roddy doesn't quite see, but senses. 'It's hard for her. She does blame you. She won't, in time, but she does.'

Roddy blinks in reply. Alice, then, has recognized where the blame lies. He's glad, in a strange way. At least someone has seen the truth, instead of reassuring him of his innocence all the damn time. 'Does Tina blame me?' he asks. It's the most important question of all, for Roddy. His future dangles from it.

'Tina asks about you,' Howard says.

'What have you told her?'

'We've told her the facts. Your spinal cord is damaged, you won't walk again, you will be able to live independently in the right circumstances.'

Roddy thinks about how much he will miss the unthinking actions of his life. Right now he wants to walk over to Howard, shake his hand, clap his shoulder, thank him for just saying it the way that it's going to be, instead of talking about compromised movement and learning to live with limitations.

'I see,' he says instead, 'thank you for being honest, Howard.' He wants to say, tell her I can still get a hard-on. I wake up in the morning and it's an embarrassment

260

when the nurses come in and see it. Instead he says, 'What did she say?'

'She isn't saying a lot.' Tina says almost nothing in response to questions. She only answers direct, closed enquiries: would you like cheese or beans on your potato, shall I put the radio on, would you like the curtains drawn. If anyone asks how she is feeling or what she is planning, she just looks at them, as if to say, what does that matter, now. The doctors talk about depression being understandable, about the guilt that survivors feel. They suggest antidepressants, but Tina just says no, and closes her eyes.

She does ask a question about Roddy. 'How's Roddy?' are her first words in the morning. Roddy was the first word she said when she came round. Her mother had run out of the room, in tears. Of course it had been the relief; but it had also been the fact that, as they sat at her bedside waiting for her to wake, they'd talked about Sam, about how they would tell Tina about Sam, about how the first thing that Tina would want to know was how her brother was, and how they would break the news to her.

But Tina said the wrong thing. And Tina kept on saying the wrong thing. She wouldn't talk about Sam, turning her face away when his name was mentioned, or feigning sleep, although the tears rolled out from the corners of her eyes. Howard kept on telling Alice that the reason for this was that there would be no change in Sam, but that Roddy's condition was uncertain, and that Tina could love Roddy without that making her love for Sam any less. But Alice couldn't see that. She had entered

261

a world that was black and white, alive or dead, done or not done, a stumbling world with no light in it at all.

The two men are silent. Howard's head is full of the gone-ness of his own son; Roddy, however broken, seems like a miracle. The rattle of a trolley in the corridor pushes Tina's father into saying what he has come to say.

'Your mother and I have been talking and we can take you to see Tina. If you'd like us to. Alice is having an afternoon at home,' Howard says, his voice stumbling a little, 'doctor's orders. We can take you to see Tina. If you want to.'

'Really?' Roddy feels the tears come. There's nothing that he wants more, right now, than to see Tina.

'Really,' Howard says. 'Apparently I'm not qualified to push you, but I know a nurse who is. Hold on.' And Roddy tries to make himself ready, not that there's a lot he can do other than reach for a flannel and pass it over his face, avoiding the place where the stitches are, push his fingers through his hair, gently at the stiff bits where the scabs have formed. And then he's being pushed along corridors, and then he sees his mother holding a door open, and then, there she is. Tina. The nurse brings Roddy close to the side of the bed, makes sure that the call button is easy for Tina to reach, and then the door closes behind her and they are alone.

Tina is propped up in bed. Everything from her waist down looks plastered and bandaged. She's wearing a pale green nightshirt. She has a cut on the side of her face and there's bruising across her neck, an almost-black line where the seat belt did its best to save her. Her hair is dull and her skin is grey and the bags under her eyes are as purple as thunder. As soon as she sees him she starts crying, violently, her lungs shuddering. And she is the most beautiful sight Roddy has ever seen.

'Tina—' he gets out, 'I'm so sorry.' She can't speak but she nods, stretches out a hand to him and it's shaking, shaking. So is his. He only dares lift one hand from the chair, so he takes her hand to the side of his face and he holds it there.

It's a long time before she can calm her breathing for long enough to say anything. When she does, she says, 'I'm sorry.' She is remembering the moment when she woke, when she had asked about Roddy and her mother had got up and run out of the room and her father had looked so serious that she had thought Roddy must be dead. Later, of course, she'd understood why they had looked so stricken: they had been preparing to tell her about Sam. In the moment of waking, she hadn't thought of Sam at all. She doesn't know why. Probably because he was always just – well, alive. Vibrant. Half of her. Nothing would ever happen to Sam.

Thinking about her twin ought to make her want to cry more but instead it makes her steady, as though the thought of him is giving her roots, strength. She nods to Roddy, as if to say, I'm done. For now. He nods back.

'I'm so sorry about Sam,' he says. 'I will never forgive myself.' He had thought that when he saw her again he would say, I'll love you enough for both of us, but now that sounds mawkish, and anyway, he has run out of breath. He looks at her clavicle, where the bruising is a rainbow of black to grey to blue to green to yellow.

'It's not your fault, Roddy,' Tina says. Her voice is rasping at the edges. Roddy imagines a tube in her throat while they operated. Not you too, he wants to say. But she hasn't finished: 'It wasn't you. It was me. I distracted you—'

'It was not your fault,' Roddy says. 'Please, Tina.'

She looks away. It's as though a lift door is closing and soon she will be gone. Roddy holds her hand tighter, in case she tries to take it away from him.

'I'm sorry,' she says.

'We can mend this, Tina,' he says.

'I don't know,' she says. She's looked back at him, but she's not really looking at him. She's looking at the wheels of the chair, the place where his hand clings to it.

'It is only,' Roddy says quietly, 'a fucking wheelchair.'

'It's not the wheelchair,' she says, 'you know that, Roddy. It's—' She shakes her head, because she can't think. There are painkillers and steroids and sleeping tablets in her system, there's a mother who cries at the sight of her and a father who's being so stoical that it physically hurts her, makes her chest clench, to look at him. There's the place where Sam is not, which she touches, gently, the way the tongue goes to a site where a tooth's been extracted: and when she does it there's a shiver and shock of loss so deep that she knows she can't stay there for long, not yet. 'I don't – I can't – I have no idea about anything. I don't know which way is up, Roddy. I've always been a twin. And if—' But she stops.

264

When she catches herself thinking of an if – if only I'd not asked, if I'd not mentioned Aurora to Sam – she simply stops, stops thinking, stops talking. She lets the 'if' fill her head or her mouth but she refuses to let it go any further. It's something that sometimes helps, in the hole of an afternoon when she is listening to her mother weep, or when she's alone and she feels as though she is experiencing every painful click and stitch of her bones knitting together.

Roddy kisses Tina's hand. She looks away. He wanted to see her so much, but hasn't really thought about how it will be to look at the damage he's done. He needs to put it right. And he realizes that he isn't going to be able to do it here, now, in a conversation. He can't pull Tina to him, he can't tilt her chin so that she looks at him, he can't talk her into being OK. He had thought – assumed – that they would suffer their losses together. He sees that Tina is locked into something, alone, and that he must wait and be ready when she is ready to come back to him. This isn't what he wanted, but it's what he's got. He looks at his legs, then up at Tina's face. When he speaks she turns towards him. 'I have to spend about six months away,' Roddy says, 'in rehab, learning how to manage. When I come back I'm going to come and see you.' There's none of the love that he feels in his voice. He keeps forgetting that his lungs lack power to send air across his larynx, and so any attempt at intonation yields nothing.

Tina nods. 'I think,' she says, carefully, knowing how much these words matter, how she will think about them later, wonder whether she got them right, 'that seems like a good idea. I don't think I've even absorbed everything yet. Sam. You. Me.'

Roddy asks, 'Will you call me?'

'I don't know, Roddy.' Tina thinks of long silences stretching out, of how hard it was to talk even when there was nothing serious to talk about.

Roddy nods. Tina closes her eyes. The tension in her hands says that she wants him to let go. He can see that she's fighting sleep, and that sleep is winning.

'Do you want me to go now?' Roddy asks.

'Will you stay until I've gone to sleep?' she asks.

'Of course I will,' he says. But he stays longer, watching her face, staring at the cut and the bruises until he can do it without flinching from what he has done.

Roddy, who has never been static for more than the time he needs to sleep, throws himself into rehab, giving it all he's got at the gym, with the physio, and over the flat paved paths in the grounds that he practises steering himself along in his wheelchair. The mental recovering he's expected to do he finds more difficult. He knows that he will never walk again. His spinal column was twisted to snapping when the driver's seat was wrenched round by the impact of the lorry, an absolute that meant that his future is like a triple-jump, nothing to be done but getting into your stride and going for it. He doesn't know whether he's entitled to think about even so much as a metaphorical stride. He has killed someone, and he has injured someone he loves more than he loves his own life. He knows this for sure, because the thought of Tina being opened up and sewn and pinned and bolted

266

back together still makes him feel worse than his own prospects. Her skin, her encased frame, her bruises are images that he keeps coming back to. The thought of them is worse than the many small humiliations that come of learning to adapt to this new way of living.

Thinking and talking about Sam is harder, but Roddy forces himself to do it, with his counsellor and with his fellow rehab inmates. Although everyone whose opinion is supposed to matter – including the lorry driver, the police and, later, the judge at the inquest – says that Sam's death was accidental, Roddy knows better. He knows the shock of a life being there then not there, from being in the stall when a horse has to be destroyed. The animal will be present and then gone, something too momentous to happen in an instant, but something that cannot happen any other way.

Tina hasn't called, but he knows that even if she doesn't, she'll wait for his promised visit. He needs to be ready to give her a life that will make up for their shared loss, his stupid complacency. Roddy Flood vows that he will never be complacent again. He'll be hard-working and devoted and matter-of-fact and strong.

'Could I ride a horse, Dad?' he asks Fred, one day. His parents are valiant in visiting, even though the rehab unit is a three-hour round trip for them. He has tried to persuade them to come less often, unsuccessfully, and stopped when one of his fellow patients pointed out that maybe they came as much for themselves as they did for him.

'Well, best to learn how to ride a wheelchair first,' Fred says.

'Fred!' Fran had said, half horrified, then half laughing when she saw her son's tired smile. And the next day, when Fred arrived, he told Roddy how he'd had a look online and made some calls and had found out about adapted saddles and carriage-racing. He hands over the printouts, tells Roddy there is more to come, with brochures in the post. Roddy knows the slowness of their internet connection, and how temperamental the printer is, too. The pages in his hands represent hours of his father's life, on top of the driving from here to home and back again. But he can't stop himself from asking the next question:

'Could I drive a car?'

'Would you want to?' Fran asks. She finds herself flinching every time she gets in a car, whether she's driver or passenger. She's being fearless with almost everything that life is hurling her way, and there's a lot coming at her. There's the sight of her non-stop son pale in a wheelchair, there are calls from journalists, and the long conversations with so many people who need to say something about Roddy, his potential, what a shame it is. There are tears from grooms, there is the thought of Alice's devastated face on the first day after the accident as she waved her away from Tina's room: I'm sorry, Fran, I just can't look at any of you. But she cannot deal with anything to do with Roddy's cut-about, twisted car. When the insurance company had called about it that morning she'd handed the receiver to Fred, mute and pale, and gone to stand in the yard until the conversation was over.

'I don't want to drive,' Roddy says, 'but I don't want to have you drive me around either.'

268

'You'll never get up the hill in a wheelchair,' Fred says with cautious, make-the-best-of-it cheerfulness, the sort that comes in handy when one of the horseboxes breaks down or a regular client decides to move their horses closer to their new home. Fran is starting to think that it might be just what they need now, too. Roddy pants out a laugh.

Fred finds out about adapted cars with automatic gearboxes and handles for pedals.

Roddy's next question is 'Could I live on my own? I mean, independently.' He has no intention of living on his own, but he wants to be able to assure Tina that she won't be his nurse. Fred finds an architect who can adapt one of the barns.

'Isn't this all going a bit quickly?' Fran asks, having just come from tea with Howard, who seems able to construct a sentence but not a conversation, and who says that Tina is saying nothing, being cajoled into move-ment and eating, being medicated into sleep. Roddy's therapist talks about shock, and delayed reaction, and a high brought on by surviving. Fran is waiting for the crash. The second crash.

'I'm alive, Mum. I can't think of a thing that I won't be able to do if I put my mind to it.'

'Of course,' Fran says. She pretends not to notice Roddy's long pauses to gather his breath between sentences, which give the lie to his brave words.

'We need to get things organized so that they're ready when I get out of here. Apart from anything else, I can't live in the farmhouse again, unless I live in the kitchen.'

'No,' Fran says. She is looking at everything on the

farm in a new light, from the height of latches on stalls to the way that tack is stored and the three steps from the kitchen followed by the narrow turn that leads to the rest of the house.

'I'm talking to the insurance people. We're nearly there,' Fred says. The lorry driver's firm has admitted liability. Now it's a question of damages, which means putting a price on Roddy's needs. No one has any idea how long it will take. Howard and Alice have opted to negotiate their case separately. Fred cannot imagine how you begin to put a price on the loss of a son.

'I'm very proud of you, Roddy,' Fran says. She has tears in her eyes, although she always seems to, these days.

'Don't be,' Roddy says. 'If I was anything to be proud of we wouldn't be in this situation.'

'It wasn't your fault.'

'You weren't there.'

Fran has tried before to tell Roddy that it's not his fault. She takes a different tack. 'It takes time.'

'Time,' Roddy says. He's never been patient. He's having to learn. He doesn't like it. He checks his phone for messages, three, four times a day, although the one person he wants to hear from is Tina. She has a mobile phone now, Fran has told him, via Howard: she has his number.

Fred says, 'That's what we all need. It will come right. As right as it can.'

They are adding a Sam-coda to every conversation. Anyone who says 'life goes on' or 'we just have to get on with things' must add, via words or facial expression, the understanding that they accept that for Sam

Randolph, life is not going on; Sam is not getting on with things; Sam was not lucky, and it could have been no worse for him. It's exhausting. Sam would give anything to be exhausted right now.

On the day Tina is supposed to go home, after two months in hospital, she has a panic attack on the hospital steps. The nursing staff and her parents say that it's too soon, and not to worry, and they re-admit her.

It is too soon. The thought of being out in the world stops time and her faltering feet and her breath. But also, she's pushing so many things out of her mind. It's as though hospital life has given her a pass to ignore the big things she needs to think about: Sam, Roddy, her own stupidity, her own wretched lack of trust. When Roddy came to see her, she had been shocked by his cut-about face and his heavy legs locking him into unfamiliar stillness. She had wanted nothing more than to go back to the tumult of his homecoming from Devon, and his easy belief in her. If she had trusted her instinct, the way he looked at her, touched her, she would have known that Aurora was nothing for her to worry about, not for a minute. In her hospital room there was no mirror. When she got back home she knew she would have to look herself in the face.

If someone had offered her the chance of staying in hospital for ever, she would have taken it. She likes the idea of having to do nothing, ever again, except eat the food put in front of her and be examined from time to time, walking on a treadmill and doing her physiotherapy to make her strong, and then sitting in a chair in

271

the dayroom watching the television jabber without taking anything in, to make her weak again. She likes it more than she likes the idea of going home, anyway. She has refused all visitors except Fran, and of course her parents, who she feels she can't say no to, as they have already lost one of their unmatched pair.

The day comes when she is driven home, though, to the place where she's lived all her life with her brother, to try to work out how to live without him, without Roddy, with her mother's soft sobbing, with her father's obsessive gardening the only movement in their new, static world.

The doctor has prescribed sleeping tablets, and she can't get used to being the last one to wake in the house. Her mother has refused medication and seems barely to sleep at all, sitting at the kitchen window, Flora always on her lap, the two of them watching the birds come and go.

But waking late is just one item on the long list of things that Tina can't get used to. There's the fat her body is gathering because she moves so little, for a start. She does her physiotherapy without fail, but barely leaves the house otherwise. Her shoulders, stomach, thighs, once hard and taut with muscle, are slackening.

She can't get used to the closeness of the air inside the house, or the dampness in the garden in this wet, subdued summer, or how long the days feel, with nothing to fill them.

She can't get used to Katrina's brave discomfort. Her friend refuses to be turned away, and then spends half an hour apologizing for almost everything she says, for fear that the mention of boyfriends, horses, even clothes would upset Tina, as though Tina has somehow forgotten everything that has happened since she got into Roddy's car with Sam and they set off for the Flood Ball, and one wrong word from Katrina will prostrate her again.

Most of all, because she was immobile in hospital when Sam was buried, she can't get used to the idea that he isn't going to drop in, call up, invite her to Oxford for something, pull her hair. It's not just because she wasn't there when he was buried, of course. It's because he has always been there. No other reason. Just that. Twins don't say goodbye to each other as much as other children, she remembers her mother saying, once, as the train pulled away from Oxford, and Tina had tears in her eyes. You went to school together, you went to clubs and choir practice together, you played together. Until you found horses and Sam found football, you were together most of the time. No wonder it feels strange to you to be without him.

The months go by, both dragging and flying, Tina in one room, her mother in another, not enemies, not at all, just too afraid to look at each other, to see each other's grief. Howard goes between them, a sad messenger, and then goes back to work, and shops in the town and brings the groceries in, so that Alice won't have to leave the house. And every evening the three of them sit around the television.

'You know the doctors did say that when you're ready you can ride,' Howard says, one day as the two of them sit in the kitchen, drinking tea. Alice is dozing in the garden.

'I can't ride,' she says as firmly as she can, so firmly that she doesn't think her father will feel it's worth arguing. The thought of getting on a horse appals Tina.

'It might help you,' Howard says.

'It won't,' she says. She gets up, such an ungainly effort that it makes the point better than words could. Horses aren't mentioned again.

Tina's first real walk is to the graveyard where Sam is buried. She goes as darkness approaches, her father silent at her side. Her bad leg drags and the muscles reknitting themselves in her hip, unused to slopes, pull and moan. It takes twenty minutes to get to the grave, which is a mound of weathering earth, a scattering of irises on the top.

Howard gathers them together again. The graveyard is flat, utilitarian, an extension from the churchyard where the graves are laid with, it seems now, no thought of how many were to follow, each death marked by space and grass and a headstone unlike any of the others. Sam, in contrast, lies behind rows that are much more uniform, granite and marble slabs for the most part, the occasional heart-shaped headstone, only now and then a flamboyant, showy angel.

'We have to wait a while longer. For the headstone. It's not ready,' Howard says, uncertainly, not sure whether to be silent or interrupt his daughter's thoughts.

'OK.'

'The earth, I mean. The earth's not ready. Not – not settled.' Her father is twitching at her shoulder, worried. 'Don't get cold, Bettina. Don't overdo it.'

274

'It's OK, Dad.' She had hoped that knowing Sam was close to her again would make her feel comforted, peaceful, or as though she had made a step towards the thing that she refuses to call acceptance. But he doesn't feel any closer. The ground feels too dense, too final.

'Why did we bury him?' she asks. 'Why not cremate him? Then we could have scattered—' Her voice hesitates when she has to choose between saying 'him' and 'his ashes'. She can't manage to say either, so she stops. And she wonders: where? In their garden, on the Isis, in the pub?

'I think your mother wanted him to – to be somewhere,' Howard says quietly.

'But . . .' Tina puts her head in her hands. The pressure from tilting her body forward is making her pelvis ache. Sometimes she thinks she can feel the metal pins grating against her bones.

She can't articulate what she's thinking without it sounding terrible, and they are all of them cautious, now, of saying things that may add to each other's burdens. But what about when you die, she wants to say, will you still want what you've always said you wanted, to be scattered in a woodland? Will you feel you have to be with Sam? Does this grave mean that you're trapped here now, and can't go anywhere else?

'We bought a plot for four,' her father adds, 'although you might not want to be here. That's a long time away.' This last is more of a plea than a statement of fact. Tina thinks of how nothing from before Sam's death counts, now. Everything needs to be renegotiated and rethought.

Her father is there, hands extended, ready to bring her to her feet.

'I know this is hard for you too, Dad,' she says, and her father nods, and they start the walk home, slowly, quietly, arm in arm. Tina thinks of how downhill ought to be easier than uphill, but it isn't.

Roddy has worked hard at getting well. It's a lot of work. There's more to being in a wheelchair than being in a wheelchair. He needs upper body strength, of course, but not just in his arms and shoulders. For the first six months the muscles in his neck ache constantly as they adapt to holding his head at a different angle. He has done exercises to strengthen his trunk, so that he can be stable without his lower body to help and support him in all the invisible, unappreciated ways that he no longer has at his disposal. His lungs no longer have the space to expand as they used to, so he has learned to breathe anew, and to think about his words before he says them, in case he wastes some of his diaphragm's forced energy and his lungs' great effort. He has taken a course in using a wheelchair on rough terrain, and after six months, when he is strong and safe enough to do everything he needs to do in a day, from getting out of bed into his chair to making a meal to taking a shower, he goes back to Flood Farm to start life in his new home.

He can, with a great deal of effort, swing himself from wheelchair to car seat and fold his wheelchair up. He refuses to let Fred help, although he does allow him to put the chair into the boot when it's folded. So he travels back to Missingham in the back seat of the car, the way he did when he was a child, and he tries not to think about that. He closes his eyes for the bend in the road where the Cosworth was sent flying through the hedge. He notices that his parents stop talking when they go round it, and wonders whether they do that every time. He feels sick.

'Can we stop at Tina's?' Roddy asks. His parents look at each other.

'Howard says that they aren't coping very well,' Fran says, as though that's an answer. 'Alice is – well, "unrecognizable" is the word Howard uses.'

'Best leave it, son,' Fred says.

Roddy says, 'I'm not really asking. I said I would go to see her when I got back. I promised.'

'We could get you home first,' Fran says, 'so you can see everything.' Roddy has refused a phased return to home life. He's managed in one of the independent-living units in rehab, and the converted barn that he's going home to has been designed with him in mind. He's sick of feeling like an invalid, he says, and he's not going to behave like one.

'Mum,' Roddy says, 'I told her that I would go when I got back. I need to see her. I have to keep my promise.'

And so without another word Fred drives them down through the village, past the Green Dragon and the small row of shops, and into the estate where the Randolphs live. Fran has seen Howard, from time to time. He's come up to the farmhouse and looked at Roddy's new home, watched the horses and the grooms who look away when they realize who he is. He's sat at the kitchen table and told Fran that things are 'difficult' and he's afraid that Alice is 'isolated' and that all of her sparkle and joy has gone. She's given up her job and she sits in the house, looking out of the window. As time has passed he's said he doesn't know how to help her. He's cried. And when Fran has asked about Tina he's just shaken his head and said, I don't know, Fran. She's quiet. She doesn't complain but she hardly goes out. She tries to talk about Sam sometimes but she can't get very far. I've stopped asking her about work, about seeing you, because all she says is that it would be better if she'd never come here in the first place. Alice will come round, Fran had said. She's had a terrible blow. It will take time. But Howard had said, bleakly, that when Alice played Martha in *Who's Afraid of Virginia Woolf* she kept up a Midwest accent for the whole of the rehearsal period, at home, at work and in her sleep. She's a determined woman, Fran, he'd added, and she's always had her way.

It's as slow a process for Roddy to get out of the car as it is to get in. Howard sees him first. He tends to sit in the living room, which looks out over the small front garden, while Alice prefers the kitchen table, the view across the back garden, watching the birds come and go. He goes to find Tina, who is in the kitchen, measuring out flour for the bread she's recently started to bake again. He puts his hand on her arm, inclines his head, and says softly, 'There's a visitor for you, Bettina.'

He'd hoped that Alice wouldn't notice – sometimes she dozes in the afternoon – but her head snaps round to look at them. 'Who is it?'

'It's the Floods,' Howard says gently, 'it's Roddy. Now, Alice—'

But Alice is up and out of her chair, Tina behind her, as they go to the living-room window. Tina's heart is swelling as her stomach tightens, as though space is being reallocated in her trunk. She's thought of this moment, often. She's thought about texting Roddy, too, but she hasn't known what she could say, apart from more apologies. One thing that she did know was that as soon as she started a conversation with him, he would want to know what they were going to do, and how they were going to progress. He would want them to make a new life. Tina still has no idea whether this is going to be possible. Her heart is like a dead thing most of the time, and when it does come to life it is with spasms that are unbearable, as she thinks about how she had distracted Roddy at the worst possible moment. And because of that, because of her, Sam was gone and Roddy's career, his passion, his easy loping stride were all gone too.

Roddy negotiates the kerb, the gate, and wheels himself down the path, Fran and Fred following. Alice is all narrow-eyed silence, her breathing as tight as a drum. Howard's hand is on Tina's shoulder. Tina is drinking him in. Roddy is just as handsome, although his mouth is twisting in concentration rather than a smile, his chest looks broader and the long, lean arm muscles that developed over years of working with horses have been replaced by bulk and obvious strength.

The sound of the doorbell rouses them. Howard moves towards the door, and Tina follows. Just as Howard has his hand on the latch Alice takes Tina's arm, a grip rather than a hold. Her nails are sharp.

'You're not going to talk to him.' It's a command, not

279

a question. Tina looks from her mother to her father. The door is open an inch.

'Now, Alice—' Howard says.

'Don't you "now Alice" me,' she replies, her voice low and full of fury.

'Tina?' Roddy's voice. It makes Tina shudder, and thrill. Howard opens the door. Alice takes a step back, as though the sight of Roddy has physically hurt her. She's still holding Tina's arm, and Tina, who still needs to concentrate in order to balance properly, stumbles away from the door with her.

'Tina,' Roddy says, 'I'm back. I said I'd come.'

'Is Sam with you?' Alice asks, her voice made of knives.

Fred opens his mouth, closes it. Fran puts her hand on Roddy's shoulder, and Howard turns to his wife: 'Alice. No.'

'Mum,' Tina says, 'I think Roddy and I need to talk.' Roddy's face lights at her words. He puts out a hand, as though he's waiting to guide her over a gangplank. She moves towards the doorway, thinks: I can step outside, I can close the door, I can talk to him. I can touch his face. But Alice's grip is tightening. She swings her daughter towards her.

'Have you no loyalty?' she asks. 'Have you no heart?'

'Alice,' Fran's voice this time, 'Alice, no. Please.'

Alice continues as though she hasn't heard anything. 'He is the man who killed your brother. He has ruined our lives. You owe him nothing.'

Tina, her back to the Floods now as she faces her mother, can hear someone crying. It might be Fran, or

280

her father. She tries to pull away from Alice, but her mother is holding her, hard, with her hand but also with the unblinking look in her eyes, the cold pleading of her voice.

'Are you so blinded by their money and their charm that you'll walk over your own brother's grave to get to them?'

'Mum—' Tina is crying. Her mother is dry-eyed. She lets go of her daughter's arm, steps past her, and stands in the doorway. She looks at each of the Floods in turn: Fred, Fran, Roddy. Howard puts his arm on Alice's shoulder but she shakes it off. For a horrible moment Tina thinks that her mother is going to spit in Roddy's face.

But all she does is say, clearly and slowly, in the same measured way: 'Do not come to this house again. Do not contact my daughter again. You people have done enough damage and you should be ashamed to show your faces here.'

And she closes the door.

'I'll be waiting, Tina,' Roddy calls through the closed door. He doesn't know whether she hears.

Over time, conversations no longer stop when Roddy enters a room and he ceases to be the centre of attention, although when Aurora goes to the Olympics and comes back with a medal people start to ask him how he is more often. He says he doesn't need the Olympic Games to remind him that he's not a world-class showjumper any more. He means for it to come out cheerfully but he knows it sounds sour.

He's as better as he'll ever get, although he tries not to think of it as better, and tries not to imagine the able-bodied Roddy standing behind him, limbs effortless and unthinking.

The depression comes, of course. Years three to five after the accident are grim. By then his life has been neatly resected and rewritten into Before the Accident and After the Accident, although Roddy talks about BW and AW, Before Wheels and After Wheels. He is living in his lovingly, expensively remodelled barn, the doorways and corridors broad, the surfaces low, the ceilings high and full of skylights.

People who know him well have stopped looking at him with what he calls the 'brave Roddy faces' and treat him as himself. He rides, with the help of a modified saddle, and he races a carriage, something that he enjoys more than he ever would have thought he could, although his competitive spirit has gone. He drives a modified car, although he doesn't enjoy that as much. He says to himself that it's because he's no longer behind the wheel of his beloved Cosworth but admits, sometimes, as he takes a corner too slowly or pulls into his driveway too fast in his desperation to be out of the car, that he's afraid of the wretched thing. He buys a new pair of cowboy boots every year, even though the old ones never wear out.

And he starts to realize a few things. Now that he doesn't need to concentrate on the nuts and bolts of every day, and his upper body is as strong as it's going to be, he cannot ignore the atrophy of his legs. With his life as easy as a determinedly positive attitude and insurance company money can make it, he has the energy again to look around and ahead. And raising his eyes brings on the deep misery that people have only recently stopped watching him for and warning him about.

When Roddy looks forward he sees nothing different. He doesn't want to compete – the desire to be better than other people left him on the day that he proved so conclusively, to himself, that he wasn't, by hurting the woman he loved, first in her own body and secondly by taking Sam from her. And, after three years of being forced to give her time and space – though he would rather find her, see her, and see whether there's really nothing more to be said – Roddy starts to think that perhaps Tina won't come back. He has heard that she has moved to France and her parents have moved, too. He couldn't blame them. He thought he saw them, sometimes, when he looked down to the grave-yard. Sometimes he takes out his photographs of himself and Tina and looks at them, for hours. On other days he is tempted to throw the photos away, sell Snowdrop and go away himself. He could take up the standing offer he has from the Fieldens to go and work with them, or move to a city and see if he could be Roddy Flood without the horses. But he knew that it wouldn't make a difference. Not really.

One night, Fran pops in when the photographs are out. She looks them over, looks at his face, puts her hand on his and says, 'I hate to say this, Roddy, but Tina knows where you are, and she always has. She would come back if she could.' They've never talked much about what Alice said that day, but they all remember it. Roddy had a text message from Tina on the evening of her mother's outburst. It had read, 'I'm sorry.' He'd thought she had been apologizing for her mother. 'It's understandable,' he had replied, 'let's meet.' But there had never been a response. So maybe what she was saying sorry for was the endless silence to come.

The next day, he starts to flirt with one of the newer grooms, and within two weeks he takes her to bed. It's the first time since the accident. He knows that he's doing it for the wrong reasons, but he doesn't care. It isn't for liking the girl, or even for wanting the sex, but in the hope that, where patience had failed with Tina, giving up – the appearance of giving up – might work in this warped universe.

Roddy's days become as dark as his nights. He feels the outside of himself hardening, like leather left in the sun. He forces himself to sound and act like himself, so that he keeps on being the man he wants to be, on the outside, at least. But the inside of him feels hollow and cold. His heart has become like his legs, something he can stick a knife into and feel nothing.

He had only done this once, and not with violence but with cool fascination. He'd taken his penknife into the shower room with him, on the cord he usually wore it on round his neck. After he'd moved himself into his shower seat and washed himself, he'd pulled out the sharpest blade – which he knew wasn't very sharp at all – and pressed it against the taut skin at the side of his knee, where it bent. He had to press hard before blood appeared at the metal tip. He took the blade away, and felt nothing. He rubbed soap over the tiny cut, and felt nothing. He sat there for a long time, letting the water chase the seepage of blood down his leg, and he thought of Tina, sitting on his bed, fresh from the shower, on one of the many mornings where such a thing was ordinary. Him saying, you've cut yourself, your leg. And her, twisting her body around to see the back of her calf, saying, I didn't even feel myself do it.

Part Nine: Throckton and Missingham, July 2013

Rufus looks Bettina up. It takes him a while to find the right places. He starts by trying to find online references to Tina Randolph, but there are numerous Tina Randolphs, and when he thinks of what else he knows about Bettina, he discovers that there isn't a lot to go on. A dead brother, some time in France, although he isn't sure whether she was still Tina Randolph or whether she was Bettina May by then. Of course the internet is loaded with Tinas, travels and small tragedies. It's only when he adds 'Flood horses' to the search that it all starts to come into focus, and make horrible sense.

1998. Kate was seven. Rufus was working long hours and quietly resenting Richenda's carping and complaints. Mealtimes were sullen. Kate was bright and sweet but didn't look much like the marriage-saving gift that Rufus had hoped she might be. He had just set up on his own and business was slow. He and Richenda bickered and point-scored, so Rufus had felt as though he was not so much walking on eggshells as crossing a minefield covered in the things. Newspaper reports about an accident in another county in which a young man was killed and two other people seriously injured had barely registered in the Micklethwaite household at the time.

But as Rufus searches newspaper archives and follows

links, he thinks that he does recall the story. He certainly remembers working late with an eye on the 2000 Olympics from Barcelona and hearing Fred Flood, trainer, mentioned every time there was an equestrian event. The commentators had made much of the fact that his son would have been expected to be there. Rufus finds pictures of Aurora Fielden with her bronze medal and her golden smile, and recognizes her as a younger version of the woman who had accosted Bettina at the fête.

And he feels his love for Bettina growing, like bread in the oven, at the thought of all that she must have gone through. He calls her and suggests that they have dinner together. 'I looked you up,' he says, 'and I'd really like to talk.'

They meet at their usual table in the restaurant. By unspoken consent, they talk the way they usually do, asking about each other's day and sharing news. The first attempt at a pecan-maple plait had been disastrous, too sweet and dense for bread, too salt for cake, so that even Josh had refused to eat more than half a slice; Daisy's cough is clearing; the purchase of the land for Rufus's house has gone through; Verity has proposed that Bettina might consider a delivery service, and although her first impulse had been to reject such an idea out of hand, she's starting to wonder about the possibilities. Rufus mentions the planning of the house to her, and something in those hazel eyes lights up as she nods but he's not sure she understands that he's talking about a house for them to share. Tonight probably isn't the night to check.

They finish a bottle of Bordeaux with their meal, and then adjourn to Rufus's flat for coffee, but decide to have another glass of wine when they get there. They take an end of the sofa each, and turn towards each other, facing but not touching. Bettina nods: Rufus takes this as permission.

'What I don't understand,' he says, because it's the thing his mind has kept on returning to, 'is how you've managed at all. I don't understand why you're not more . . .' He flounders, trying to find the right word.

Bettina helps him out. 'Damaged?'

'No! Yes. I wouldn't have used that word. But people get – distorted – by things that happen to them.' Rufus is thinking of steel buckling from pressure in the wrong place, tree roots breaking concrete. 'When terrible things happen, they can – twist you. You don't seem twisted.'

Bettina considers. 'I don't think I'm twisted. But I think I might be stunted. My life stopped growing. Not altogether.' It's been a long time since she's permitted a conversation about herself that doesn't stick to what's visible from the outside. So she's careful with her words. She thinks about them before she says them, knowing that Rufus will take them seriously. He waits. 'But it did go different ways. My life was more feeble, afterwards.'

He decides to let the 'feeble' pass, for now, but he has every intention of letting her know, in word and deed, how much he admires her strength in becoming the woman that she is, free of self-pity, focused and strong. 'Did you ever talk to anyone?' Even as he says it, it seems like the wrong question, the wrong place to start. But they have to start somewhere.

'You mean, a therapist?' Rufus nods. 'No. Well, sort of.' Rufus waits. He thinks of the counsellor Kate sees, less often and with less impact now, but a godsend when the post-natal depression had hit.

Bettina takes a mouthful of wine, a breath. Another mouthful. Another breath. She has known that this conversation would need to happen ever since she gave Rufus her old name. She's wondered if, in the speaking-aloud of these old griefs, she would cry, but her eyes are dry. 'I tried,' she puts down her glass and her hands knead the air in her lap, 'but – I've never had to talk a lot. Horses. My mother used to say that Sam talked for both of us. Bread. And then there was someone I really loved—'

She pauses, looks at Rufus, checking that he knows she isn't talking about him, that he isn't offended. 'I understand, Bettina,' he says.

'We didn't talk a lot. Me and Roddy. His name was Roddy.'

'Roddy Flood? He was the one who was driving the car?' Rufus says.

'Yes. He was my – he understood me, not exactly the way Sam understood me, but better than anyone else. He just let me be, and he behaved as though I was all he needed, just by being there.' Her voice is softening, sweetening, just a little, but enough for Rufus to see the truth of her past that wasn't written in newspaper reports. He wonders whether he has ever loved the way Bettina has, although he suspects that he knows the answer.

'Yes,' he says, because she is looking to him to say something.

'I couldn't see how to start talking about something so big. And there were no words for it. Losing a twin, it's like—' Tears are tightening her larynx now, making her voice thin.

'I understand—' Rufus says.

'But that's the thing. You don't understand.' She can feel tears on her face, although there are no sobs to go with them: it's more of a sadness overspill.

'No, no, that's not what I meant.' He touches her knee, lightly, leaves his hand there. 'I meant to say, I understand that there couldn't be any words for that kind of loss.'

Bettina pats the back of his hand, twice, leaves her palm on the backs of his fingers. 'Yes, that's it. Thank you. So, when someone came to talk to me, and tried to get me to talk, I felt trapped. You see it in horses sometimes, when their eyes roll back and they can feel pain, but they don't understand the pain they're in, don't know why it's there or where it's come from. It was like that.'

Rufus nods. He doesn't trust his voice.

'And there were things that words couldn't fix. My mother – she blamed Roddy. Roddy blamed himself. I blamed myself. It was – it was such a mess, Rufus. Not talking about it seemed best. And my parents decided to move away from Missingham, and so I made a run for it, to France.'

They fall silent. He is thinking of how it must be, to lose everything, so swiftly. The closest he has come was the night Kate almost drowned, and that had been unbearable, and it had been oh, so brief, and she had survived. So even such a terrible experience has no magnitude at all next to what Bettina has lost.

She knows that Rufus wants to talk more. She can see it in his face. But she's so tired, in so many ways. She can't think about herself all those years ago without feeling an echo of the pain in her body so real that she's not sure she'll be able to move. But her limbs and joints unfold as she wants them to, and she stands. Rufus stands too.

She's so close to leaving, wanting to be in her own bed, on her own, because Rufus knowing about all this means that being with him is no longer an escape, though not yet a comfort. But his face is all kindness and her heart is all sore, and she knows that if she is going to stop living half a life, she must start doing things differently. She sees how he is cautious with her, and she is determined not to spook. 'Can we go to bed,' she says, 'and talk some more another time?'

Both Bettina and Rufus are used to their own beds, their own space, their own habits. Most of all, though, they are both used to their own way, Bettina fiercely and Rufus passingly so, and so they are having to work hard to find a common way to live. Bettina sometimes wonders whether it would have been easier to move in together than to do things the way they are, every small step a courteous negotiation. She wonders about the house he is planning, and whether it's meant for the two of them. She shakes her head free of the thought. It wouldn't be. It's too soon.

Bettina had woken at three from a dream that she

couldn't remember. Knowing that she wouldn't get back to sleep, and not wanting to lie and think in the not-quite warmth of the not-quite morning, she had risen and left Rufus's flat for her own flat, a shower and fresh clothes, and then her kitchen domain. As she moves into the quiet rhythm of her work, she can see that this settling-in is only to be expected, and wonders how they can manage it better, or if it's simply a question of time and mature compromise. She can see that having something to think about other than her mother is good for her.

She's been surprised, in the two weeks since her mother's funeral, by how many spaces in her life Alice has left. In the days when, one Monday a month, she would walk back to the train station from the nursing home, trying to find some blessings to count, she would acknowledge that what she was doing was slowly coming to terms with the loss of a mother who was already mostly lost. But now she is discovering just how often she stored up things to tell Alice, even though Alice might not acknowledge them.

She catches herself noticing the birds in the garden behind the bakery and the brightly coloured shoes that some of her customers wear, and realizes that she's filing these observations away to give her something to say to her mother that might just spark an almost-gone connection. She still puts aside newspaper articles that she thinks Alice would enjoy having read to her.

Every day, Bettina is tripped up by a baker's dozen of memories and reminders that she's motherless. The fact that there has been so little mothering for the last few years doesn't seem to matter as far as her feelings are concerned. This grief is different to any she's experienced before – she doesn't feel mauled by it, she isn't chewed and broken apart in its jaws. No, grieving for her mother is like wandering a maze, a dead end every time she comes to a thought of Alice. It's exhausting, and dispiriting, and made worse by the twin difficulties of not sleeping well and being honest with Rufus. Almost honest. Although she doesn't remember what her dreams have been about, she thinks they might be to do with Roddy appearing at the Green Dragon after Alice's funeral: certainly she wakes with the same sense of agitation and disappointment. Certainly she replays their conversation, over and over, wishing for a different outcome, although she's not sure what that should be.

But here in the kitchen, all is as it always is. Bettina is getting close to perfecting her new recipe, a honey and lavender loaf baked in a tin so that it can easily be sliced, put in a toaster, and eaten with olive oil and more honey, or butter flaked with salt. Once she's certain of it, she'll write it up and add it to Simon's file, and he will scale the quantities up and the loaf will be added to the repertoire of Adventures in Bread. Bettina will work out how often to put it in the cycle of baking, depending on how popular it is – although she prefers to under-supply, just a little, so that her customers feel lucky when they find their favourite loaves on the shelves. ('You should be running a small dictatorship, not a bakery,' Rufus had said when she'd explained what she was doing, one evening. 'Architects could never get away with that. You can't under-deliver on light.') Once it's a regular product, Simon will make it in one of the two big mixers. But for now, Bettina is testing the recipe by hand. She's making these loaves in readiness for today's bread-tasting.

She starts with the leaven – the plump, spongy wild yeast that she feeds every day and bakes from twice a week. She has other batches for the other days, each delicately different, although she knows that only she would really notice or care that the flour that feeds one is half rye, and another has a tablespoon of wild local honey added once a fortnight. The fact that only she knows makes it more special. She adds flour to the leaven, two-thirds white and one-third wholemeal, and pours on a steady trickle of water that she's boiled and cooled to blood heat. With the hand that isn't holding the water jug, she mixes, feeling the ingredients move from wet and dry to a warm, squashing whole. Once enough water has been added, she moves the mixture from bowl to bench and she begins to knead, scooping and slapping the dough until it becomes first consistent, then smooth, then a silky elastic that never stops being a miracle.

She pushes two fingers into the centre of the dough and adds runny honey – she thinks she's finally got the measure that makes for a flavour of honey without it being too sweet – and a tablespoon of dried lavender. She's experimented with drying and using the flowers from the plants that Rufus brought her, but they seem to lose their taste after baking, so she's bought culinary lavender instead and that's just right. It keeps its smell, and has an almost sour tang that balances the honey.

Now Bettina kneads again, changing the motion this time so that instead of picking up and turning the dough in mid-air she's folding it over and then pushing it away with the heel of her hand. Then it goes into an oiled bowl to rise. In a few hours Bettina will knead it again, divide it into loaf tins and leave it to rise again. When the mound of the loaf is above the edge of the tin, she'll bake it. Next year, or the year after, she might be baking some of her bread in the wood-fired brick oven that she is starting to research. For now, the kitchen ovens will have to do. The bread will come out plump and crisp and bursting with good smells and the promise of crunch without, softness within.

And then, after lunch, when it's still warm, she'll try it out on her customers and see whether she's got there at last. She needs the bread to be something that they love, exclaim over, and go home and talk about. Until it's that good, she won't be happy.

Almost as soon as the dough is out of her hands and into the bowl, Bettina feels something slip away from her: control, or peace, or both. And then she sits down and lets herself cry, and cry, because she knows she's just had the best part of her day.

When she's calm again, Bettina looks around for the next thing to do. Over the last fortnight she's cleaned and re-cleaned and re-ordered and re-labelled, and the bakery is more efficient than it's ever been. Rufus says it's understandable that she wants to keep busy. Bettina agrees, but what he doesn't know is what she's trying to keep her thoughts from. It's not grief or shock that are troubling her so much as an overwhelming sense of disorientation. In this world, everything she has dreaded has happened. First, her mother has died and left her the last one of the family, when after fifteen years she still isn't used to being a solo twin.

Then, the thing she had feared since she moved from Missingham has happened: she has seen Roddy again. And Roddy couldn't care less, and they had nothing to say to each other. And now that that dread has gone, Bettina has no idea of what her world is. She thinks, maybe this is just what life is like, when what you've been hoping for and dreading for so long happens, and turns out so . . . flat. Not even crushed, or broken. Just nothing.

On Sunday afternoon, Rufus had brought Daisy over. As the rain hammering on the window had put paid to their planned walk-and-duck-feeding at Butler's Pond, instead they had mixed up fairy cakes in the kitchen and watched cartoons while they waited for them to cook. It had been a warm, sweet time, but when Daisy giggled at a cartoon character who ran off the edge of a cliff, Bettina felt as though she was watching herself.

She needs to keep moving, keep moving, to avoid that moment of stillness that is the preamble to the plummet. When she's feeling bravest – or perhaps when she's most tired, or least able to keep up her resistance – she sees that the absence of dread is also the absence of hope. So she keeps busy. She bakes and she cleans and she does her best to please Rufus, who she knows will love her if she lets him, and who she thinks she might love, a little, in a pragmatic, realistic, only passingly romantic way.

She wishes she could stop being tired for long enough

to see clearly. She wants to step out of her life, just for a minute or two, to get the measure of whether she's being pragmatic or giving up; whether she is doing the best thing, or the wrong thing, or is too damaged ever to be able to do the right thing.

But because that isn't possible, she starts to prepare the ingredients for a chocolate orange cake, which Rufus loves. Then she imagines how pleased he will be when she tells him that she made it for him, as though he's adding it to his bundle of evidence that she loves him, although she can't say the words. And so even the baking of a cake, which should be simple, comes with an aftertaste.

Almost everyone who comes into the bakery as the lavender bread is cooling raises their nose to the air like a hound on a trail and says, what's that smell, the way they do when the Christmas stollen are baking.

Bettina has written on the board in careful capitals: 'Bread-tasting at 2pm, all welcome.'

She's glad to see a group of people already gathered around the central table, as she brings out the bread: earlier, she'd put butter (salted and unsalted), honey (runny and on the comb) and olive oil out, along with plates and knives. Bettina has also set out the tray of small bowls with the ingredients, so she can talk through the process. She loves to see people understand the simplicity of bread, which is no more than flour, water, salt and alchemy. The pleasure is starting to outweigh her fear, although she has looked over her prompt cards while she ate a quick lunch, and written out a new one for her lavender loaf.

As Bettina puts down the bread and everyone gathered looks at it, she can see who she recognizes, and decide whether she can put names to faces or whether she'll ask people to introduce themselves. Elizabeth, who runs the quilting group, is here with her mother-in-law, Patricia. Elizabeth made the tea-cosies for Adventures in Bread and she champions Bettina's wares at the hotel where she works. Bettina often feels that if she had ever got the knack of making friends, Elizabeth would be one of them. Bettina knows that Patricia will mention that she bakes her own bread; knows, too, that she will quietly buy a Scarborough Fair loaf to take home with her. Then there's the recently retired headteacher, and the woman who breeds beagles and sits on the council; and there's another woman she doesn't recognize as a regular customer but who reminds her of Fran Flood. She goes back to the counter for napkins. When she turns back, she sees the woman has got up and followed her.

It is Fran. Older Fran, more tired Fran, Fran with kind eyes and her tawny-grey hair cut short. Bettina waits to be shocked or upset, but she's comforted. Fran was never anything but kind and understanding, and she was a friend to her father. If Bettina was an easy embracer of people, she would put out her arms. She smiles, instead.

Fran smiles in return, but it's a half-smile, dimmed by nerves. She says, 'I hope you don't mind. I came to see you. I should have called. I didn't know there was a tasting.'

'Of course I don't mind,' Bettina says. She takes a look

in her heart and finds that she really, truly doesn't. 'I have to do the tasting, though.'

'May I stay for it?' Fran asks. 'Or is that too much?'

'Yes, stay, please,' Bettina says. Her pulse is a little skippier than usual as she sits at the table and prepares to launch into her welcome speech, as written on card one.

The sight of Fran is such a warm, friendly thing, answering the homesickness that Bettina has felt since she looked at her name in the visitors' book at the nursing home. But the worry about what's brought her here, the sense that this is never going to be over, gnaws. She hands out pens, paper, plates, knives, concentrating on her hands and the hands she is passing to. She asks the group to make their introductions, and she talks about how her bread is made, talking through the work she's done in the kitchen this morning. And then the tasting proper begins. Bettina is glad that she wrote out the new card.

'This is a sweet lavender loaf. I started wondering about it when a friend brought me some lavender plants in pots. My father loved lavender. He used to say that you didn't get the scent until you crushed it, and that people are the same, only showing what they're made of when they're under pressure.' Bettina looks around the table and sees that Fran is nodding, solemn, not looking at Bettina. 'The bread is still a little warm, so it's easier to tear than to slice. I'd like us to try it toasted and untoasted. Let's start with it untoasted, and then we can try toasting it when it's cooled a bit more.'

'My John used to say that it's criminal to toast fresh bread,' Patricia offers.

'Well, he was right, I'd rather have it fresh and un-toasted too.'

Vindicated, Patricia nods. Elizabeth catches Bettina's eye, smiles. Bettina is trying very hard not to look at Fran, without making it obvious that she isn't looking at her.

And then Fran speaks. 'You can tell such a lot by the way the crust breaks,' she says.

'Yes,' says Bettina, 'yes, you can.' She breathes in, out, slowly, focuses her attention on Elizabeth as she talks. 'Take the bread in your hands,' she says, 'and tear a piece off. Try it on its own first, then with one of the butters, and see what you think. You can tell me, you can write it down. It's up to you. Please don't tell me what you think I want to hear, because that won't help. I'd value your honest opinions, even if you think this is the worst thing you've ever tasted.'

She watches the eyes; even risks a glance at Fran, who, whatever her reason for coming, is treating the bread with every seriousness. Bettina's urge to cry is growing, building, as she looks at the woman who, unknowingly, threw her a lifeline by teaching her how bread could be made, and how the making of it was an everyday love, a way of making peace with each new morning that comes.

She has lost one mother, and, watching Fran out of the corner of her eye, realizes that there was another mother she has missed out on for fifteen years. She brings her heart back to her breathing and her attention back to her bread.

Watching her testers' faces is like watching a series of

303

lights come on. One for the crust, one for the texture, one for the smell, one for the first hit of honey, one for the tang of the lavender. Bettina knows all she needs to know, about the bread. She itches to know why Fran is here.

'Very good,' says the retired headmaster. His shirt is missing a button. Bettina remembers that his wife died, not long after he stopped working.

'I'd like to try this with goat's cheese,' says Elizabeth. 'If you have a spare I'll take one to work for the chefs to play with.'

'Of course,' Bettina says. She is carefully slicing the other loaf now.

She puts the first four slices in the toaster, and steps away to ask Angie to bring a platter of cheese over. She realizes that she's breathing too quickly. There's sweat in her hairline and on her lip. She remembers the panic attacks of the early days of her recovery, brought on by the sound of a car backfiring or the screech of wheels on a television programme or even too many people in a room at once.

She puts her head against the door of the fridge, reminds herself that she doesn't need to panic now. Fran, as far as she can see, is joining in, talking to Patricia about making her own bread.

At last, the tasting session is over, with an all-round thumbs-up for the lavender and honey loaf, and Bettina nicking the tip of her index finger on the breadknife in her hurry to clear away. She uses the blood as an excuse to go upstairs and clean up. While she's there, she changes into a T-shirt unembellished by flour, washes

304

her face in the coldest water that the bathroom tap can manage, and brushes her hair. She isn't upstairs for long, because she knows Fran will be waiting.

And she is.

'Someone to see you,' Angie says, voice full of curiosity. 'She's sitting round the corner. The woman from the tasting. I don't think she's been in before.'

'Can you manage if I take her upstairs?'

'Of course I can manage. Do you want me to stay on until you're done?'

'Yes, please.' Josh hasn't been on his own in the shop yet. So with everything under control, Bettina rounds the corner.

'Tina,' says Fran, rising.

Now Bettina looks at Fran, properly, and sees tears on her face; feels her own eyes tingle and burn. She says, 'Fran. Why don't you come upstairs? We can talk there.'

Rufus's blue silk tie is on the table. He'd left it the last time he'd stayed, and Bettina had put it there to remind her to take it with her when she went to meet him for dinner, but had still forgotten to pick it up. She squashes her impulse to hide it. I'm thirty-five, she says to herself, I'm allowed to be in a relationship. But still, she wishes she wasn't. Or at least, she wishes Rufus's tie away for the duration of this conversation.

'Have a seat,' she says.

Fran takes the end of one of the sofas, settles back and waits for Bettina to sit, diagonally opposite on the other sofa, before she begins.

'Your father and I stayed in touch for a long time,' she says. 'I don't know whether he told you.'

'No, he didn't. We didn't talk about you.' Bettina corrects herself, 'My mum wouldn't, of course, but I – I couldn't. He tried to tell me what was happening, but I couldn't—' Roddy was in the newspapers, the Sunday supplements, from time to time, though. She remembers Alice reading an article out, in a tone at the fulcrum of heartbreak and malice: although Roddy's agenda was clearly to promote a charity he was working with, the focus was very much on his bravery and determination after the terrible tragedy he'd suffered, the support he was getting from his family and friends, from Olympic hopeful Aurora Fielden. (She used to be 'fellow Olympic hopeful', and Tina had wondered if Roddy had felt the loss of that one word as acutely as she did.) He's not the one who's suffered the tragedy, Alice had said when she'd got to the end of the article, and Howard had said, come on, Alice, the lad's paralysed. Alice had sniffed, as if to say, well, I'd hardly consider that to be a tragedy. Tina had taken the newspaper from the bin, later, and smoothed out and examined the article: she'd seen how tired he looked, how Aurora had a hand on his shoulder, and she had hoped for his happiness because she knew that she had lost hers. 'I saw you all in the papers, sometimes,' she says, and then she adds, 'My father never told me that my mother had vascular dementia, either. He was very protective.'

'I think that's maybe when we lost touch,' Fran says. 'He used to call me, or email, every few months, and we'd meet up. But I suppose he wouldn't have been able to leave your mother.'

Bettina remembers Fran as assured, comfortable,

confident, but the woman in front of her now seems anything but. There are tears on her face; her palms are pressed together, rubbing, an anxious prayer. 'We weren't – we weren't equipped, were we? None of us,' Fran says. 'When I look back on it – your poor brother – I just wish I could go back and tell us all that we don't have to do anything immediately. We don't have to decide now. All those decisions we made, when we were least fit to make them.' She looks up, her hands suddenly still, as though Bettina is the person she's been praying to.

'Yes.' Bettina reaches back to herself in her bedroom the day Alice had turned the Floods away. She had been tired and tearful, sorry and so very sad, thinking about how she had to choose between her mother, who had lost one child already, and Roddy, who had sat at the doorstep with his parents solid and strong behind him. In the next room her mother had wailed like an injured child, with part hurt, part confusion. She had heard her father, remonstrating at first then crying too. Bettina had made the only choice she could. She reaches back to that Bettina, that day, and she wishes she could – what? That's the question. Should she tell herself not to keep away from the Floods, not to go to France?

'Fred won't talk about it at all,' Fran continues, 'he never has. Can you believe that? He's never said a word. Not in all these years. I know what he'd say. He'd say talking about it won't put things right. But it might have helped me.'

Better surely to go further back and tell herself not to apply for a job in the stables, not to let Roddy get under her skin?

'To be fair,' Fran doesn't seem to have noticed that Bettina isn't saying anything, doesn't seem to mind; continues, 'Fred has done a lot. Everything Roddy needed, he's found. Physios, trainers for carriage-riding, everything you can think of at the right height. Fred has made it all happen. Roddy decided that he was going to live the best life he could because – well, because he thinks he owes it to Sam and to you, I think. Fred will do anything to support that. Except talk to Roddy. Or to me.'

Bettina nods.

Fran keeps talking. 'Someone said they thought they'd seen you, at the church, and I went down and looked and I realized that your father had died. And your father always told me how you were, and what you were doing, and I didn't realize how much I needed to know that you were all right until I no longer had any way of knowing. I never told Roddy I was seeing your father, because I didn't want to get his hopes up. The last thing I heard, you were in France and working in a bakery, and I knew you moved around a lot. I googled you every now and then, but of course all that comes up is the accident. I never thought about you changing your name.'

'It is my name, still. I didn't change it.' Bettina, who knows that she ran away and hid, finds that she doesn't want Fran to think that she ran away and hid. Fran doesn't even acknowledge that Bettina has spoken; she's in a quiet fever of confession, of years of unspoken words finding an exit route at last.

'And then Aurora said that she'd seen you, here, in

Throckton, and I thought, at last, I can find you. I came here, one Monday, but the shop was closed, so I thought I'd come back. But of course Aurora had told Roddy as well, and you'd said that Alice was in a nursing home, so he decided that it would be a place you could travel to easily or you may as well still be abroad. He and Fred called everywhere until they found her, and then when I saw that Roddy was hell-bent on going, I insisted on going with him. I didn't know whether it was the right thing to do, but I wanted to see Alice, and I wanted to be there just in case.' She shakes her head, and doesn't seem able to articulate just in case of what. Bettina knows exactly what she means. 'I'm sorry if it was the wrong thing to do, Tina.'

Bettina waits for the next wave of confession, but it doesn't come. She shakes her head in an echo of Fran's feeling of hopelessness. 'It's all right. She was past – past being upset. She didn't always know that Sam was dead. She used to say, "Lovely boy, Roddy."' Although Bettina thinks about her mother a lot, she rarely speaks of her; and so when she does, when she hears the past tense out loud, she startles herself into tears. Fran moves to sit next to her, and takes her hand.

'It was nice to see her enjoying her birds still. She was a lovely woman. I remember her as being . . .' Fran searches for the word, 'bright. Lovely clothes, and a big smile, and laughing.'

'Yes. Once.' Bettina thinks of Alice, so wan from the moment Sam died.

'Of course.' Bettina has forgotten Fran's ability to do this: to understand not just words but what's behind them. She catches herself thinking about how much easier the aftermath of the accident and Sam's death must have been for Roddy: no lost brother, no lost mother, just understanding and honesty. No. No. Don't be this person.

Fran presses a tissue into Bettina's hand. She dabs and blots at her face.

'I thought she recognized me,' Fran says quietly, 'but it was hard to tell.'

'She mentioned Roddy,' Bettina says.

'Did she? Well, that's something . . .'

'None of it meant anything. She sometimes recognized me as myself, she sometimes thought I was her sister. She used to ask where Sam was. There was no way of knowing what was real to her.'

'I can't imagine how awful that must have been. For her and for you,' Fran says.

Bettina nods. 'She never mentioned my father. If you showed her a photograph of him she couldn't tell you who he was.' There's relief in saying this to someone who knows just what it means, because they'd known her parents as the people they had been.

'I'm sorry. I've never forgotten your father. He was a lovely man,' Fran says.

'Yes,' Bettina says. They are quiet for a minute, two. She asks the thing she most wants to know: 'Why didn't Roddy come here? Once Aurora told him?'

'I think Roddy thought that if he saw your mother, if he could make peace with her, then you wouldn't have a reason not to speak to him. And of course once we'd seen her again – and realized . . .'

'I'm sorry,' Bettina says, though she's not sure what for. She feels sorry, though.

'I persuaded Roddy to do nothing until I'd been to see you. But then Aurora rang Roddy because Verity told her that your mother had died—'

'Verity did?'

'She came into the shop and asked for you, and they told her.' Fran pauses, finds her place again, and Bettina remembers coming into the shop the day after Alice had died, and a cheerful note from Verity scrawled on the back of a *Throckton Warbler* compliment slip waiting for her. 'And, well, I'm sorry he came to the wake. I'd have stopped him if I'd known. Which is why he didn't tell me, of course.'

Bettina nods. She lets her tears dry on her face. They make her skin cool and contract. She quite likes the sensation. It's not unlike the feeling of opening a hot oven door, or riding on a windy day.

'I'm so glad I've found you,' Fran says.

'Why did you want to find me?'

Bettina thinks of Roddy's indifference, at the wake. This fever of searching makes no sense when he was so formal, so cold. Back in her memory sits the sight of her mother, crying, saying 'I don't want to talk about it'; her father, shaking his head, 'let sleeping dogs lie'. Fran seeking her out when their shared history is so grim seems perverse.

'Tina, I don't think you ever understood that you were like a daughter to us. You were part of our family. We thought you would always be part of it. Roddy was so serious about you, so devoted. And then you were gone, and although you, understandably, didn't want to see us, we still cared about you.'

'It wasn't that I didn't want to, but my mother found it very difficult—' Bettina says. She hears how defensive she is. 'You remember that day.'

'Oh, I remember it,' Fran says. She thinks of the welcoming committee at the stables, dismissed by Roddy's scowl; Roddy wheeling himself around his new home without comment, hauling himself into bed, not coming out into the air for three days, while she told herself to be patient and sat in her kitchen with worry and loneliness for company.

'My mother always saw things as being very simple. Even when they weren't. She was always a bit like that.'

'They were good people, your parents. We were all good people.'

'I wasn't. I distracted him. In the car.' Bettina's impulse to confess is sudden and unstoppable.

'What?' It's taken Fran by surprise, too.

'We were talking about something, and he thought I was upset, and he kept looking at me even though Sam told him to watch the road, and the next thing we knew—' And the next thing we knew, she thinks, was nothing.

The tears, again. Fran is holding both of Bettina's hands. 'Listen to me, Tina. We were all good people. We none of us did anything wrong. It might have been easier if someone had. Then we could blame them, instead of all blaming ourselves, and each other.' It sounds as though Fran is crying, too. When Bettina looks at her, her eyes are dry, though her face is mournful.

'Roddy seems – all right.'

'He is, I think. Though—' Fran looks at Bettina, deciding, 'though he was upset after he saw you at your mother's funeral.'

'Really? He didn't seem upset. He was very – matter-of-fact.' Her heart still shrinks at the thought of it.

'Oh, come on, Tina, you know he was never matter-of-fact about you. I don't believe you've forgotten a thing about him.'

'I didn't know what to think. I—' remembering, Bettina is determined to do better, to find words that will say something real, 'I couldn't find a way to start talking to him, because I was so thrown by him being there, and then he was going, and—'

Fran sighs; smiles, her face as gentle as the morning, before the sun comes up. 'I'm sorry. I didn't come here to rake over the past. I came to say how sorry I am for everything you've been through. And that I wish there had been a way to resolve things.'

'I'm not sure that we could have done a lot differently,' Bettina says, although when she thinks about her past it's nothing but an endless ribbon of 'if only'.

'I didn't mean—' Fran shakes her head. 'I'm not saying anything as well as I could. I know nothing was going to bring Sam back, that's not what I meant. I meant – I wish we'd been able to help each other. That you and Roddy had been able to—' Fran is crying like someone who has nearly used up their life's allocation of tears, without sound, without volume, but with feeling.

'It was a long time ago,' Bettina says. She has picked up Rufus's tie, and is twisting it through her hands.

313

'Well, yes, but that doesn't matter, does it, when you live with the effects every day of your life.'

'I suppose not.'

'Really, what I came to say was – I'm sorry about so many things, but I'm really sorry Roddy came to the funeral. I hope he didn't upset you. I'm glad you've moved on. Maybe now Roddy will.'

'I don't know that I've moved on.' Bettina has a vision of herself: never very assertive before the accident, she has since moved from place to place simply by waiting until to move was easier than to stay.

'You're married. You have a child. I'd call that moving on. And there's nothing wrong with that.'

'What?'

'Aurora saw you with your family. A little blonde toddler, she said, a man with good shoes.' She smiles; her eyes say, typical Aurora.

'Oh, no, that wasn't my little girl – I'm not married.'

'Roddy said you were wearing a wedding ring.'

'It was my mother's ring. They took it off her when she died and gave it to me, and I put it on my finger—' Bettina doesn't want to start explaining about her lack of a jewellery box, the holes where her ears were pierced closing over because she didn't wear earrings from the time when, presumably, the ones she was wearing for the ball were taken out when she went into surgery.

Her hands are bare now. She hasn't yet had the courage to go through her mother's personal effects, collected by courier from the nursing home. But she did take out Alice's jewellery box and put it on her bedside table, and put her wedding ring in it. She holds her hands out to

314

Fran, turns them over, as though they are evidence, as though merely saying that she's not married isn't quite proof.

'But there's someone?'

'Well, yes. Rufus.' Bettina holds out the tie. It is as good as the shoes. More proof.

'That's good.'

'I don't know.'

'You're allowed to be happy, Tina. We all are.'

'Yes,' Bettina says, feeling as though Fran has said something theoretically true but that seems utterly irrelevant, like the laws of physics that hold the universe together. 'Are you happy? Is Fred? Roddy?'

It's Fran's turn to hold her hands in front of her, her palms up. 'I don't know. Sometimes. Fred seems to be trying to work himself to death. Roddy acts the same as he always did, but he has never forgiven himself for the accident—' she tries again, 'for what happened to Sam—' once more, 'for Sam's death. Roddy has never forgiven himself for Sam's death.'

Bettina almost smiles. It's on the tip of her tongue to say, I've missed you. But Fran is talking again.

'Are you happy with Rufus?'

'I don't know. He's kind.'

Fran nods. 'I see.' She looks as though she's going to cry again, but instead she picks up her handbag, takes something from it.

'I brought you something. I've no idea whether I should have or not. It seemed like a good idea when I set off, when Aurora said you seemed happy and Roddy said you were married. But it's up to you.'

She hands over an envelope, thick and smooth.

'It's the ball next week. We didn't do it the year after Sam died, and the year after we were still getting Roddy sorted out. But the third year, Roddy said he wanted to do it again, but none of us wanted to go back to the Coach and Horses, and we couldn't have it on the same date, so we have a marquee in the bottom paddock and we do the whole thing there, on the anniversary of us buying the place to begin with.'

'That's good,' Bettina says.

'Really? I've never been sure.'

'Well—' Bettina wants to say, life goes on, but can't quite bring herself to. Instead she offers something that's definitely true: 'When I think about your place, I feel as though I'm watching a film. It feels like another world. It always did, a bit.'

'You mattered to us. We missed you. We still do.'

Bettina has opened the envelope. She sits with the card in her hand, looking at it as though it will tell her the answer. It doesn't.

'I don't know, Fran.'

'When I came here, I thought you were settled. I thought you might like your husband to see the place where you worked. We were a big part of your life for a long time, Tina.'

'Yes.'

'I can see it's a bit more complicated than that. But you'd be welcome.'

'Does Roddy know you're here?'

'Yes.' She makes a sad sound that is probably meant to be a laugh. 'I gave him such a going-over for not telling me that he was going to Alice's funeral, I couldn't have avoided telling him even if I'd wanted to.'

'Does he want me to come?'

'Roddy thinks you're married.'

'Yes.'

Fran reaches up and cups Bettina's cheek, running her thumb across the hollow under her cheekbone. Her skin is rough and chapped. The feel of it is familiar, as though Bettina has, somewhere, logged the shape of Fran's fingertips and waited to come into contact with them again. 'Isn't it time you started pleasing yourself, Tina?' she says, gently. 'It's allowed, and it always has been.'

Bettina nods. She can't say anything; there's no one sentence she can pull from what she's feeling.

, At the door, Fran turns.

'I know you might not come to the ball, but can I tell Roddy that Aurora was wrong about the toddler, and that you're not married?'

The answer is simple, and complicated. Bettina's past and future wait, breathless, for her to speak.

'Yes,' she says, 'tell him.'

'Fran Flood came by today,' Bettina says to Rufus later. 'Aurora told her about seeing us. They have a ball every year and she brought me an invitation.'

'That was good of her. She must have thought a lot of you.'

'Yes, I think she did, then.' Bettina adds to herself: before she saw how I broke.

Rufus smiles. He really does have the most beautiful

teeth, straight and white. Kate has them too. 'I'd better get my tux cleaned.'

'Oh, I hadn't decided about going.' A technical truth. Bettina makes it sound casual, but she's thought of little else.

The Bettina of the last fifteen years wishes she had ripped the invitation in two and put it in the bin before Rufus arrived. The Bettina she is striving to be sees no reason why she shouldn't go. It's not going to do any more harm, she reasons, and maybe it will help her. Fast on the heels of that thought comes another, audacious in speed and content, a thoroughbred of a thought: maybe she deserves help.

'Why wouldn't we go?' Rufus laughs an uneasy laugh. 'You're not ashamed of me, are you?'

'No, I'm not.' And Bettina knows that she isn't; but she is ashamed of herself, for her life that has run through the channels where the earth is softest, while Roddy has, it seems, gone fearlessly forward.

'Shall I book us a room at the hotel,' she asks, 'then you can have a drink.'

'You want me to drive us there?'

'Yes. It's only carsickness.'

'If you're sure.'

'I'm sure.' Bettina forces her hands to be still in her lap as she says the words.

'I love that you trust me, Bettina. Thank you.'

'Don't thank me. You have nothing to thank me for.'

Rufus makes the face that means: I know that your mother just died, so I'm letting that pass, but we both know that it's not true. He gets up, going to retrieve his laptop cable from his briefcase, which he left by the door when he arrived. He touches her shoulder as he walks behind where she is sitting, and pretends that she doesn't flinch. Bettina decides that this isn't the evening to explain about seeing Roddy again. They are both tired, after all.

Bettina has one dress that she thinks might be suitable for a ball. She had it made during her third year in France, and it's long and she thinks it's beautiful. She asks Rufus if he'll tell her what he thinks of it, because she doesn't know how much it will have dated, how it might date her, or whether she might be too old for it. So one night, before dinner, she goes into the bedroom and puts it on. There isn't a full-length mirror in the flat, so she can't see all of herself, but she can feel that it still fits – if anything, it's a little too big around the bust – and she looks down at herself and remembers how the sea-green of the silk catches the light. It's a strapless shift, the bodice lightly boned and the skirt flaring softly at the hips, so that she can walk and move as comfortably as she once did in jodhpurs. Putting it on again feels better than she imagined.

'What do you think?' she asks Rufus, stepping through the doorway: but she can see the answer in his face.

'You have exquisite taste,' he says. 'It's beautiful.'

'I lost the wrap to go with it.'

'It's a lot easier to match a wrap to a dress than it is to find a perfect dress in the first place.'

'It's not too dated?' She doesn't want to be flattered: she wants to be reassured.

'It's not too anything,' Rufus says, 'honestly. You asked me to tell you what I think, Bettina, and I think you look beautiful in it. It isn't dated, or too young for you. Really.'

'Thank you,' she says. When he uses her name it always sounds like a reprimand, somehow. 'I have some black satin ballerina pumps, somewhere.' She adds, 'I can't wear heels.'

'Perfect,' Rufus says, again. The next night he brings a black silk wrap, plain and soft and fine, which is exactly what the dress needs, as well as being exactly what Bettina needs to feel comfortable in the dress.

The day of the ball dawns warm and soft around the edges. On the drive towards Missingham, Bettina forces herself to open her eyes and look as the familiar countryside approaches. She keeps her head still, her eyes on the rise of the road in front. Rufus is quiet, and there's music – Rachmaninov, she thinks he said – which she is starting to like.

Being in the car makes Bettina feel as though she's an arrow shot from a bow, sucked forward on a course she can't change. She doesn't like the feeling. But then again, she doesn't like anything much, at the moment.

Seeing Fran was like having a visit from her young self, the Tina who was growing in confidence and learning to love and starting to wonder and hope that what was happening with Roddy could be real, and true, and lasting. That Tina wouldn't think much of the half-life her older self was living now. Even the baking of bread feels like a failing. Bettina has chosen a life that means she is awake when others sleep, that she can work in silence, and the only hands that matter are her own.

And this feeling is bound in with the fact that she still hasn't told Rufus that Roddy came to the funeral. She's been waiting for the right moment, knowing that such a thing does not exist. Rufus has been coaxing details of her past out of her, and he's done it with genuine interest and concern, nodding at things she's said as though he's an archaeologist just given another piece of a skeleton that helps him make sense of a whole. Of course, he thinks he's dealing with someone from her past, not someone who's written right through her. She wonders if he'd be quite so forensic if he knew how much time she spent wondering what Roddy might have said if she hadn't been wearing her mother's wedding ring.

As if to confirm this, Rufus says, 'I've brought some sketches, for our house. I thought we might have time to look at them tomorrow, as we'll have the morning together.'

'Our house?' Bettina says. She and Rufus have talked about the house that he's planning to build. Bettina has lived in a lot of places, so she has lots to say about build-ings, about space and light and practicality. It's becoming a joint project, but to Bettina it's just an extension of what they did when Rufus advised her on the bakery and café. So she repeats his words not with warmth, or excitement; she says them with surprise mixed with panic. And even allowing for the fact that they're in the car, so he's not looking at her but concentrating on the road – it's one hell of a bend on the way down into Missingham – he knows with a plunge of his heart that he's misjudged this whole situation. He says 'our house' in his mind and heart, but always 'my house' when he's talking to Bettina.

'I mean "my house",' he says. 'I suppose it feels like our project, that's all.' He half laughs. 'Don't worry. I'm not going to ask you to move in.'

And Bettina, who doesn't believe him but cannot think how to say so, says nothing. She thinks about pointing out the place where the accident happened, but this feels too private for Rufus to know and anyway, her throat has seized. The church and the graveyard flow in and out of view, and then they've arrived.

'You look lovely,' Rufus says, later. They're standing side by side looking at themselves in the mirror in their hotel room. They've got ready in a hurry, because Bettina had stayed to help Angie to clear up and, perhaps, to avoid the necessity of giving Rufus a guided tour of Missingham. But Bettina is prepared to concede that she does look good, in a grown-up, elegant sort of a way. Rufus is as immaculate as ever, and his eyes are shining as he looks at her via the mirror's reflection. He's been quiet since they arrived, although to be fair there hasn't been much of a chance for conversation, between taking turns in the bathroom and the general working-round-each-other of two people used to getting ready on their own.

'I should have bought you something,' Bettina says, as she strokes the soft stole, which she suspects is, along with the dress, probably the single most expensive item of clothing she's ever possessed. Rufus makes noises about the recession but she's seen the receipt for his new shoes. 'I'm a hopeless—' but she stops – there still isn't a word she can find for their relationship. And anyway, what she should be saying is: I'm a terrible person because my instincts were right, and even before Roddy rode in I knew I'd never love you. Yet I'm standing here letting you think that I might.

Rufus and Bettina walk up the hill, quiet among the pairs and trios of excited partygoers around them. They don't arrive late, but the marquee is already noisy and a little too hot. A string quartet plays near the entrance. There's champagne for them as they wait to be greeted by the Floods.

'Nice place,' Rufus says.

'Yes, it is,' Bettina replies. The Flood farm feels both exactly the same and entirely different. The serenity and solidity of the farmhouse are the same as they ever were, but there's a new indoor riding school behind it. The wooden gates have gone and metal ones with key-pads and codes have replaced them. The smell and sound from the yard is like a mother's heartbeat. Here is the place where Bettina meets herself again. Her legs feel weak. She doesn't know whether she wants to sit down, or run away. She remembers Fran telling her that she was one of the family. She has run away once and all that running turned out simply to be a long loop back to the place where it all began.

'Tina,' says Fran when they get to the front of the reception line, 'Tina. I'm so glad you're here.'

'Yes' is all Tina can manage.

Fred says nothing at first; but rather than the genteel

323

peck on the cheek that he's giving to the other women in the line, he wraps his arms around Tina, suddenly, so that, unprepared, she is standing with her arms pressed to her sides as he holds her. His beard is sharp and warm against her cheek. She hears Fran and Rufus introducing themselves to each other: and then Fred says, 'Welcome home,' his words low and gruff and full of heart, and she's released. She steps away, and sees Roddy waiting, the third in the welcoming line.

'We didn't know whether you'd come,' he says.

'I didn't know,' Tina says. Oh, for more words, for better words, or the time and space to think of them, say them.

A peck on the cheek to a man in a wheelchair isn't the easiest thing Tina has ever done, all the more so because, as their bodies move closer, Tina's body remembers what Roddy's body can do to it. The shock of the memory wobbles her, so that Roddy needs to steady her, his hand running up her forearm as she lurches forward, not so much kissing his cheek as pushing her face against his face, which is smooth – she knows it must be less than an hour since he shaved. Her lips stop at the side of his ear, so if there was a secret for him, she could whisper it. She straightens up. He holds on to her left hand, and his thumb rubs across the base of her third finger where she had been wearing her mother's ring the last time he saw her.

'Sorry,' she says.

'Don't be sorry,' he says, 'Tina.' She's sure he says her name that way on purpose, almost a whisper; she knows that he would say it exactly that way if they were pressed

324

together in the dark and he wanted to know if she was awake or not. She wonders if he's doing it on purpose. A look into his eyes, serious and still, tells her that he is. Roddy's eyes are telling her that the reins are ready for her, if she wants to take them. Something in her stiffens, locks, preparing for the jolt and the forward swing.

'I'm Rufus Micklethwaite,' Rufus says, extending his right hand while sliding his left arm around Tina's waist, 'hello.'

'Roddy Flood,' Roddy says, 'pleased to meet you.'

And then they've been moved on by the next people in line. They make their way into what is not so much a marquee as a room, with chandeliers and a solid floor, and the sides rolled up to let the summer air move through. Rufus looks around for people he knows. Bettina looks, by turns, at Rufus's tie and her own blunt fingernails, at the tips of her shoes and the champagne in her glass. Every now and then, she takes a discreet look around the marquee to see who, if anyone, she recognizes. The Fieldens are out in force. She sees Edward and Arabella, Aurora and at least one of her sisters, tall men who might be their husbands, children of different heights but all with the same dark hair. They have formed an enclave at the far end of the marquee. Tina thinks she should be able to keep out of their way.

Rufus's excitement at being here is palpable. He scans the marquee too, but for a different reason: all he needs is someone to recognize him to make it a perfect occasion. Well, that and Bettina being less preoccupied. Still, it must be a big thing for her, to come back here. And he can see how strongly she is tied, still, to the

Floods – he of all people can recognize unfinished business when he sees it.

He looks at her. She's looking at a group at the other end of the marquee. He looks at Roddy. He's still glad-handing, but whenever there's a break his eyes come to rest on Tina, and he has the look of a man who cannot believe what he is seeing. She's not looking at him, at least, and Rufus is relieved, until he sees how deliberately she is keeping her eyes away, as though a look will burn her. He moves to face Bettina, knowing that in doing so he will block her line of sight.

'Stables convert so well,' he says, 'they're so solidly built to start with.'

Bettina rouses herself to say, 'I don't think the Floods will be converting theirs any time soon.'

'True,' Rufus says, 'but barns are the same, perfect dimensions for living. I often wonder what the people who built stables and barns would think of them being used as homes.'

Bettina startles. Rufus puts out a hand to her, and realizes that she's watching a woman in a badly fitting black dress stride past as though she's wearing wellies underneath it. 'Sorry,' she says, 'there are a lot of people here I haven't seen for a long time, and—' She shakes her head.

'Would you like to leave?' he asks. At least he will be able to say that he's been. And at least, if they leave, she will be a long way from Roddy. He wonders if how he's feeling is how Richenda felt when she knew that he was looking elsewhere. Despite his new shirt and newly cleaned suit, he feels shabby.

'No,' she says, too quickly. It doesn't make him feel any better.

Once the reception line has dwindled away, the string quartet stops playing and Fred, Fran and Roddy move to the area in front of the stage which must be intended for a dancefloor, as there are no tables there. As Rufus watches the Floods progress, he sees that the slightly odd layout inside the marquee, with tables dotted rather than clustered, means that a wheelchair can go anywhere, with ease.

Fred clears his throat and taps his glass with his wedding ring. His guests let their sentences fade, and turn to look at him. 'Thank you for being here,' he says. 'It's an honour to welcome old friends and new. I'll keep this brief, and then we can eat, drink and be merry.' There's polite laughter and a shout of 'Yes please!' that causes more laughter still. Fred waits for it to fade, smiling an amiable smile.

'This year we're proud to be training world-class competition riders as well as providing lessons for the next generation of riders, both amateur and professional.' He pauses and waits for the applause to stop. 'And we're glad to be in good health and good heart.' More applause. 'We won't say a lot, but we will make some toasts, and then the debauchery will begin in earnest.' Applause, laughter. 'Let's raise a toast to our equine friends. Long may they tolerate and teach us.'

'Equine friends,' calls the crowd. Bettina chinks her glass with Rufus.

Fran is next. 'Flood Farm wouldn't be what it is without all the people who work with us, support us, and cheer us on. We're honoured that so many of you have joined us tonight. Thank you. Here's to you.'

The guests look round at each other, chink glasses, nod, smile, say a few words. 'Here's to you, Bettina,' says Rufus. He kisses her, on the cheek just above the ear.

Then Roddy speaks. He pauses long enough to let the chattering die away again. He seems, too, to search out Tina as he looks around the room. Once he's seen her, he raises his glass.

'To absent friends,' he says. Roddy is looking straight at her as he touches his glass to his lips. His eyes shine, brim. Tina's mirror him. He nods. She nods. The murmur of 'absent friends' goes round the room, a more sombre sound.

Rufus is saying something, but Bettina isn't listening. His hand is on her waist and she knows that to move away from his touch would be churlish. And then Aurora is at the front, saying something else that Tina can't listen to because she can't look away from Roddy, who is looking at her still. It feels as though they are doing all of the looking, all of the longing, that they've missed. She had known that Fran would tell Roddy everything that they had discussed on the afternoon Fran came to see her. She wouldn't have been surprised if Roddy had turned up in Throckton the next day. But he hadn't. She'd been disappointed, at first, but then she'd realized, in the car on the way, that it's up to her to come back to him. She was the one who left, however sound her reasons had seemed, however much she'd wanted to protect and please her mother, make up for the loss of Sam, and apologize to Roddy for ruining his career and his life by, first, not trusting him and then punishing herself.

A trio of small children – Aurora's, Bettina presumes, they all have the hair and the confidence – follow their mother and break the eyeline between Tina and Roddy. They present wine to the Flood men, and flowers to Fran. Tina thinks about how little Fred and Roddy need more wine and how Fran dislikes cut flowers. She feels for them, all their effort and attention met with little more than thoughtless, hurried goodwill.

Soon there's wine instead of champagne, and food more substantial than the barely-a-bite canapés that have been doing the rounds so far.

'Would you like to sit down?' Rufus asks, and Bettina nods.

The bravest guests are already dancing. The covers band is loud enough that it's OK not to talk.

Bettina and Rufus have found a bench for two at the side of the marquee. They are a little way away from the action. Bettina watches as people move between groups and conversations, easily, cheerfully.

She could imagine her mother here. Sam would be good at it too. She and her father would have sought each other out, and they might have sat here, together. Her father would have watched her mother, proud of her for being herself, and so different to him. Tina would have watched Sam in much the same way.

Rufus turns to Bettina and takes her wine glass from her, putting it with his at their feet. He takes hold of her hands. His thumbs rub across her knuckles, although she doesn't think he notices that he's doing it.

'What I said about the house being our house, Bettina—'

'Rufus—' Bettina says, but she stops, because she doesn't know what she can say that will even begin to explain this properly. There have been so many steps, each in themselves understandable, each in themselves forgivable, which have put her in the right place at last, but sitting next to the wrong man.

'I'm sorry,' Rufus says, 'it was too much, too soon.' Tina, not expecting this, looks straight into Rufus's face. She knows what kindness he's capable of, and that once, such kindness was enough. There are two paths; she takes the harder one, for a change.

'Rufus—'

But Rufus hasn't finished. It's as though he's watching her shape-shift, and has only this chance to take hold of her, to stop the magic making her into something unreachable. 'But you must know how I feel about you, and—' she's opening her mouth to speak again: he holds up his hand, 'please. Let me finish. I know that you don't feel the same way about me. Not yet. But I think that we have something, and I think that, in time, it could be something that makes you happy, if you can give it a chance.' He stops. He's watched her this evening and he's realized that he might not be able to compete with memories, with passion, but he might be able to appeal to Bettina's pragmatic side. Now he's started saying his piece, it feels threadbare against his heart.

But she's still listening, or seems to be. Her hands are still in his hands.

'I'm not stupid. I know you have unfinished business

with Roddy.' The way her face changes at the mention of Roddy's name tells Rufus that he's as good as gone from her life. There are words in his mouth, about old relationships not being able to compare with the memories of them, and how none of us can truly go back and there's no use in trying. He swallows them back, where they join other words, things the man he was before he met Bettina would have said: has she really thought what being with a man in a wheelchair might be like, does she want to be a nurse for the rest of her days, does she even know that he is still a man. But it seems that Rufus is a better man for knowing Bettina, more patient, more clear-sighted, more self-aware. When she looks at him he feels as though she can see everything that there is to him, and he wants her to see something that's worthy of her.

The hubbub of the party is getting louder. Bettina leans in to speak. 'Rufus, I think what you want is someone to love, and I don't think it has to be me.'

'But you're—' It's her turn to hold up a hand.

'Please. You've said that you know I don't love you.' Her words are hard but her eyes are soft, telling him that she isn't trying to be hurtful. And, oddly enough, it doesn't hurt, not really, because all she is doing is saying what they both know. It does occur to Rufus that anyone looking on – Roddy, say – as she puts her hand to his face, will think that this is a lovers' conversation, intimate and absorbing.

He nods. She continues, 'I think I wanted to prove that I'm not damaged. I don't think that's a basis for a relationship.'

'Probably not.' Rufus fights to remind himself how much he loves Bettina's honesty. Half of the reason that he began to love her was that sense she gave him of not dissembling. He takes a breath and realizes that, actually, he is the one who has joined the dots the wrong way, and has wanted this to work so much that he's taken every small sign of progress and multiplied it to make something that isn't there. She is the one who's given as much as she can to him; he is the one who's failed to see how insubstantial it was. But he can't help trying. 'We have such a lot to give each other. In time—'

Bettina shakes her head. 'I'm sorry, Rufus.'

'Please. Hear me out,' he says. 'I think you're good for me. You bring out the best in me. I'm good for you, as well. We were getting somewhere. But then your mother died. And—' he gestures, half wave of the hand, half shrug, 'well, this.' He feels his hold on Bettina sliding away; he stills his urge to scrabble, to cling, to make a noise louder than the sound of his heart falling like a rock down a mountainside.

But then again, one last attempt can't make things any worse. He doesn't want to have to go back to his flat and take those photographs off his fridge and start again. 'Doesn't the fact that we can talk like this make you think—'

She takes his hand. 'I thought I was free,' she says, 'I wasn't. There was always someone else.'

And there really isn't anything to say now. He sighs, a great sigh that empties him and leaves – well, it's too early to say. Bettina is touching her eyes. Her face is

332

turned away and he can't see if she's crying. He hands her his handkerchief and she takes it, touching his hand. He thinks he might cry, later.

'I'm going to get another drink,' he says. 'Would you like one?'

'No thanks,' Bettina says, 'I'm going to get some air.'

'I could bring it out to you.'

'No, Rufus,' Bettina says, as kindly as she can without being encouraging. She stands and steps away, towards the entrance, feeling sorry, feeling free. Rufus goes in the opposite direction, to the table where wine glasses are being filled, row after row of them. Rufus toys with taking two, in case she comes back in to find him, but he knows that she won't. As he turns round, he sees that Roddy is behind him.

'Rufus,' Roddy says with a nod.

Rufus takes a deep breath. 'She's gone outside,' he says. 'I think she's waiting for you.'

'Thank you.' Roddy nods and turns. Rufus waits for the satisfaction of his own generosity to make him feel better. He takes a second glass of wine, because he thinks it might take a while.

Tina hasn't just gone outside. She's gone down to the place to the left of the gate, above the bottom paddock, where the land falls away and there's a clear view down to the church and the graveyard. The bells have just struck nine-thirty. The stone of the church has a honey hue to it, clinging to the light a little longer than the buildings around it. It's not long since the longest day of the year. Everything on the farm that once was mud, or gravel, or track, is paved and smooth; there's a bench here that wasn't there before, but Tina leans on the fence that she remembers, although she imagines that every plank of wood will have been replaced since she last stood here.

When she sees the horse coming towards her, her first impulse is to back away, but she doesn't, because something in the way the animal moves holds her attention. Of course, she reminds herself, it's a long time since she's seen a pedigree horse up close. It's easy to forget how they look, so effortlessly elegant, their movements as smooth as their coats. And then the animal comes nearer, and nearer, and then he's standing next to her. His face is older, and his coat is not so sleek and plentiful as it was. But there's no doubt that it's Snowdrop.

Tina's hand, forgetting that it belongs to a person who cannot bear the sight or touch of horses because they remind her of everything she's lost, rubs him between the eyes, the way he likes it. He drops his head so that she can put her hands around his ears and stroke them, the way she used to. He knows who she is. She's sure of it. He puts his nose against her shoulder; she feels his face against her ear, wonders if she's dreaming him. But he's here, all right. And so is she. He nickers into her neck. She does the maths: he's twenty-two. It's a good age for a horse to reach, though not surprising as he's had all the benefits of good stabling and good care.

'Hello, old boy,' she says, 'I didn't think we'd see each other again.' Her heart is nineteen again, almost tearing apart with the joy of being next to this animal, who seems above all others to understand her. The pulse in her throat is calming at his nearness.

'He seems happier out here, so we leave him out when it's warm enough, with a couple of his mates.' She turns. Roddy is there, as handsome as ever in the half-light. 'I think he's been waiting for you to come back,' he says.

'I didn't hear you coming,' Tina says.

'I keep my wheels oiled,' Roddy says, and he smiles. 'It doesn't fool the horses, but it keeps the people on their toes.'

Tina laughs. She isn't sure why, or if she should. She is disoriented in this world, back where she started, different but the same. 'I can't believe Snowdrop's still here.'

'You didn't think we'd part with him, did you?'

'No, but—' She doesn't know how to explain that she'd locked off this part of her life so thoroughly that any evidence that it's been living and breathing still is like walking with ghosts, living in dreams.

'He's still yours, you know. I never gave up, Tina.' There's no reproach in his voice.

'I did.' Tina sits down on the bench. Roddy brings himself next to her, so they are side by side, looking out over Missingham. She thinks about touching him, but doesn't dare. 'I'm sorry, Roddy.' Her heart is beating in her throat. She's not sure whether he heard or even whether she's speaking aloud. She thinks of how many conversations she has had in her head, over the years. Roddy, Sam, her father, her mother. So much better to have said it all out loud.

'On the day Sam was buried, they all stood here,' he says. 'We were both in hospital.'

She shivers at the thought of it, of those awful days of trying to understand how it was that she was a twinless twin, how such a thing could even be.

'My parents come down here still, a lot. So we put this here. Even the new people who don't know the story know that this is a place to come and be quiet.'

'That's good.' Sometimes what seems most unfair is the lack of a mark that Sam made on the world. He didn't have time enough for much that would outlive Tina and her memories. So she likes the idea of a quiet place for the most unquiet of brothers.

'I suppose it is. Nothing seemed to be enough.'

'I know,' Tina says.

'Of course you do,' Roddy says. Then, after a moment where they watch Snowdrop as he watches them, 'I'm sorry I hurt you, Tina.'

'I'm all right,' she says.

'You lost your brother. You limp. You had an impossible choice. You felt you had to run away.' Roddy makes a point of not wishing for legs that work, but right now, he would do anything to be able to kneel in front of her, look up into her face, understand better what she's feeling from the look in those eyes that, it turns out, he has remembered perfectly, in every detail. She's not looking at him now. He could ask her to, but he decides to keep talking instead. Thinks of being curled into her back, the side of his face resting on the back of her head, talking into her hair.

'Those things are not your fault,' she says. She is

336

thinking about the wheelchair, and how often she has thought about Roddy in it: Roddy stuck, Roddy limited, Roddy unmanned. Something else she was wrong about.

'I'm so sorry,' Roddy says, quietly. She glances to the side. He is looking straight ahead, but sensing her, he turns to look at her. 'I didn't think you would take Aurora seriously—'

'I was just afraid,' she says. 'I never had – what you had. That fearlessness.'

'And look where that got us. I thought—' Roddy's voice sounds quieter now, because he's pushing his words out through a set, unmoving jaw; his hands are clenched on his lap. 'I thought we would be together always. I couldn't imagine life without you. That was how I knew.'

'I just thought I was lucky,' Tina says. 'I used to watch you sleeping and think, it's only a matter of time.'

'You were the love of my life, Tina.' That 'were' hurts; balances the fizz and pop of the rest of it.

'We were young,' she says. Her own voice is soft, now; scared.

'Yes, we were. Are you going to tell me that that means what we felt wasn't real?'

'Of course not, Roddy. It was always you.'

Geese fly overhead, calling. From the marquee comes a round of applause as a song ends. There's a count of one-two-three-four and then the music starts again.

'Before this,' Roddy strikes the wheelchair with the flat of his hand, 'I took everything for granted. Including you. I thought I'd always have you.'

'I know you did. I didn't dare hope for that.' She's crying. She uses the edges of her wrap to blot her tears.

'I know. That's why we worked. I was too sure and you were too doubtful, so we balanced everything.' He smiles, though he looks as though he's about to cry, too. 'I've had a long time to think about this. Years and years.'

'You didn't say anything, at my mother's funeral. You were – friendly. I thought—' Roddy's head and shoulders kick back in a mirthless, soundless laugh as he remembers what that friendliness cost him, his guts aching for all the time they spoke.

'You were wearing a wedding ring,' he says, his voice quiet. Snowdrop leans over the fence, ears forward, as if to hear. 'I'd screwed your life over once. I wasn't going to make it hard again. I thought you'd moved on.'

Tina gets up and goes back to her horse, to touch him again, but also to give her a reason to turn and look at Roddy, drink him in. She has forgotten how easy it is to be around him, and how difficult it is to be close to him without touching him. 'Not really. I ran away.'

Roddy comes towards her and reaches for her hand. He takes it and lifts it to his chin, where he holds it against his face. 'It's hard to move on when you know you'll never have it as good as you did.'

Her thumb finds the notch in his jaw, sits there feeling his blood beat. 'Yes.'

'I'm so sorry about Sam,' Roddy says, after a moment. 'I know.'

'I wanted to talk to you. I waited for you. Your mother was in such a terrible state, but I thought it would pass.

338

Not that she would stop missing Sam, or blaming me, but I thought she would let you find your own happiness.' He remembers Fran saying how you could never predict what grief would do to people, but he had hoped that he could. He'd been wrong.

Snowdrop turns and makes his way down the field, away from them. Tina nods. She doesn't seem to have any words. She doesn't like looking down at him. So she takes back her hand, goes back to the bench and sits. Roddy follows, but this time he puts himself at right angles to her. They can look each other in the face, and if they lean forward, they can clasp their hands together, which they do.

Roddy says, 'I've spent all these years having conversations with you in my head, and now you're here, and I can't seem to find anything that means anything. There isn't a way to say it all. It all sounds—'

'I know what you mean,' Tina says, then, 'We had everything, and we didn't really understand.'

'You're right there,' Roddy says. Then: 'What about Rufus?'

'Oh,' in this collision of her old life with her old self, everything Throckton seems a long way away, 'that's – that's not what it looks like. He's not – he's my neighbour, really. I let him think there was more. I thought there might be. Until you came to the wake and I thought you didn't care. And then I thought, well, if you don't care, then I'll try not to care. And now I know how much I do.'

'Are you sure?' he asks.

'It was always you, Roddy,' she smiles.

Roddy needs to be sure: 'Really?'

'I've told Rufus that there's not going to be anything. I told him tonight.' Her face is serious. 'I should never have let it start.'

'So it's just us?' She has always remembered the openness of his face, his bellwether eyes. But remembering it is different to experiencing it, here, now, with everything that there is to him in front of her, waiting to be understood. She can't believe that so many years have passed since they last sat so close to each other. She thinks of the question she never had the chance to ask her father: how he managed to look after her mother, love her, even as her spirit then her health left her. It seems as though the answer is here. Roddy is the same to her now as he always was, and she to him. Love is love. Everything else is sortable.

'It's just us.' He smiles. That smile. He's leaning towards her, pulling her towards him. She's never forgotten the look that's in his eyes now, sheer joyful lust and longing. She thinks of everything she has thought about saying to him, if she ever has the chance: 'But, Roddy, I need to say some things.'

'Fair enough.' God, he wants her. But he's waited this long. Now that he knows she isn't married to the man with good shoes – Aurora has never got any more tactful – Tina can talk or be silent or anything, for as long as she wants to. Now that she's in reach again and they have no one to stand in their way, Roddy doesn't care what Tina does, as long as she doesn't disappear.

'When we were together, I loved you, and when we were together, I knew you loved me, although you never said so.'

'Didn't I?' He looks perplexed; the man who has come home to find his front door open, but sure that he closed it behind him.

'No. You didn't.' Of course, she hadn't either. It seems so ridiculous now, so trite, as though saying that you loved someone made it the truth, and not saying it meant that you didn't love them at all.

'But you knew that I loved you?' And then he can't resist it; he lifts her hand to his lips, kisses it. 'Love you?'

'Yes. Almost.' Tina brings his hand to her lips now, kisses it back, her heart vaulting. She can't believe that this is happening. She's going to do it better, this time. 'I love you too,' she adds. She curves her hands around his face. Her face hurts with the width of her smile. Her eyes are stinging with the need to cry. She wants to kiss him and never stop. He slides his hands up to cover hers, then pulls them down and holds them, tightly, in his, against his knees. He sighs the sigh of the man who has been holding his breath for more than a decade.

He knows that before Tina will let him talk about the future, she needs to finish her turn at talking about the past. 'What was the almost?'

'When you weren't there, it was harder. I kept thinking about how you should be with someone – different.'

He laughs. 'You spent more time trying to fix me up with Aurora than anyone else did.'

'Maybe,' she smiles, but then her face becomes serious again, 'but after the accident – everything was different. I had no Sam. It was like – like – Sam used to say, when people asked what having a twin was like, that you never

341

really thought about it, like you never thought about your arm. It's hard to explain.'

'Like you never think about your legs, until they don't work. All you can focus on is the loss.' Roddy still experiences a shadow of this feeling, every day, as he puts socks on to as-good-as-dead feet.

'Exactly,' Tina says, 'and my mother – you know she blamed you. So when I missed you – when I wondered how you were – I couldn't ask anyone, because she was always there, or listening, and if your name was mentioned, she'd – she just – it was awful.' If Tina closes her eyes she can still hear the wailing.

She smiles a sad smile to match Roddy's, and then she's crying again. 'When I got better, every time I put one foot in front of the other, I thought about you, and how you'd never walk, and I'd done that to you.'

Roddy reaches inside his jacket and hands her a handkerchief. 'My mother always cries, at some point during the ball,' he says. 'I like to be prepared.'

Tina blows her nose and looks away, past Roddy, down to the graveyard.

'It wasn't your fault,' Roddy says, gently.

Tina's gaze is fixed on the place where her brother and her parents lie. She feels as she did in the car with Rufus: hurtling, on course, heading faster, faster, faster to the place she's aiming for. 'I just couldn't see how we could get past it all. And my mother was so – furious and so desolate – and my father was so stoical, and I walked around thinking that they must be thinking that the best twin had died, because Sam was so much more – everything – than me.'

'That's crap, Tina.'

'That's what I thought, though. And I mentioned you to my mother, it must have been nearly two years after the accident, when I thought things might have healed, a little, for her, and she said I should be thinking about losing Sam, not losing you.'

Roddy makes a sound that's somewhere between growl and cry, frustration and anger and sadness for Tina, and for the thought that she has suffered all this without him, and because of him. Tina looks away from the graveyard and into his face. 'I just couldn't upset her. I didn't dare. I didn't think about the long-term consequences. I wasn't thinking of you and me and our future, because there didn't seem to be a future any more. I just thought about keeping my mother calm. All we did, Dad and me, was try to stop her from hurting.'

'I can understand that,' Roddy says.

'And then—' Tina doesn't really know what she is going to say, but she knows it's coming from somewhere true, and so she lets it. Roddy has taken her hand again, or she his. She's given up on wiping her face, letting the tears shiver down her cheeks in the cooling air. Roddy is crying too, quietly, and she hands his handkerchief back. 'Once I realized that I'd lost Sam, and I'd lost you, then nothing really mattered. And I liked making bread because it was such a basic, uncomplicated thing. And being able to do something made me feel that I could be useful. This all sounds so stupid now, when I say it like this. It sounds more thought out than it was.'

'It's not stupid.'

'And then we decided to move, because my mother

wouldn't go out in case she saw one of you, and I thought I would go away. It felt as though she couldn't bear to look at me, so I went away to make bread. And that was it, really. I drifted. I got to be not unhappy.'

'Oh, sweetheart.' He holds out his arms, she stretches across to him, but there's the arm of the wheelchair in the way, and the end of the arm of the bench poking her under her ribs as she leans, and it's like trying to embrace someone through a window. So now they are laughing, and crying, as this first lovers' embrace of their new beginning won't work.

'How do we do this?' Tina asks.

'Sit on my lap?' Roddy says. So she does, arms looped round his neck, the crook of her knees over the arm of the wheelchair. They are still crying. Still laughing. Snowdrop meanders back over to look at them again.

'This is about as comfortable as your old sofa,' Tina says.

'I still have that sofa. My mother had it reupholstered though, so it's not the same.'

'Thank goodness.'

'Will you stay tonight?'

'Yes please. I don't need to be back until tomorrow evening.'

'Good.'

She settles her cheek against his hair. Their breathing quiets, stills. People are starting to leave the marquee, not to go home yet but to find places to smoke, or kiss, or whisper. The summer darkness has turned, at last, from grey to black; Tina has forgotten how close the stars seem, here.

'I'm sorry you had such a lousy time,' Roddy says quietly.

'Don't feel sorry for me. I could have made a better job of it all.'

'We all could have made a better job of it all, if we hadn't been dealing with it.'

'Your mother said something similar. When she brought the invitation.'

'I'm glad you came,' Roddy says. His fingers are in her hair, gentle; her scalp sings.

'Me too.'

Roddy nods. He rubs her arms, which are pimpling in the cool air. 'Do you want to come back to my place?' he says. 'I've got a barn conversion, you know.'

'Not just yet,' she says, 'if you don't mind.' There's such peace here, such calm. There's going to be such a lot to do, think about, decide, learn and relearn, and although Tina cannot wait to do it, for now she is happy just with this: Roddy, Snowdrop, stars.

'Get up a minute, will you?' he says.

'Of course.' She stands, quickly, afraid that she's hurting him. But he leans forward and wriggles out of his jacket. His shoulders are broader, now. He holds the jacket out to her.

'I've got my wrap,' she says.

'It's not enough, though.'

'No,' and Tina puts on Roddy's jacket, and she settles herself back into his lap. 'That's better,' she says.

Epilogue

Missingham, 2014

Fʀᴀɴ ᴀɴᴅ Fʀᴇᴅ come for tea on most Sundays. Tina bakes, Roddy sets the table, and they have leaf tea and use their china tea set, which had belonged to Roddy's maternal grandmother. Even six months after Tina moved in there's a sense of excitement, as though none of them can quite believe that they are here, like this: that, despite everything, and with no disrespect to what has gone before, they have made a happy ending.

Fran has brought a batch of granola.

'You don't have to bring things,' Tina says.

'Tina,' Roddy says, 'don't say that. She has to bring this.'

Tina laughs. They do get through it at an astonishing rate. At breakfast, Roddy picks out the raisins and puts them into Tina's bowl. Tina trades him for hazelnuts.

Today there are ginger scones and lemon cake, and black olive bread with blue cheese and sun-dried tomatoes to go with it. It's the first really warm spring day, so they open the French doors and enjoy the warm air, and all of its promise.

'I'd ask how business is,' Fred says, 'but if this is what you're baking, I don't think I need to.'

'It's fine,' Tina says, 'Angie is doing a great job.' Her former deputy had taken the promotion with great energy, bubbling with ideas and training up her own assistant with aplomb. Tina goes over once a week, to check on things: Fran sometimes drives her, if Roddy can't free up the time in his schedule. So long as she takes her medication she's not sick, and she's getting used to the journeying, although even with a fair wind it's a four-hour round trip.

'Have you found anyone for the flat yet?'

'Well,' Tina says, helping herself to a scone and sliding a smiling look at Roddy, who grimaces, 'funnily enough, Rufus's daughter is looking for a place.'

'She says she just happened to bump into him and they went for a coffee,' Roddy offers. Fran laughs.

'I said,' Tina says, 'that he left a note for me in the shop inviting me for a coffee, and I was very happy to see an old friend. And he happened to mention that Kate was keen to find a place. So, that's good.'

'You just need to find somewhere here, then,' Fred says, 'for another shop.'

'Yes,' Tina says. When she'd moved in with Roddy, a month after the ball, she'd been adamant that she wasn't going to be a spare wheel, as she put it. She would start the second Adventures in Bread here in Missingham.

'That might need to wait,' Roddy says.

'Well, best to get the wedding over,' Fred says. Tina laughs. The wedding is two weeks away. It will be the four of them plus a dozen friends, a register office ceremony followed by drinks here at Flood Farm, where, as Roddy says, we will all drink champagne until we fall

350

over. Tina is having a dress made by a friend of Fran's, something draping and delicate, with the final fitting already booked. She's bought silver shoes and pale cream lace underwear. Roddy has made her a gift of a princess-cut diamond pendant that matches her engagement ring. Roddy has a new suit, the caterers are booked and the wedding cake has been made since Christmas, and is now wrapped up tightly in foil and waiting in the dark of the cupboard under the stairs.

'The wedding is really taking care of itself, Fred,' Tina says.

Fran, who never misses much, says, 'I see you've passed on the blue cheese, Tina.'

'I don't see what that's got to do with anything,' Fred says, and as the rest of them smile and Fran starts to get out of her seat, her arms already reaching out to embrace Tina, who's sitting next to her, he adds, 'This is why I like horses.'

'Dad,' Roddy says, 'the bakery is on hold and Tina is passing on blue cheese because she's expecting.'

Fran is making a noise that's half-shriek, half-purr. 'When? But can you—' she says, 'I thought—'

'I'm twelve weeks. I'll have to have a C-section,' Tina says, 'because of the way my pelvis healed, but apart from that, everything should be normal.'

Fred's on his feet, shaking Roddy's hand, clapping Tina's back, then putting his arm around Fran's shoulder and squeezing her until she laughs. 'You and Tina are going to have a baby,' he says. 'Well, that's the best news I can imagine.'

'No, Dad,' Roddy says, 'we're going to have two.'

Acknowledgements

It sometimes takes a while for me to get from the idea for a novel to the real story, so I often quiz kind people whose contribution never makes it to the page. I'm grateful to them just the same: they are part of finding the path. So I thank Dennis Hetherington (Mr Insurance), Joanna Sothern who found out lots of things about planning permission for me, and the various architects and eventers I have stalked and interrogated.

Sometimes the opposite happens. I went to see a baker with a vague idea that my heroine might have a little business. Listening to him talk about bread and the everyday magic and meaning he finds in it helped to inspire and create Bettina. Andrew Smith of Bread and Roses in Northumberland, thank you.

My dad helped me to find Roddy's Cosworth and work out how it all went so wrong on that road. I spoke with Stacey Davison about being a twin, and Rachel Pearce and Margi McAllister about mothering twins. I hung out on twin message boards, horse-related message boards, and message boards for people who use wheelchairs (particularly the apparalyzed forum).

Thanks to everyone who answered my rookie questions. Thanks too to the good people of Twitter and Facebook who are always happy to help with writer research requests. My nieces, Hannah and Emily, also helped a great deal with the horses.

This book was written in near secrecy, because I was very protective of Bettina. But Alan Butland, Emily Medland and Susan Young read every word. Thank you.

I have a brilliant agent, Oli Munson at A. M. Heath, who is supportive and insightful and makes my writing life easy. And three bright and clear-sighted editors have guided me into making a real book from the lump of words I presented them with. Thank you, Emma Buckley, Harriet Bourton and Bella Bosworth. Deborah Adams has copy-edited this and my previous novel with intelligence and insight. Thanks, too, to the team at Transworld, whose passion for books is something to behold.

I'm blessed with friends and family who are prepared to listen to me as I try to work out plots and people, and who still talk to me even though they know I might well steal little bits of their lives to brighten up my pages. Thank you especially to Alan, Ned, Joy, Mum, Dad, Auntie Susan, Lou, Scarlet, Emily, Jude, Rebecca and Diane.

Three recipes from Adventures in Bread

(Bettina makes the breads using her own leaven, but
I've substituted dried yeast.)

Fran Flood's Everyday Bread

Equipment:
1 x 2lb loaf tin
A freestanding mixer with bread hook *or* a mixing bowl
and wooden or silicone spoon
A baking tray and a small ovenproof bowl or ramekin

Ingredients:
500g strong white bread flour
1 tbsp (approx. 8g) fine salt
1 tbsp (approx. 8g) dried yeast
300g water, boiled and cooled to blood heat
A small amount of flour for dusting work surfaces and
hands

Method:
1. Put the water into a bowl. Put the flour on top, and
   add the salt at one side of the bowl and the yeast at
   the other.

2. If you are using a mixer, start it slowly and once the mixture is roughly incorporated turn up the speed and leave to mix until the dough appears silky and smooth, and has an elastic quality when you stretch it.

3. If you are mixing by hand, first mix with the spoon and then, once the mixture has come together, tip it on to a floured surface and knead it. The easiest way to do this is to put a little flour on to your hands and then bring the edges of the dough into the middle and push it down. Do this again and again, turning the dough as you go, until it becomes silky, smooth and stretchy. It will probably take about 10 minutes. Put the dough back in the bowl.

4. For both methods, cover the bowl with a plastic bag or damp tea towel and leave it to double in size. The warmer the place you leave the dough, the more quickly it will rise. You could make it in the evening and leave it somewhere cool overnight, or put it somewhere warm for a couple of hours.

5. When the dough has doubled in size, knock it back: take it out of the bowl and knead it on a floured surface for 5 minutes or so. Shape it into an oval roughly the size of your tin, and put it in the tin. Cover it with the bag or tea towel again, and leave it to double in size once more.

6. When the bread has doubled in size, heat the oven to 400°F/200°C/gas mark 6. Slash the top of the loaf with a sharp knife and sprinkle it with water.

7. Put the bread tin on a baking tray along with a small bowl of water. (The steam from the water on the

bread and in the bowl will stop the crust from forming too quickly.) Put the tray on the middle oven shelf.

8. Bake for 25–30 minutes. When the bread is done it will be browned on top and smell fantastic. Turn it out of the tin – it might need a little shake but it should get itself free fairly easily. Knock on the bottom and it will sound hollow.

9. Leave your loaf to cool on a cooling rack. Feel free to test a slice when it's still slightly warm . . .

Scarborough Fair Cob

Equipment:
A milk pan
A freestanding mixer with bread hook *or* a mixing bowl
    and wooden or silicone spoon
A baking tray and a small ovenproof bowl or ramekin

Ingredients:
300g semi-skimmed milk
1 heaped tsp each of dried parsley, sage, rosemary and
    thyme
300g strong white bread flour
200g wholewheat bread flour
1 tbsp (approx. 8g) fine salt
1 tbsp (approx. 8g) dried yeast
A small amount of flour for dusting work surfaces and
    hands

Method:
1. Put the milk in the pan and add the dried herbs.
    Bring it to the boil, switch off the heat, and leave it
    to cool. If you can leave it to infuse overnight, so
    much the better.

358

2. Pour the herby milk into a bowl. Put the flour on top, and add the salt at one side of the bowl and the yeast at the other.

3. If you are using a mixer, start it slowly and once the mixture is roughly incorporated turn up the speed and leave to mix until the dough appears silky and smooth, and has an elastic quality when you stretch it. It should be a stiffer dough than for Fran Flood's Everyday Bread.

4. If you are mixing by hand, first mix with the spoon and then, once the mixture has come together, tip it on to a floured surface and knead it. The easiest way to do this is to put a little flour on to your hands and then bring the edges of the dough into the middle and push it down. Do this again and again, turning the dough as you go, until it becomes silky, smooth and stretchy. It will probably take about 10 minutes. Put the dough back in the bowl.

5. For both methods, cover the bowl with a plastic bag or damp tea towel and leave it to double in size. The warmer the place you leave the dough, the more quickly it will rise. You could make it in the evening and leave it somewhere cool overnight, or put it somewhere warm for a couple of hours.

6. When the dough has doubled in size, knock it back: take it out of the bowl and knead it on a floured surface for 5 minutes or so.

7. Divide the dough into two portions. One should be about two-thirds of the mixture, the other the remaining third. Shape both pieces into balls and flatten them slightly. Put a piece of baking

parchment on your baking tray and arrange the pieces of dough with the smaller on top of the larger. Cover it with the bag or tea towel again, and leave it to double in size once more.

8. When the bread has doubled in size, heat the oven to 400°F/200°C/gas mark 6. Slash the top of the loaf with a sharp knife and sprinkle it with water.

9. Put a small bowl of water on the tray with the bread. Put the tray on the middle oven shelf.

10. Bake for 25–30 minutes. When the bread is done it will be browned on top and smell fantastic. Turn it over and knock on the bottom – it will sound hollow.

11. Leave your loaf to cool on a cooling rack. This bread goes really well with cheese.

Rufus's Favourite Chocolate Orange Cake

Equipment:
3 x 21cm sandwich cake tins (if you don't have 3, you
   can bake in batches)
3 circles of 21cm baking parchment
A pan with a lid, big enough to hold two oranges with
   a little bit of space around them
A freestanding mixer with paddle attachment *or* a
   mixing bowl and wooden or silicone spoon
A food processor or stick blender (or if you don't have
   these, see the suggested alternative, below)

For the cake:
1 orange, of a thin-skinned variety, such as Valencia
25ml orange juice
250g butter, at room temperature
250g caster sugar
4 medium eggs, at room temperature
250g self-raising flour
40g cocoa powder

For the frosting:

1 orange, of a thin-skinned variety, such as Valencia

25ml orange juice

100g 72% cocoa solids dark chocolate

100g butter, at room temperature

100g full-fat cream cheese, like Philadelphia, at room
  temperature

400g icing sugar, sifted

a tablespoon or two of milk

Method:

1. First, prepare the oranges. Put them in the pan,
   whole, and cover with boiling water. Let them
   simmer for 20 minutes, then take the pan off the
   heat and leave them in the water for another half-
   hour. Take them out of the water and leave them
   until they are cold. (You could do this the day before
   you plan to make the cake.)

2. Set the oven to 350°F/180°C/gas mark 4. Put the
   baking parchment in the bottom of the tins and
   grease the sides. (You could wipe round them with
   the wrapper from the butter.)

3. Cut one of the cooled oranges into quarters. Take
   out any pips you can see. Put the quarters (rind on)
   into the food processor or bowl of the stick blender
   with the orange juice, and whizz to a pulp.

4. Mix together the butter and sugar until the mixture
   is light and pale.

5. Add the eggs one by one, mixing between each
   addition and adding a tablespoon of flour each time
   you mix.

6. Add the rest of the flour, the cocoa powder and the blended orange, and mix gently together.
7. Divide the mixture between the three tins, or if you are baking in batches, put a third of the mixture into each tin and put the rest to one side. (You don't have to be completely accurate.)
8. Put the cakes in the oven and set the timer for 15 minutes. The cakes are done when the mixture springs back when pressed.
9. Leave the cakes to cool in the tins for 5 minutes, then run a knife around the edge and turn them out on to a cooling rack. Leave them to cool completely before peeling off the baking parchment.
10. Now for the frosting. Melt the chocolate, either in a bowl over a pan of hot water, or in very short bursts in a microwave. Leave it to cool while you do the next bit. Beat the butter until it is soft. Stir in the cream cheese and then gradually beat in the icing sugar.
11. Add the cooled chocolate and milk. You should have a soft, spreadable mixture.
12. Take the second orange and do exactly what you did with the first one: cut it into quarters, take out any pips you can see, put the quarters, rind on, into the food processor or bowl of the stick blender with the orange juice, and whizz to a pulp.
13. Now assemble the cake. Put one of the three cake layers upside down on the serving plate and spread it with half of the orange pulp, then a third of the chocolate frosting. Put the next cake layer upside down on top of the frosting and spread it with the

other half of the orange pulp and another third of the chocolate frosting. Put the third cake on top, right side up, and spread the last of the chocolate frosting on that. Turning the first two cakes upside down means that the orange pulp can sink into the sponge more easily.

14. Serve on pretty plates, with cream on the side if you feel like it.

Alternative, if you don't have a blender:

Instead of using oranges, buy a jar of thin-cut good quality Seville orange marmalade (a standard jar is about 340g). Add half to the cake mixture in place of the orange. Spread a quarter on each of the cake pieces instead of the orange pulp.

Letters to My Husband

Stephanie Butland's heart-wrenching and powerful first novel

'An immensely powerful, and ultimately uplifting, debut novel'
KATIE FFORDE

'Gorgeous. I had to take a deep breath and let out a big sigh when I'd finished'
JULIE COHEN

Dear Mike, I can't believe that it's true. You wouldn't do this to me. You promised.

Elizabeth knows that her husband is kind and good and that he loves her unconditionally. She knows she hasn't been herself lately but that, even so, they are happy.

But Elizabeth's world is turned upside down when Mike dies in a tragic drowning accident. Suddenly everything Elizabeth knows about her husband is thrown into doubt. Why would he sacrifice his own life, knowing he'd never see his wife again? And what exactly was he doing at the lake that night?

Elizabeth knows that writing to Mike won't bring him back, but she needs to talk to him now more than ever . . .

How much can you ever know about the people you love?

Originally published in hardback as Surrounded by Water

Do you love talking about your favourite books?

From big tearjerkers to unforgettable love stories, to family dramas and feel-good chick lit, to something clever and thought-provoking, discover the very best **new fiction** around – and find your **next favourite read**.

See **new covers** before anyone else, and read **exclusive extracts** from the books everybody's talking about.

With plenty of **chat, gossip and news** about **the authors and stories you love**, you'll never be stuck for what to read next.

And with our **weekly giveaways**, you can **win** the latest laugh-out-loud romantic comedy or heart-breaking book club read before they hit the shops.

Curl up with another good book today.

Join the conversation at
www.facebook.com/ThePageTurners
And sign up to our free newsletter on
www.transworldbooks.co.uk